A Respectable Man

A Respectable Man

Printed in the United States of America

First Printing, 2016

ISBN 9780997109115

MAEMARIE, LLC

Note: Some passages in this book contain quotations and allusions from "Pride and Prejudice" by Jane Austen.

Warning: This book contains references and inferences to non-graphic sexual harassment, mental and physical abuse.

Table of Contents

Chapter One

September 20, 1810 (one year prior to canon Pride and Prejudice)

Alma, although the proper way to address her was Mrs. Younge, had already explained her wish for Georgiana to call her by her Christian name, for they were *friends*, had already explained to Georgiana that it was right and proper for her to receive and entertain George Wickham. He was an old family friend--almost like a brother, Alma had reasoned, citing the old, past time childhood memories that Georgiana had shared with her on more than one cold, damp, lonely evening.

 It was that reasoning that led Georgiana and Mr. Wickham, now seated on a blanket on the ground, out in the warm sun. Alma had left them less than half an hour ago, and now, the would be lovers had all the time in the world.

It was here that her brother, Fitzwilliam, came upon them. Georgiana had hardly known what was happening. She and George had made up a game, where one would think of a particular memory, and the other would ask pointed questions as to what the memory was about. It had to be a memory that both shared. It was Georgiana's turn. She had thought back to the first time she could properly remember George--which was long after her mother had passed beyond this world, at her birth.

Fitzwilliam had not yet arrived from his boarding school in London, and her papa, from what she could remember of that time, had already cloistered himself in his study, burying himself in matters of the estate. He was, to her, a tall figure dressed in mourning black.

Georgiana had only been a little girl then, and frequently raised her nursemaid's ire by escaping her, often going into her mother's heavily shrouded room. The first few times, she thought it empty and cold. But she had kept going, and soon discovered it a different world, in the right light. In the right light, it was a paradise. It reminded her of heaven, beaming in bright light and white.

This was where a young George Wickham had found her-- laying her small head upon the same pillow that her mother had left this world on. He had laid a rough, but gentle, big hand on her shoulder, startling her, for she had trained herself to hear the angry, rising, exasperated tones of her beloved nursemaid. Georgiana turned, only to see what she thought, could only be an angel.

It was George, his smile easy and affable, his light hair shining, though it was as black as a raven's feather. He was light, he was blinding. He was her mother, come back to her. He was George Wickham. He helped her down from the huge bed, without one hint of reproach, and took her by the hand outside the room.

He offered her a sweet from his pocket, one that he had gotten from the cook in Pemberley's kitchens. Georgiana remembered biting into the sweet, feeling its flavor wash over her mouth. It was a vivid sensation, one that would never leave her, nor the warmth of George's hand enveloping her small one.

Georgiana had begun the game by giving hints as to her memory, answering George's questions when Fitzwilliam came. She had not heard his approach, and there had been no Alma, nor her lady's maid to tell her of her brother's approach, for her to be able to properly receive him, as her brother, his sister. All she was aware of was George suddenly stopping off, in mid question; mid jest, making a rather hurried apology and promise of a swift return, and he was gone.

Georgiana was about to rise and follow after his rapidly

retreating back, as she knew Alma would encourage her to not allow her almost lover leave without a proper goodbye to either of them, when a looming shadow fell over her seated form. She turned.

"Fitzwilliam!" she exclaimed happily. "I did not expect you for another fortnight. What a happy surprise!".

Fitzwilliam Darcy's countenance was grim, anger rolling off of him in waves. Georgiana noticed that he was stiff, almost unwelcoming as she finished her greeting with a warm hug.

"What is the matter, Fitz?" she asked worriedly, as she saw his gaze turn, and remain fixed in the direction that George Wickham has so neatly escaped to.

His gaze turned to her, softening, while desperately searching her face and figure. "Did he hurt you, Georgiana?" he asked.

Georgiana drew back from her brother, her eyebrows furrowed in shock. "What is your meaning, Fitz? George would not--".

"George?" he interrupted her sharply.

Georgiana felt a blush color her face. Although George and Alma had insisted on the informality of her addressing them by their given names, George and Alma, respectively, and, in return, she felt the obligation to give her permission to call her by her given name, under her elder brother's piercing gaze, she felt like a young child, not yet out of the nursery, nor from under the sharp eye of her nursemaid..

"F-forgive me brother, it was a mere slip--". Fitzwilliam cut her off. "We must take this indoors, Georgiana.". He cast a look around.

"Where is your companion, Mrs. Younge?". Without waiting for her stammered reply, he led her wordlessly back to the lodgings she shared with her companion. They were upon Mrs. Younge before she knew it, Georgiana flying to her, already ahead of her brother.

"Mrs. Younge---!". that was all she managed to get out before her brother took over.
"Mrs. Younge," he said, his voice almost booming, "I would like an explanation as to how I have arrived here, in the lodgings that I have paid for yourself and my sister to stay in, and come to find an reprehensible rake and scoundrel, such as George Wickham, not only in my sister's company, but unchaperoned at that!".

Alma seemed to shrink into herself with every word. Georgiana's strength seemed to rise with each and every word, and thus, she could not be silent. She would defend her caretaker, her friend; her brother, her lover. Her soon to be husband. He was to be Fitzwilliam's brother, not just by the bonds of love and affection, but by law. She knew then, that he sensed something was wrong. Improper. In a way, it was.

Georgiana did not necessarily want an elopement. She wanted her brother and her family see her marry the love of her life in the very rectory that they would serve their God, and their family in.

Not a long and uncomfortable carriage ride to Scotland, with only Alma, and perhaps one of George's numerous friends to serve as witness. No, she would tell Fitzwilliam, and he would understand that she was not a child any longer, she was a woman grown, and was prepared, and ready for her marriage.

So she told him, knowing it would have a twofold purpose-- knowledge of why George was with her, unchaperoned, and the happiness that George had brought to her in such a short time. To Georgiana's shock and dismay, as she told the tale, beginning to end, her brother's visage only darkened, further and further, the more she said. He then, to her surprise, snapped at Alma to stay seated, rang the bell for her maid, and ordered Georgiana to her room until he sent for her.

A numb Georgiana went to do as she was bid from her normally taciturn, yet loving elder brother, when he suddenly pulled her into a tight hug. She felt herself fold into his embrace, as a babe to its mother's breast. His chest was warm, his heart beating rapidly in her ear. Fitzwilliam drew a ragged breath, and asked her, in a gentler tone, to go to her room until sent for. She acquiesced with a small smile, no longer worried. Fitzwilliam had had a bad shock to her news. It was not surprising.

George Wickham was the son of their father's old steward. He had nothing really in the way of money--they were to take residence at the living that their father had promised George, and would use her dowry as well. They would not have as much as though Georgina had married a titled gentleman, like her cousin, the Viscount of ____, but they would be comfortable together. They would have each other, and that was what mattered. What she wanted. And George would tell Fitz, and it would be understood.

Georgiana sat at her vanity, absentmindedly rearranging the small collection of combs and perfumes laid out. A small smile reached her lips, as she reached for the comb she thought would best suit her hair on her wedding day. Yes, Fitzwilliam would understand that she was in love and wanted to marry. He would understand and give permission. Her mind drifted, to much more pleasant thoughts, as she awaited her brother and her love.

*****

When Georgiana was first taken away from Pemberley, from her own dear home and brother, she had been inconsolable. Pemberley was where she belonged. There was nothing that she could not undertake nor learn in the matters of her education, such as history, sums, languages, literature, and of course, music, that she could not learn from the comforts of her own home.

Her governess, Miss Worth, had been the person to awaken the love of the pianoforte within her. Why, oh why, was her dear brother so determined to send her away? And to London, at that! Later, when he relayed his plans to send her to Ramsgate, with a new companion, a Mrs. Younge, her thoughts were much the same: Why? A smile now touched her lips, as she considered the outcome of such a trip.

*****

Some weeks prior.....

"Georgiana, come my dear, you must awake!"

Georgiana's eyes drifted open, blearily focusing on the face of her new companion, Mrs. Younge. All at once, she was aware that the carriage had stopped, and suddenly she was aware that she was much too cool. She put her arms about herself, shivering.

"Are we at the cottage, Mrs. Younge?" she asked hopefully, wanting to get out of the carriage, out of the cold.

Mrs. Younge smiled, "Yes, my dear, we have arrived at the cottage."

Georgiana returned her smile uneasily. She was not yet at ease with Mrs. Younge, as she had only known her a few weeks past since her brother had hired her to be her companion while on holiday. Even then, that time was spent mainly with her brother and cousin.

He and Cousin Richard had take a few weeks from their daily duties to spend time with her at their London townhouse. So while Mrs. Younge had accompanied them on outings, they had not much time to interact with each other. And now they were alone, and would be for two months.

"My dear, are you cold? You are a shivering little mouse!" Mrs. Younge laughed gaily at her little joke. Georgiana let out another smile, and shivered again, for emphasis. She simply wanted to be out of such a confined space with Mrs. Younge, and into a place with a hot meal and bath.

Mrs. Younge, sensing Georgiana's distress, helped her out of the carriage, and together they walked to the cottage. A mere hour later, Georgiana had taken a nice, hot bath, changed into a fresh outfit, and was now sitting at a small table, eating a simple and delicious meal of beef stew. Afterwards, Georgiana was led to her room by her companion, where she wished her a peaceful night.

Once in bed, Georgiana thought that she might lay awake for half the night, due to her nap in the carriage, but to her surprise she found herself drifting away--not fully aware that she was even asleep, until suddenly her eyes open, and there was a shadow looming above her; everywhere else was slowly glowing with light. She jumped up in shock, until the shadow spoke.

"My dear Georgiana, I am so sorry. Did I scare you, dear?"

It was Mrs. Younge. Oh dear merciful God, Georgiana thought to herself, and then answered timidly "A little bit, Mrs. Younge. I am sorry. I am not yet used to having--.".

Mrs. Younge waved away her concerns with an airy hand. "It is no matter, dear. Now, come come. I know that it is a bit early, but I wish to take a walk with you around the beach. Simply to stretch our legs before breakfast, after that long carriage ride. Although I suppose you are used to the length of the trip." Mrs. Younge left the room before Georgiana could say anything else, and was quickly followed in by her maid, Letty.

Georgiana was glad to see Letty, if only for someone who was close to her in age, and not quite as familiar with her, as Mrs. Younge was. Her brother had wanted to send for a maid from Pemberley, as the school she attended in London hired their own maids for the ladies attending, but in the end, it was determined by Mrs. Younge and her brother, that Mrs. Younge would look for a maid that worked near the cottage.

As she found last night, Letty was perfectly punctual and cordial to her new mistress, but not familiar nor warm. It was just as well. Georgiana was not particularly familiar with any of the Pemberley maids. She had been under the charge of her nursemaid up until the time her brother sent her off to school in London, and from then on, was served by strangers.

With Letty's help, Georgiana was quickly dressed and out the door of her room. Downstairs, Mrs. Younge awaited her in a chair near the door. Smiles were exchanged, a walk was taken. Tea was poured. Biscuits were eaten. Mrs. Younge questioned.

Touched Georgiana's arm.

Smiled.

Smiled endlessly, at every expression, every deed that Georgiana wore or did. Nothing seemed to matter; nothing brought them close. They were two strangers, living together in a pantomime of a respectable family unit.

Georgiana couldn't, not much longer--not for the entire eight weeks, as her brother wished. Little had she known, that feeling of discomfort would soon change.

Georgiana let out a small sigh as Letty dressed her before her morning walk with Mrs. Younge.

"Something the matter, Miss?" Letty asked. Georgiana minutely shook her head. "It is nothing Letty. I believe that I

am simply not in the mood for a--.”

Her words were cut off by a knock to the door of her room. “Just a minute, ma’am.” she heard Letty say. Georgiana compressed her lips into a small scowl as Letty hurriedly finished dressing her, and let Mrs. Younge in.

Mrs. Younge gave her another one of her smiles. “I’m so sorry dear. You and I will not be able to take our walk today. I am afraid something came up with my late husband’s business affairs. I must meet with my solicitor this morning. I shall be back in a few hours. Perhaps Letty can accompany you on your walk?” she asked, with a glance toward Letty. Letty dipped her head in response.

“I’ll have to grab my shawl from my room, and then I shall be ready Miss.”

Georgiana paid no heed to the change in plan. Letty was much more tolerable company than Mrs. Younge, even if she did not know her well. Most of their days together passed in near silence, punctuated by the occasional question and answer--generally to do about her toilette. At least she now had a quiet walk to look forward to.

Mrs. Younge left, Letty retrieved her shawl from her room, and their walk began. It was a normal walk, filled with the beautiful but familiar scenery. Perhaps it was just her ill humor at being in Ramsgate, so far from Pemberley. From her brother.

 The walk was normal. But then it was not.

Georgiana and Letty had just stopped to take in the majestic, crushing waves upon the beach, when Letty noticed that a man was walking towards them. As he drew nearer, she alerted Georgiana, as it seemed that he would not alter his course to avoid them. When Letty alerted her, she thought it rude.

What sort of a gentleman would be so rude and improper to two young women, of whom he did not have any prior acquaintance with? Georgiana stepped aside, determined to ignore this rude, rude man, when she heard her name. But not from Letty. From the man. How could--.

Georgiana whirled around in shock, but instead let out a girlish shriek that surprised even herself. It was George! "George!" Georgiana was in a state of disbelief. She had not seen George since she was twelve years old, in the few months leading to her father's death. Afterwards, he seemed to have disappeared. She had been very sad, as George was her best friend. Her only friend. She had not been as close to her brother then, as she was now. Then, she had only George and her nursemaid.

"How is it that you have came upon me, Geo--I apologize, Mr. Wickham?" she asked formally, her cheeks tinging as she realized that she had not been entirely proper, even within the sanctity of her own mind with Mr. Wickham. Mr. Wickham was just as happy to see her, his easy smile lightening Georgiana's spirits.

"It is no bother, Miss Darcy. We are old friends, you and I."

"How is it that you have come, Mr. Wickham? Oh, how I have missed you! Did my brother tell you where I was, and send you? I confess that I have been rather morose in the few letters home that I have sent him."

Mr. Wickham answered those questions with an easy smile, that had belied the harsh truth of his words. "No, Miss Darcy. Unfortunately your brother and I are not at the best of terms at the moment. Come, let us walk, and speak in private." Georgiana turned to her maid, slightly uneasy. It was not entirely proper for her to walk with a man who was not a relative, unchaperoned at that! In her haste to be rid of Mrs. Younge for even a few hours, she had quite forgotten that even with her maid, it was still improper. She knew her brother would not want her to be alone with a man, unchaperoned.

But this was not simply a man. This was Mr. Wickham! Her brother's brother. Her brother. Although people outside her family might not understand the relationship, she was quite sure her brother would. And with that--she invited Mr. Wickham to their cottage for breakfast and tea. A chance to speak privately. Perhaps she would be able to give Mr. Wickham insight into the disagreement between himself and Fitz, thereby mending the breach.

Georgiana and Mr. Wickham had settled in at the cottage, when Georgiana heard Mrs. Younge's arrival into the breakfast room. Mrs. Younge was shocked; it was understandable to Georgiana.

Chapter Two

The early death of Lady Anne Fitzwilliam Darcy had left both Fitzwilliam and Georgiana bereft of normal, familial companionship. His father had left the raising of Georgiana to Fitzwilliam's former nursemaid. While she was more than competent at the task of taking care of Georgiana, she had been getting on in years, and obedience, rather than the normal mischief of a child, were the order of the day. She had turned into a stern taskmaster, than the motherly figure of Fitzwilliam's childhood.

While Fitzwilliam had gotten into the normal mischief a child concocted on a daily basis, answering to his nurse and mother was something to look forward to. He and Richard, his favorite cousin, had spent the majority of their boyhood waiting for the shrieks and stern warnings from his pliable nursemaid, the disappointed looks that melded into a giggle and a small smile from his mother as she half halfheartedly lectured them on their behavior, and then sent them into the nursery for tea and scones.

That idyllic childhood, full of scrapes and sweets, had not occurred for Georgiana. With their father buried in his work, all that was left for Georgiana was to be an obedient, still child. Such a thing did not come naturally, as with any other youth. As a tender footed young child, Georgiana had been an inquisitive, somewhat meddlesome charge. His father never addressed Georgiana's existence in his letters, except to note her general health, and their lady mother's room. As his father's health worsened, his letters became shorter and shorter, until all correspondence from Pemberley was eventually written in the hand of its steward--Old Mr. Wickham.

After their father had died, Fitzwilliam had come home from university, to take his place as the master of Pemberley. The portrait of an mischievous imp had dominated his thoughts of his sister--an image he welcomed. However, when he first laid eyes upon her, he knew he and cousin Richard had quite an endeavor before them. Georgiana had been altered, in the severest fashion. In all respects, she was a properly attired and well behaved young lady, as befitting her stature and rank.

Shortly before the church service that would lay their father next to their mother, Fitzwilliam had taken the time to study his sister. As she quietly sipped her tea, while giving him a small, obliging smile, he saw in her eyes not just his lady mother, but a stillness, a silence. She had retreated into herself, and Fitzwilliam vowed then and there that she would never need to do so ever again.

As much as it had pained him, the only way he knew to give his sister genuine companionship, was to send her away to school. As much as he had disliked it, in order for her to move within their society as a young lady, she would need to learn how to interact with others. Fitzwilliam was not surprised, when Georgiana made only sycophantic acquaintances, which was his experience until he found a true friend in Charles Bingley.

So much so, while he had stressed the importance of the applicant's references and work history, he had ultimately chosen a young widow, who was only a year or so younger than he, to be Georgiana's companion while on this holiday from school.

He had hoped that it would bring Georgiana out of her shell somewhat--to be close to someone who was young, although not her own age, who would not only help her build her own self confidence, but also be a dependable ally, until such a time came that he took a wife.

Fitzwilliam leaned his head back with a sigh, slowly, in the heavy armchair found in the cottage's small library and study. It was not to be. It was wrong. Foolish. He knew it then, before the insipid woman had ever even opened her mouth to speak. Mrs. Younge, whom he was quite sure was not even a "Mrs." Younge, no matter what she said to the contrary, was in league with Wickham.

Any speculations on the contrary were erased from his consciousness from the minute he marched into the drawing room and saw her face, before she had registered that it was

him. When she had thought that it was an overexcited
Georgiana barreling into the room.

It was a gleeful, anticipatory look, a look that told him that
she had expected to receive a considerable portion of his
sister's dowry. Georgiana thought that she had made friends,
had made a second home for herself in George Wickham
and Alma Younge. She had not, and as soon as he dispatched
Wickham and that wretched woman, he would tell her.

Fitzwilliam settled more uprightly into his chair. Shortly
after directing Mrs. Younge to pack her things, he sent his
driver into the small town of Ramsgate to fetch the
magistrate. Thankfully, after a few minutes of a terse,
discreet conversation, the magistrate had agreed to bring
Wickham in to him.

Not surprisingly, the magistrate was a sympathetic ally
when Fitzwilliam had spoken to him, being that Wickham
owed all of the vendors in town a sum of over five hundred
pounds, and he had scarcely been in Ramsgate a solid
month! After assuring the magistrate that he would settle
Wickham's debts, the man was much more obliging, and set
off, to oversee the matter personally.

Fitzwilliam walked to the window. The sky was a clear,
boundless blue. The color of his mother's eyes. It *had* been a
beautiful day. Perfect for a picnic. He crossed over to the

small desk that contained port and brandy, his hand lightly trembling after pouring a small quantity.

He was well aware that he was after the conversation he would have to have with Wickham, and then with Georgiana, he would be decimating the only happiness she had felt since leaving school. He would write to Richard to come immediately.

Family obligations had prevented Richard from surprising Georgiana, as Fitzwilliam had, and it was only God's grace that Fitzwilliam had finished his business early, and had come.

*****

George had been taking a load off at Swinton's Pub when the blasted magistrate himself came to pay him a visit. Of course, that nancy, uptight arse Darcy had called the magistrate, and, like a leaderless tin soldier, the fool had obliged. Flashing his most charming smile, he tucked back the rest of his drink and said lightly, "Lead the way, boys."

Unsurprisingly, he was treated in a rather rough manner. George scoffed. It was not as though he was a murderer. So he owed a little bit of money to people here in town. It was not any of Darcy's business, and if the shop owners had a problem with someone owing them money, then maybe they should not be so free with their credit.

The men dragged him to the now familiar cottage, and practically threw him into the little library, where Darcy waited for him. George sneered at the cold look on Darcy's face--a look he was well familiar with, due to the fact that they had both attended the same university. Darcy had done his best, in those days, to impede his fun, either by refusing to lend him more money, or by warning his newly made friends that he sometimes had some complications in squaring away his debts.

 Honor debts, they were called, and yet none of those blackguards seemed to have any. They had all been born with silver spoons in their mouths, while he had to work for what he was given. Being the favorite of old Mr. Darcy was not as easy as it seemed.

George straightened himself. "What do you want, Darcy?" he asked.

Darcy had been surveying him with the same cold look, not saying a word. After a moment, Darcy gave him his answer.

"I do not wish to hear a single word from you, Wickham, other than the word, 'yes'." I have made arrangements for your debts to be paid off, in this town. Undoubtedly you have other debts, elsewhere. I will seek them out, and pay them."

George felt his grin return, as he licked over his top lip. He glanced over at Darcy, whose gaze was studiously fixed on the wall behind him.

"And what have I done, to merit such.....generosity?" he asked with a teasing lilt to his voice. Before he knew it, a burst of pain filled his vision. Darcy had hit him so hard, he fell to the ground.

"What is wrong with you?!" he shouted indignantly, holding his jaw. His mouth was starting to bleed.

"You think me a fool?" Darcy hissed, as he hauled George up by his lapels, pressing his face very close to George's.

"I know your game, Wickham. I know you. I know that you are not as big a fool as you pretended when you cooked up this scheme with that woman! So I will tell you now. You will leave my sister be. If you think you are getting your hands on my sister's fortune, think again. I will not allow it. Not now, not ever. Do you understand?"

Wickham returned Darcy's glare with a teasing smile, but inside his mind was racing. He was no fool. Even if he convinced Georgiana to run away with him to Scotland tonight, after witnessing her blasted brother's ire at him, it would be all for naught if Darcy was not going to release her dowry to him.

Sure, he could go to the courts, but he did not fancy his name being bandied about in the London papers for that length of time. Too many.......unsavory characters would come looking for him, far beyond the scope of what he was comfortable with. But he had to get his crack in.

"Perhaps you will learn not to be so free with your sister, eh Darcy?"

Darcy's grip on his lapels tightened, warningly. George ignored it, as his face was so white he looked as though he was about to faint. Darcy knew he was correct.

"I did you a favor. That is what High Society will do to your fool of a sister. Handsome, titled young men will bow over her hand and laugh at her insipid games, her dull conversations. They will spend the entirety of their courtship reminding themselves of what she is worth, in an effort to--."

A sharp, feminine gasp was heard. It was Georgiana. She was trembling, her sky blue eyes welling with unshed tears. He looked at her wanly, with none of the warmth she was used to. Georgiana Anne Darcy was a pathetic, plain little girl who thought she was a woman.

George pushed a shocked Darcy away from him and scoffed, brushing past Georgiana without even a backwards glance. He would have his money, his debts paid off, and an exciting new prospect in the Army. Perhaps he would met a lovely widow or heiress, tempted by his striking new uniform, to share his bed and her coffers.

*****

She couldn't breathe. A tightness spreads to her chest and belly, and she couldn't breathe. She is not sure that she wants to breathe at all. Her brother's face, with George a visage of wrath and anger, has now transformed into a portrait of understanding, love, and guilt. Georgiana's chin quivers minutely as she considers the ramifications of what she had nearly done. A lone tear slides down her cheek before she can help it, and she stops thinking.

*****

There was nothing else for Fitzwilliam to do, but to talk. It was not a conversation that he had ever intended to have with his sister, especially not in this circumstance, and he now regretted the necessity that precluded it. Regretted that he had not adequately protected her from the adversity she now faced, simply because he did not wish to taint the only object of happiness and affection she had from her younger years, while he was away at university. He could see that he had been wrong. Georgiana was not yet ready to be wed, especially to a man such as George Wickham, but she was not a child.

His continual treatment of her in that area, as though he were her father, had contributed greatly to their current situation. Fitzwilliam silently vowed to himself that he would never again keep something of such importance away from Georgiana again. They were all they had of each other, and divided their house would fall.

He started hesitantly.

"I did not wish to taint your memories of George Wickham, Georgiana. I am well aware that he was the source of all your happiness during your childhood. I-I know that Father was not present, not in the way that he had been for my childhood and youth, due to Mother's death coinciding with your birth. It took you and I quite a period of time to get this place in our relationship--as brother and sister--although I fear that I behave more like your father in some areas."

Georgiana started to protest. Fitzwilliam held a hand to calm her softly. "No, sister, the fault lies solely within myself, and I need to explain. I wanted to protect you, and in protecting you in this way, I held open the gates for men like George Wickham to ruin you."

Drawing in a ragged breath, Fitzwilliam started again. "As you are aware, Wickham and I were childhood friends--his father being the steward of Pemberley--and our own excellent father being his godfather. As children, we were forever getting into scrapes with each other--stealing apples from the orchard, a scone or two from the kitchens......

Wickham, Cousin Richard, and I were the best of friends. All of that changed once Wickham and I left Pemberley for university."

Fitzwilliam stopped to study his sister's face. Her face was ruddy and streaked from crying, her eyes red and heavy from the short nap she had taken after running to her room, after overhearing, at least part, of the conversation and bribery between himself and Wickham. After today, she would no longer be a child. She was a woman grown.

"While Wickham and I had both been mischievous young boys, constantly getting into trouble with Mother, our nursemaid, and occasionally, Father, we were very different. Had very different upbringings. Father put aside a few hours a day, once I had reached the age of ten years, to teach me some aspect of managing the estate. By the time we had gone away for university, I was quite studious in a way that very few students were, especially ones of my position. And I was quite shocked to discover that Wickham and I were not to be as brothers, let alone friends, once I had refused to become his personal banker."

Darcy paused here, not simply for Georgiana's benefit, but for his own. He and George had been all but blood brothers. Indeed, when they had been children and young men, he had been convinced that it did not matter. George may not have been his brother by blood, but he had chosen him as his family, as had his father, and would treat him as such.

It had....been quite a shock for him to discover what George had really wanted from him. Not his company or friendship, but his money and name. Besides Richard, George had been his closest companion, one he had expected to keep close until death parted them.

"Unknown to myself, Wickham had used my name to get close to the sons of some of the London's wealthiest and titled scions--mainly for gambling and other activities." Fitzwilliam finished lightly, trying to treat carefully. Another one of George's outside activities had been consorting with prostitutes.

"Once I had refused, and warned the others that Wickham had no money, relations between us soured to the point to where we would not speak or look at each other. I heard sometime later that Wickham had quit his studies,and had left London. I did not wish to find him until Father became quite ill, this last time, and wanted to see him before death claimed him."

Georgiana's face began to take on a sense of foreboding dread. It was as though she knew what he was about to tell her, and Fitzwilliam then wondered what George had told her. What excuse had he given, as to why there was a rift between himself and Fitzwilliam? He could only surmise it to be a twisted version of the truth, as George had been fond of sprinkling small lies over the truth.

"I used an agency to track down Wickham--sent word that Father was dying and wished to see him. I thought that even if Wickham had hated me, he would go and see Father. But he would not come. Not even after I offered to pay for his travel and lodging. Father died without seeing him. And then, when news of Father's death had been published throughout the papers, Wickham came to Pemberley, and announced that he would not suit the Church, and wished to have the equivalent of the living bestowed upon him, right now, so that he could go and study the law. I admit, Georgiana, I was angry. So angry. But I wanted him gone and out of our lives, so I gave him the three thousand pounds, and told him that I never wanted to see him again. That he was not to come near myself, you, or Pemberley, so long as he lived. And until yesterday, I had not seen him in five years."

Tears welling within her eyes again, Georgiana opened her mouth to explain how George had tricked her--Fitzwilliam stopped her. He did not need to know--it did not matter to him. It was over and done with, and his sister would never again be tricked like that again from a dissolute man.

"Darling sister, I will write to Richard. We shall go to our townhouse, he will meet us there, and we will take in a few plays. Go to the park. We will be fine. You will be fine. No one else will ever know, and Wickham will not bother you again."

Fitzwilliam took her face within his hands, and looked into her eyes. Georgiana was still pained. She was slowly reverting back to how he had found her--a shrinking little girl, only known to herself.

"You will get married, one day, sister. And it will be to a man who will court you as you deserve to be."

*****

Georgiana closed her eyes, and leaned into her brother. She did not believe him, but she had no wish to make him ill because of her. So she could do nothing but be agreeable to all that he said. And that is all she did, hoping it would be enough.

That he would not see.

Chapter Three

A few weeks later.....

Mr. Bennet leaned back in a most ungentlemanly fashion in the driver's seat of his carriage, not particularly concerned with the actual handling of the reigns to the carriage. The horses took up a plodding pace, instinctively knowing when to follow the bend in the road. It was the eldest Bennet girl's birthday, and this was his fatherly deed to her, for the year. She had wanted a ride around Longbourn and Netherfield, and he had obliged.

The entire family was to go, but Mrs. Bennet had stayed behind to entertain her sister, Mrs. Phillips, Mary retired to her piano, and the two youngest had used the excuse of the carriage excursion to ride with them part way, and then walk the remainder into Meryton—no doubt to expose themselves as silly, twittering young girls to the officers. His Lizzie walked a ways behind the carriage, too stubborn to change her ways. When there was a chance to walk, she did so. He chuckled to himself, catching his Lizzie's eye as he leaned his head backwards for a brief moment.

"Papa, be careful."

Mr. Bennet turned his head into the low, worried tones of

the eldest female Bennet, Jane. Ever dutiful, serene Jane. He
remembered when Lizzie had been born--Jane had been
nearly three years old, and a little lady, much to Mrs.
Bennet's delight and expectation. It was not to be with their
second daughter--his Lizzie had been recalcitrant from the
womb. Mr. Bennet had been convinced that she was to be
born a boy, being that Mrs. Bennet's confinements between
this pregnancy and her first were as different as night and
day. A smile touched his lips, he received something better
than a boy--his Lizzie.

Lizzie may as well had been born a boy. From the moment
she could walk and talk, she was forever exploring, always
pushing the boundaries. While Jane had been content to stay
in her nursery and play with her dolls, as their mother had
so ordered, Lizzie always had to sneak out of the room and
visit her Papa, or go to the kitchens to slip a sweet or two
from the cook.

Once they were older, Jane did her best to mind the younger
girls, while Lizzie did her best to get them all into some
mischief.

Or so Mrs. Bennet so shrieked, in another fit of nerves.
Her Jane, his Lizzie. Her Jane sat and did her embroidery
without a token complaint, while his Lizzie escaped outside
to explore the countryside.

Her Jane had never defied her, except for one instance, an instance in which Mrs. Bennet was not even aware. When she was fifteen, a young man had had pressed his suit towards Jane. Mrs. Bennet had been thrilled, that a young gentleman of such means had been interested in her Jane. From the moment this young man had expressed a preference for her Jane, Mrs. Bennet had pressed Jane to do her best to secure him. Mr. Bennet had largely stayed out of it, until Jane had come to him one evening before going to bed.

Their conversation had been brief, and he had taken care of the matter. Mrs. Bennet did not know, and would not know. She had expressed her regrets to the gentleman when he had announced he was leaving the area, and Mr. Bennet had hoped that would be the end of it. It had not been--as they all had the distinct pleasure of reacquainting themselves with Mrs. Bennet's nerves. However, in that moment, she was his Jane.

He turned to Jane, with a small smile, and a tease on the tip of his tongue.

And then it all went black.

*****

Jane's birthday celebrations had been going well up until

now. It was her twenty-second birthday, another year by which she had to listen to her Mama's worries about her marriageability. Every year, her mama became more and more vocal. Thankfully, Aunt Phillips was here to listen to Mama, while she, Lizzie, Lydia, and Kitty went for her birthday ride. Of course, Lydia and Kitty had begged Papa to be allowed to walk to Meryton.

Sitting next to her papa, feeling the cool air gently wafting by, Jane frowned. She was worried that Lydia and Kitty were becoming entirely too forward, especially for their age. They were not yet out, although she knew that they would soon wheedle Papa into allowing that as well--they and Mama. Jane resolved to speak to Papa about that--perhaps later today. He generally was in a better mood on such a day of celebrations, and he may listen to her. For today.

She didn't want Lydia and Kitty to get hurt. Or commit to a union for which they were not ready. They were so young, Lydia especially. She was only a year or so younger than when Jane had been pressured by Mama to encourage a young man that had paid her suit. While Jane had been initially flattered by such attention, she had quickly felt overwhelmed. By him, by Mama--especially Mama--who had already begun to plan their wedding at the table, while they ate their meal, the morning after he had shown her a preference.

Jane had no wish to disappoint her mama, but she had no

other option. So she went to Papa, and explained the situation as best as she could--how she felt. He'd patted her on the hand, and told her that he would take care of the matter. Papa hadn't spoken of it to her afterwards, nor had she seen him speak to her would be suitor, but some time later the man had left. Mama had been inconsolable, and Jane did her best to comfort her, while inwardly comforted.

She smiled, turning to her Papa, who was not watching the road.

"Papa, be careful."

Her Papa turned to her, every line in his face highlighted not just by the sun's rays, but by his small smile--and then she could not see anything.

*****

Aunt Phillips had immediately left their home to go to Meryton to retrieve Lydia and Kitty. Elizabeth thought, rather uncharitably, that she had left because Mama had already started wailing about her nerves and how they would all starve in the hedgerows, because Mr. Bennet was *dead*. Elizabeth watched, her face impassive and desperately trying to hold in her tears as Mr. Hill laid her Papa out on his bed, for the apothecary. Papa was....not himself.

Although he spent the majority of the day shut away in his library, he was not a sound sleeper, and even the slightest noise would awaken him. To see him like this, so still and quiet, it was unsettling and *wrong*.

Elizabeth knew that Mama would be of no help in these next few, critical hours, as she fluttered and clucked around the doctor. Elizabeth hurried over to Mary, who had been fluttering uselessly at the edge of the room.

"Mary," she murmured quietly, "go see to Mama, please. Take her to her room, and help her get ready for bed. I shall have Kitty bring in some tea once she gets in from Meryton. Perhaps you could read to Mama, from her favorite novel, until then."

Mary nodded mutely, and in a moment of strength, neatly and efficiently dragged an unwilling, hysterical Mrs. Bennet from the room.

Elizabeth watched the doctor do his work, mutely, wanting to ask, wanting to help. She couldn't do anything. The apothecary thrust her from the room.

"Go fetch Mrs. Hill, I have need of her. Tell her to bring hot water and rags."

Elizabeth hurried to do so, grateful to be of some use. Mrs. Hill was in Jane's room, tending to her. Entering the room, Elizabeth felt tears prick her eyes once again.

Jane, mercifully, was not conscious, but her face was swollen and purple. Elizabeth swallowed thickly, willing her mind to *stop* conjuring up the images of her sister being thrown face first into the ground, the carriage following shortly afterwards.

"Mrs. Hill, the apothecary needs you. Have Mr. Hill fetch you some hot water and rags to bring to Papa."

The older woman nodded, seemingly nonplussed by the seriousness of the situation.

 "Miss Bennet's ankle has been wrapped, miss. All she needs now is a cool bath an' some laudanum for the pain when she wakes up. You'll stay with her then?", Mrs. Hill asked brusquely, and then continued on at Elizabeth's hesitant nod. "Don't move her too much, we don' want to upset that ankle until Mr. Jones can look at it." Elizabeth nodded again, and so the older woman left her to her own devices.

Elizabeth nervously moved towards the bed, and laid a hesitant touch on Jane's shoulder, feeling how hot her skin was. The touch burned her fingers, so she quickly withdrew her hand, and moved to the small bowl of cool water on the bed side table. Lifting the soft rag, she gently dipped it into the cool water, wrung it out, and draped it over Jane's swollen face.

Pausing for a reaction, any reaction, she calmed somewhat as Jane's features remained serene. She did not want to cause Jane any more pain. And began to drag the cloth over her face and neck.

When Mr. Jones had been brought in to assess Jane and Mr. Bennet, he had quickly determined that Jane's only ailment was a broken ankle and, perhaps, a concussion, and that after the bruising and swelling went down, she would be good as new. Elizabeth supposed that this was because Jane had been awake when they had finally brought her and Papa in from the road. Awake, but in so much pain. Elizabeth wished she could take back some of the annoyance she had experienced earlier in the day.

Mama had spent the day alternatively upset and clucking over the fact that Jane was now twenty-two years old and unmarried, and then fretting over the fact that her second eldest child was not like the first. Not as demure and proper as her elder sister. Which had led to her announcing that she would take a short walk after breakfast.

Of course, Mama had latched onto that, as evidence of her stubbornness and folly (oh, that she should have been a boy!). Her dear sister had tried to ease Mama's nerves by suggesting a carriage ride, but the damage had been done.

After gently washing and dressing her sister's battered body,

Elizabeth laid a cool hand upon Jane's head, and prayed fervently that all would be well.

*****

The day began as it always did. William Collins woke as though a hot poker had been thrust at his feet, agonizingly white-hot, as he hurriedly splashed cold water on his face, and dressed. His own excellent mother, Mary Delaney Collins, a pious woman of excellent faith and charitable works, had been dead and buried for nearly ten years.

 To that end, his own honorable father, James Thomas Collins, in all his senior wisdom had shifted all the work, normally endowed by their great Creator, to the lady of the house, to himself--his father's only child and heir. For whom else could know better his own father's wants and needs, but his own son? And although his father could be rather difficult and somewhat ornery at times, William Collins contented himself in the knowledge that his good deeds, his utmost attention to his duty would be rewarded to him in heaven.

With these thoughts, William Collins hurried to make a small morning meal of boiled eggs, oats, and tea. Tea was made and poured; the table was set. It would have to do. Mr. Collins, his excellent father, took his seat at the head of the table, and breakfast was eaten in their normal, perfunctory way. There was work to be done.

Thankfully, this morning William Collins did not have to prepare a second pot of tea to his father's liking. The previous morning, it had apparently been steeped for far too long, his own fault, he dared to admit. The bitter tea had caused his father to be attacked by a fit of what must have been apoplexy, which had sent his father into a confused humor--throwing the pot and the cup to the ground.

As a good son does, William Collins had immediately jumped up--after getting over his own shock of course--and immediately placated his dear, suffering father with apologies, assuring him he would, to the best of his knowledge get down to the bottom of this situation. Obviously the blame laid with the disreputable shop that had sold him the tea in the first place.

Although William Collins had told his father that the tea had perhaps been steeped for too long a time, thereby casting the blame upon himself in its entirety, he was quite certain that the shop had been cheating him. Of course, it was his Christian duty to set things to rights, and then show the fruits of his labors to his father--but only then.

Only afterwards, when the deed was finished.

William Collins shuddered in remembrance of an incident

that had taken place with the maid that his good father had employed in the last few years of his dear mother's life. His father was good in that way, thinking of his dear wife's dwindling strength, failing health--by, unfortunately, hiring a harlot of a woman to clean their good, Christian home. He had been around thirteen years of age at the time, when he had found the harlot maid in an embrace, with a man to whom she was not engaged to, let alone joined in holy matrimony with, in their family garden.

To this day, he did not have any idea as to the man's identity--he wished he had, so he could warn the local parish, as he did with the new maid. He had not been able to find his father, after the incident occurred, so he had ran his news to the parsonage, which was separated from his own home by a mere lane. Of course, the rector had been very gratified to hear his news, and had sent him home, after some tarts and a cup of tea--to this awaiting father.
He thought that his news would serve to make his father proud, but it seemed to only anger him as he began to question William. His father had asked him rather pointed questions, such as whether or not he had seen the face of the gentleman or the face of the woman, for that matter. William had been forced to admit that he had not actually seen the faces of either the maid or her lover--but he was certain that it was their maid, because he recognized her outer garments, as belonging to that of their maid.

He had opened his mouth to tell his father of his visit to the parsonage, when his father slapped him to the ground, immediately delivering worthy instruction about what one should do when one sees something like that--namely to confirm all parties before warning other, decent Christian folk.

Of course, it had to do with his dear father's ailments. He was soon to lose his beloved wife, and was overwhelmed with the prospects of raising William Collins, his heir, on his own.

He forgave his father, as God had commanded all Christians to do, and resolved to obey his father in all things--hence taking morning walk to pick up the post, and to speak to the shopkeeper about his abominable tea. He would demand that the shopkeeper throw out the obviously defective product, under his own supervision, receive his payment for the product back in full, and then present the evidence to his father.

While he was there in town, he should also search about for other shops, for he and his father to now purchase from. He was certain that he nor his father would ever again patronize this particular shop. With this in mind, William Collins whistled a jaunty tune, keeping in with the lightness of his steps. All would soon be well.

******

In all other ways, his walk went extremely well. William Collins enjoyed such brisk walks. Exercise was rather good for one's health, and it gave one an opportunity to gaze upon the wonder of God's beauty and majesty. What He had created. He hoped the estate that he was to inherit upon the death of his dear Cousin Bennet, as well as that of his own dear father, that the new Mistress of Longbourn would endeavor to pay such attention to her health, as he was wont to.

 His cousin Bennet's inferior seed was long overdue for supplanting. As his father had always said--his dear Mother had only ever given him one son, one heir, but that it was more beneficial to have only a single heir, as opposed to a houseful of females--for which, as the head of the household, one is bound by the rules of society to provide a dowry for each female child, for when she is to become of marriageable age.

Cousin Bennet had five daughters--he remembered his father becoming agitated each time their dear cousin had written with news of an impending birth. His beloved mother often had to calm his father down, each time such a letter came from their cousin. Of course, he did not fault his dear cousin's efforts in siring a son.

Were he in the same position, God Almighty forbid, he imagined he would do the same. Yet, he also agreed with his excellent father--it was rather a lot of money, money that could be spent elsewhere--enhancing the estate, for example.

But there would be time for that, in the future, William Collins thought as he reached the end of his walk. By next Easter, he would be a fully ordained parson, and would take his orders. Frowning under the now bright, shining sun, William Collins' eyes squinted as he searched out the shop he was looking for. He had a man to speak to.

Chapter Four

Six weeks later......

Light filtered through the white and pink embroidered curtains that adorned Elizabeth and Jane's shared bed; a gift from their Aunt Gardner from a few years past. Even as little as two months ago, Elizabeth would have welcomed such a sight--the sun's rays striking down upon her, beckoning her from her bed, to go for an early morning walk. In times past, only herself and Papa had been up, both eager to face the day on their own terms.

Now, Elizabeth wished to bury herself under the coverlet and never come out. Papa was not dead, but he may as well be--a coma, the apothecary explained. A sleep from which the apothecary had no idea when he would awake from. He explained that it could be at any time--now, six weeks from now, six years from now, or, alternatively never.

Elizabeth burrowed deeper into the covers, concealing herself from what lay beyond her bed. Aunt and Uncle Gardner had arrived only three weeks before, when it was obvious that Papa was not going to wake up any time soon, and so Elizabeth had taken it upon herself to write to her aunt and explain what had happened, especially since Mama had not progressed passed needing her smelling salts on her person, in order to function throughout the day.

Normally, Elizabeth of course would have been excited to see her favorite aunt and uncle, as well as her young cousins, but now none of it mattered. As Mama constantly shrieked and moaned, their futures were all but ruined, being that the estate was entailed. Together, Elizabeth and her sisters would have only have two hundred pounds to live on, and no hope for anything more than what her beloved Aunt and Uncle Gardner would give. Although she had always known that this would most likely be her fate, being that she had vowed to herself to only marry to marry for the deepest love, she mourned for her dear sister Jane.

For what she could have done, who she could have met, who she could have married. For the tiniest instant, Elizabeth had fervently wished that Jane had married the young man who had courted her ardently. Because now, there was nothing left for her. And for that, Elizabeth mourned.

A slight rustle of the coverlet beside her, pulled Elizabeth from her private thoughts. She turned to her sister,

"Jane, are you ready to get out of bed?" she asked carefully, her tone friendly and untroubled.

Jane, sweet and pleasant as ever nodded graciously at her sister, and with some slight difficulty, pulled herself up into a seated position, pushing the coverlet to her waist. Elizabeth quickly moved from the bed, feeling a pang of guilt that she quickly pushed aside to face her sister, and offered Jane her arm.

With some difficulty, as she was still terribly bruised, Jane swung her legs to the end of the bed, gripped Elizabeth's arm, and carefully stood up, taking care to keep her weight off of her right leg. Elizabeth carefully helped her sister to their small armoire and chair, which Jane sank gratefully upon, her face heavily taut with pain.

She turned to her sister with a tight smile,

"I do hope that my ankle will eventually hurt less, in the future. It is quite painful to walk upon it, even with my cane." she said, nodding towards the black and gold cane that their uncle had procured for her.

Elizabeth gave her sister a matching smile, and then quickly turned so that her sister could not see the tears forming within her eyes.

"What shall it be today, Jane? The grey or lavender?"

Being that Mr. Bennet had not passed on, Elizabeth and Jane had made the decision for they and their sisters to wear lighter mourning colours, in terms of grey, purple, lilac, and white. Elizabeth remembered ruefully that that it was the only thing that stopped Lydia and Kitty in their complaining.....

*****

3 weeks earlier....

Elizabeth made her way downstairs for their morning meal, her normal, everyday walks being forgoed in order to be with Jane when she woke up every morning, and to see her Papa before Mr. Hill came to wash and dress him for the day.

Her Aunt and Uncle Gardner had arrived the previous day, and she supposed that she should be glad for it. Aunt Gardner especially was a buffer between herself and Mama, who had not yet gotten out of bed, yet insisted on calling all of her daughters to come attend on her.

A crash came from the next room, a wry smile made its way to Elizabeth's lips, despite her mood. Her younger cousins never ceased to behave as the children they were. Making her way into the breakfast room, Elizabeth watched as her Uncle Gardner drew one of her cousins, the eldest child, James into a different room for a private conversation regarding his behavior.

Elizabeth smiled, and almost went after her uncle to plead with him to be a little more lenient.

Their family and household had gone through a tumultuous

time, a time that would not end until Mr. Bennet was dead and buried, and they were left having to decide what their options were, yet James had behaved remarkably well.

For in previous visits, including their home and his, Elizabeth and Jane had often gone to bed to discover a frog or lizard stuck under the coverlet. One memorable time had included several spiders. That had not occurred during this visit, leading Elizabeth to believe that he did indeed understand the serious nature of what had happened to her father.

Moving over to the table, Elizabeth busied herself by fixing a tray of Jane's favorite foods to bring to her. By the way that it seemed her cousins had the room to themselves, Elizabeth knew that her Aunt Gardner was already up in her Mama's room with a tray.

Hopefully she could persuade her to get out of bed, and face what was happening with a calm and steady head. Piling some fresh, hot rolls onto a place, along with some plum cake and preserves, and made her way back to their room, casually ruffling her cousin Phillip's hair while he concentrated, most seriously, on smothering his bread in as much butter as he could before his father returned to the room.

Elizabeth sat with Jane, taking small bites of the cake that Jane insisted she eat, when a small knock on their door was heard.

"May I come in, dears?" It was their Aunt Gardner.

"Of course, aunt," Elizabeth said as she got up from the chair that she had put beside the bed. She opened the door and allowed her aunt in, gesturing that she should sit in her own chair. Mrs. Gardner waved her concerns away.

"No Lizzie, I am quite fine. I shall only be a moment. I was just thinking that Jane should get out of bed, and come downstairs. Mr. Gardner himself shall carry her downstairs, and I think it would be good for her to not be so contained from everyone. I know that her cousins wish to see her, especially Eliza Jane. And we must all speak of how you girls shall move forward, in terms of mourning. It is an unusual situation, but I feel, and I am sure you do as well, Lizzie dear, that you all must show some degree of mourning."

Unable to do anything else, Elizabeth and Jane simply nodded their assent. Mrs. Gardner simply smiled sadly and said,

"Well, I shall leave you to your breakfast, and for you, Jane to get dressed for the day. I shall come back in half an hour with Mr. Gardner, if that is all right?"

Again, they nodded, and Mrs. Gardner left, shutting the door gently behind her.

Half an hour later, Jane was dressed in a white gown with

small, dainty pink flowers embroidered upon it (the most somber that Elizabeth could find, under the circumstances), and seated at the same table that had most recently held three rambunctious children with their morning meal.

Elizabeth watched as her Aunt Gardner shooed a stubborn Eliza Jane from the proceedings, or, more accurately, her Cousin Jane.

"You will see your cousin Jane in a bit, Eliza Jane. Your father and I have to speak with her and your other cousins, about something to do with Uncle Thomas. We will be done quite soon. Go out into the garden and play with your brothers."

With a small pout, the little girl left the room. Mrs. Gardner made her way to the table, settling herself between a squabbling Lydia and Kitty--who did not stop their dispute, despite the fact that their aunt had physically separated them. No, they simply began to dispute in a greater volume, over who owned said bonnet--

"No, Lyddie, it is mine! I bought it at the milliner's in Meryton, a fortnight ago! You said it was ugly, and would not ever wear it!"

Lydia countered with,

"Yes, I shall have it! For I ripped off the hideous ribbon and re-

trimmed it with a prettier ribbon that I bought with my own money!"

Kitty interrupted, her face going a blotchy pink-red color--

"I did not ask you to rip my bonnet to shreds! Tell her, Aunt Gardner--"

Mrs. Gardner did not have a chance to respond, as Mr. Gardner arrived in the room, and interrupted them with a, "Lydia, Kitty, enough about such frivolous things. Lydia, go and sit next to your sister Elizabeth, Kitty you stay right where you are. There are more important matters at hand, than whose bonnet belongs to whom, and we must discuss them."

Kitty burst into tears, her face going redder still.

"No one ever takes my side, not even Papa! Why should I allow her to have what is mine!" she wailed, uncaring of her uncle's stern glare. Lydia flounced to Elizabeth's side, making a face at her sister as she did so. Kitty let out a fresh batch of tears, and Mrs. Gardner offered her a handkerchief.

"Dear, we shall resolve this later, but now we have more important things to discuss, things that neither you nor Lydia can afford to ignore anymore." she said, referring to the fact that Lydia and Kitty spent the majority of their time in their

shared room, never speaking of what happened to their father, nor attending upon their mother, unless forced.

Kitty shrugged her acquiescence, not caring any more. She would get Lyddie back, no matter what.

Mrs. Gardner nodded for her husband to speak.

"I would first like to tell you girls that I have written to the current heir of Longbourn, Mr. James Collins, as well as his son, William Collins. I have explained the situation, your father's condition and...." here he paused delicately, "....his expected outcome, and have invited them to stay at Longbourn."
Mrs. Gardner kept the conversation going, at his inelegant pause,

"Girls, this is a delicate situation, for which the social graces and protocols do not prepare for. However, to be on the safe side of the law, your uncle and I have determined that it would be best for Mr. Collins and his son to stay, so it does not look like your family is trying to hide your father's condition. For now, it is the best decision to make."

Elizabeth glanced around the table to see how her sisters were taking the news. Lydia and Kitty, of course, were generally uninterested. At fourteen and fifteen years old, respectively, they should have realized how significant and desperate their situation was at this time. Not for the first time, Elizabeth cursed their lack of preparation for adulthood and society at large. They would soon learn, and not within the safe confines of their beloved family.

Mary sat back, her face studious, hanging onto every word that came from her Uncle Gardner's lips. Mary knew better than anyone what was happening, and would most likely attempting to lecture Lydia and Kitty on the subject later, as she had done in previous days over their lack of care towards their father and mother. It was Mary that spent the majority of time with Mama, reading to her from her favorite novels.

Elizabeth was grateful that Mary seemed to put aside her care for more virtuous reading material, in favor of calming down and entertaining their Mama, although their mama was ungrateful about Mary's sacrifice. She could not do it--not while Papa and Jane were in so much pain.

Elizabeth faced Jane, whose face was carefully blank. She reached for her hand, squeezing it gently at Jane's confused, yet concerned frown. She hoped she would see the real Jane soon, not this careful, easy, affable Jane that she has been showing everyone she came into contact with.

Elizabeth turned to her uncle Gardner,

"Have you informed Mama, of this uncle?"

Mr. Gardner indicated "yes" with a nod of his head.

"Yes, Lizzie. I thought at first that I should not tell her until Mr. Collins wrote back, but upon reflection with your aunt, she suggested that I tell her straight away. We thought that perhaps it may induce her to get out of bed and calm her. I told her this morning, after she had finished breakfast. Mrs. Hill is with her now, getting her ready to come downstairs. She seems to be in somewhat better spirits."

Mrs. Gardner continued on with,

"Now we need to speak to you about your clothing, as hard as it is to speak of such things."

At the word clothing, Lydia perked up visibly, while Kitty gave a loud pout that was instantly quelled by her uncle clearing his throat.

"I believe that under these unusual circumstances, a half mourning would be wise. We shall need to go through all of your clothing and bonnets to see what shall match. We may need to go into town---"

At Lydia and Kitty's both excited gasps, Mrs. Gardner added a--

"Of course, it would be inappropriate for any of you girls to be

seen buying fripperies so soon after what has happened to your father, and dear Jane--"

Here, with an almost silent gasp, Jane slipped her hand out of Elizabeth's, and clasped hers together.

"--it would be best if I would do the shopping. If we spend the next few hours doing this, I shall be able to get to the milliner's this afternoon. Then we can begin making up some appropriate gowns for you, once you are fit to receive visitors and friends who wish to express their condolences." Mrs. Gardner ended on a slightly awkward tone of voice.

Elizabeth winced as Lydia and Kitty hurriedly let the room, their voices telling the entire household that they would be the ones to tell their Aunt Gardner first what they wanted for their new gown.

*****

After Jane had finished dressing, Elizabeth handed her the cane that still lay propped up against the wall. Jane gingerly got up, pain etched on her face as she put her full weight onto her ankle. As she watched her, Elizabeth could not help but feel sorrow. Her beautiful sister would never be able to walk again without such an aid as a cane, and would never be seen as the same again. Their own friends and neighbors, with the exception of dear Charlotte, had already begun to treat her differently, paying more deference to Elizabeth herself.

Walking beside Jane, they began their slow descent downstairs to the dining room, where they would eat their morning meal with their family. Mama had finally gotten out of bed the day that they had decided to go into half mourning, and had enthusiastically began helping with the sewing of their clothing, gossiping and giggling with Lydia and Kitty. Elizabeth would have been furious if she had not known that Mama had also taken to badgering Mrs. Hill over the contents of Papa's food, and whether or not it was good for him, would help him wake up again.

Elizabeth helped Jane settle into her chair next to Mama, who insisted on having Jane next to her as much as was humanly possibly. Elizabeth sat next to Jane, and filled her own plate, Mama having taken over in that duty as well. Nibbling on a piece of bread with butter, Elizabeth watched as Mr. Hill brought the mail in to her Uncle Gardner (who sat at the head of table, a fact that never stopped causing her pain whenever she saw it), who went through it disinterestedly, until he came across one such letter that made his face widen in surprise.

"It is a letter from Mr. Collins, I shall read it aloud to you all." he announced.

At this news, Mama made a disgusted face, and began to tell

everyone at the table exactly what she thought of such a letter---

"Well!" she said, flourishing her statement with an abrupt clatter of her cutlery onto her plate.

"I do not wish to hear anything that man says. My dear Mr. Bennet has rarely spoken of such a man, but from what he told me, I should not be sorry to never seen him in my life! Never has a more miserly, miserable, heartless man ever lived! You know he flatly refused to stand up for Mr. Bennet at our wedding! You remember, don't you Edward, my dear brother?!"

Mr. Gardner nodded uneasily,

"Yes, Fanny dear, I remember--."

Mrs. Bennet cut him off.

"To think that he was so angry that Mr. Bennet was marrying me, and had an opportunity for his own heirs to supplant his own. I should be entirely disgraced to be angry that my own dear cousin was marrying, and might have a son or two to inherit his own estate! A disgraceful man! If I had my own way, he would not step a foot in my house! For all we know, dear Edward, that man is going to throw us all out of Longbourn to starve in the hedgerows!"

Her voice took on a shrill, desperate edge, as she allowed herself to imagine what would happen to them.

"My dear Jane, my poor Lydia! What shall become of myself and my girls?!? I shall not be able to rely on yourself indefinitely, as well you know, Edward!" she reminded him primly.

Mr. Gardner held up a hand to calm his youngest sister down.

"Allow me to read the letter first, Fanny. Perhaps it is not as bad as you think."

Mrs. Bennet humphed, but allowed him to read at his leisure.

Mr. Gardner began reading the letter aloud, noticing that it was very short and abrupt.

Mr. Gardner,

My condolences to the Bennet family. I shall be traveling with my son and heir, William Thomas Collins, to arrive at Longbourn within the fortnight. I expect our arrival to be prepared for.

Signed,

James Thomas Collins, Heir of Longbourn
Mrs. Bennet let out an undignified shriek, and left the room. No one stopped her. Mr. Gardner frowned, noting,

"This letter is not dated. The letter I sent informing him of the situation was sent only three weeks ago."

Before he could turn to his wife, she stated,

"Well, I shall put Mrs. Hill on notice that the two Mr. Collins shall be arriving here sometime in the next fortnight, and have her and Maria clean the spare bedrooms."

Mr. Gardner nodded, and she left the room, to perform her errands as she said.

To Elizabeth's surprise, it was Mary who spoke next.

"What will happen next, Uncle Gardner?"

Mr. Gardner nodded brusquely, worried about the contents of the letter.

"I am not quite sure Mary, although I will not lie to any of you. What your mother said was true--your father and Mr. Collins were estranged for many years because of the fact that your father was the heir of Longbourn. Mr. Collins is only the heir now, because your father never produced any sons with your mother. He has made various threats over the years, especially in the early years of your parents marriage, and has only backed off recently because his own son is eligible as the Heir of Longbourn. I find his letter troubling, the animosity he felt from many years ago is just as present as it were twenty years ago."

Looking at their worried and concerned faces, he made quick efforts to reassure them.

"Now girls, do not worry. If the worst comes, know that you are always welcome at our home at Gracechurch Street, no matter our circumstances. We will never abandon family, you all know that."

Elizabeth, in her heart knew that it was true, yet worried that it would come to that. She prayed fervently that it would not, for while her uncle made quite a good income, she knew he was not equipped to handle six females who came with only two hundred pounds a year between them.

Chapter Five

Two weeks later....

"Excuse me, what did you say, Mr. Collins?", blustered Edward Gardner. These were the tones that Elizabeth heard, as she pressed her ear upon the door of her father's study, intently listening for anything, everything that would explain to her their new situation.

Elizabeth had always scolded Lydia and Kitty for listening at doors, but when they had sent her youngest cousin, Eliza Jane, to to tell her to come downstairs and listen to James Collins and their uncle speak in their Papa's study, Elizabeth could not resist, nor did she have the heart to scold them at this time. So she went, pushing them to the side and shushing their giggles, and shoved her ear into the door.

At first, their voices had been too quiet, low murmurings that she could not hear, especially with Lydia and Kitty giggling and whispering to themselves in her other ear, and she was about to push them away so she could hear better, when her uncle's scandalized tones reached her ears.

Elizabeth heard movement, realizing they were coming near the door, and so she quickly grabbed Lydia and Kitty by the hand, and dragged them from the door, and into the next room where they busied themselves in front of the fire, pretending as though they were doing some useful task or other. That did not matter, as her uncle and Mr. Collins took no notice of them, and carried on with their argument, moving into the dining room.

Of course, Elizabeth followed them to the door, listening in, and pushing Lydia and Kitty back.

"We most certainly shall not! My sister and her children are going through a tremendously difficult--."

Mr. Collins oily voice interrupted her uncle. Elizabeth shuddered to hear it. The two Mr. Collins', father and son, had arrived to Longbourn in the middle of the night, with no prior notice, excepting the letter that had been sent to them a fortnight ago.

*****

The previous night.....

Jane's ankle was bothering her, causing her to toss and turn throughout the night.

Subsequently, Elizabeth did not get any sleep at all. She would be more put out by this, if it were not for the fact that she knew that Jane was in a great deal of pain, a lot more pain than she let on. Especially for her to be physically tossing and turning with her sister in the bed beside her.

"Lizzie?" she heard Jane's soft, hesitant voice next to her.

Elizabeth turned her head to look at her sister,

"Do you need some laudanum, Jane?" she asked worriedly, as she saw that Jane was perspiring a great deal, her blonde hair plastered on her forehead and neck. Due to Jane's pain with her ankle, the laudanum was now kept within the confines of their room, for easy access.

Lighting a candle, she went to the drawer that it was kept in. Pouring out a small amount into a glass with water, Elizabeth handed it to her sister, who drank it down gratefully. Going to the small, water filled basin, Elizabeth dipped the small rag in it, wrung it out, and attended to her sister.

"I am fine, Lizzie." Jane said in between gasps. "Just a little hot."

Elizabeth wiped her sister's face and neck, and waited for her to fall asleep, this time for good. Hearing her sister's breathing slow down, she was about to blow out the candle, and climb into bed next to her, when she heard a loud banging coming from outside. It must be the dreaded cousins, but it couldn't be! It was in the middle of the night.

Even so, Elizabeth knocked on the door of her aunt and uncle, waking her uncle to explain the situation. Pulling his robe on, he immediately went downstairs. Elizabeth went to her room and pulled her wrapper on quickly, before following her uncle's footsteps.

It seemed as though the entire household was awake, except Jane, and her Papa, of course. Uncle Gardner unlocked the door, and opened it to reveal a tall, reed thin man, and a younger, heavyset man who was a few inches shorter.

Due to his resemblance to her father, Elizabeth surmised that this must be the dreaded cousin, yet why had he arrived in the middle of the night, well past midnight?

Her uncle Gardner hadn't said a word. The man, James Thomas Collins' surveyed them all--all bleary eyed and somber, dressed in their night clothes--his eyes going narrow. His lip curled, as he brusquely said,

"Am I to assume that you lot want my heir and I to freeze outside the manor until Cousin Thomas. "--this was delivered with as much disgust and envy as one could muster in a name--dies on us?"

Elizabeth felt her uncle stiffen at the insult, and contained her own gasp. Papa had never spoken of his cousin, James Collins to her. The only information she had of him were things overheard at the door of his study, and delivered to herself and Jane, by way of Lydia and Kitty during their weekly jaunts to Meryton and the shops.

Generally, the subject of his cousin had only been brought up when Mama would get worried about their futures after their papa died, and would thus require Papa to soothe her nerves.

She had only known what Mama had said at the table some weeks before, when Uncle Gardner had told them all that he had written.

Uncle Gardner motioned all of them to move away from the door to allow the two men inside. Mary had been nearest to the two men, and so Mr. Collins withdrew his coat, and thrust it in her arms. Elizabeth recoiled at the insult and blatant disrespect, and moved forward to tell him so, when her Aunt Gardner subtly moved forward, taking the coat from Mary's arms.

"I think you girls should get to bed, go on. We shall do proper introductions in the morning, I think. Go on."

With a meaningful look to Elizabeth, she then focused her attention on Mr. Collins and his son--who had been oddly quiet at this point.

*****

Elizabeth sat on the divan, pretending to listen to the young

Mr. Collins read to them aloud from *Mr. Fordyce's Sermons*.

Although they, with the exception of the elder Mr. Collins and, perhaps Mary, were pretending to be interested and listening to the younger Mr. Collins read (even Lydia and Kitty, although they had been soundly chastised by their aunt when they had carried on with their giggling and whispering to each other) no one was listening. Elizabeth certainly wasn't.

Their morning meal, and what had occurred afterwards still had Elizabeth on edge with dread for what would happen to them, especially after their aunt and uncle left for their home in Gracechurch street in a few short hours.

The day had begun as always, although Elizabeth was a bit tired, having been unable to fall asleep until the wee hours of the morning due to her fretting. It had evened out because her sister had slept in a bit later, due to the laudanum, and woke her up. She helped Jane dress in her newly dyed grey and white dress trimmed with lilac lace, and then they both went carefully down the stairs.

Taking in the scene at the dining room table, Elizabeth knew that their first impressions of the elder Mr. Collins would not be expunged. He sat at the head of the table, with his son and her uncle on either sides. Mama had been in her customary place, and did not look happier for it.

His son, she decided then, was a fool. While he certainly was not as bad as his father, nor quite so rude and angry, there was something desperately silly and foolish about him. No common sense. Something that he and his father had shared, no doubt, as he had openly gawked at Jane's leg, covered by her gown. She looked at her Uncle Gardner, a silent plea for help.

Elizabeth returned his look with one of her own, and began to sharply retort when her uncle involved himself, stating,

"Miss Bennet was injured in the carriage accident, as well you know, Mr. Collins. I informed you myself that her ankle had been crushed."

It was then, that the younger Mr. Collins spoke, his voice taking on an excited fervor.

"I would hope that the eldest Miss Bennet would thank our Lord God that her own life was not forfeit during such an adventure. Such a wonderful example of our Lord's graciousness and mercy, that he should spare her life, and--."

He looked at them all 'round the table, his voice growing more and more excited, until he reached his father's grim, unsmiling face, and grew silent.

Elizabeth could not forgive that, even as Jane reached under the table, and gently squeezed her hand in warning, her own face open and gentle, as she smiled beatifically at the father and son, along the table. She said, coolly,

"You are correct, Mr. Collins. I shall endeavor to remind my sister of that very thing, as our friends and neighbors speak of her as though she were not in front of them."

The younger Mr. Collins had blustered, only stopping, again, at a look that his father gave him. Elizabeth would have felt sympathy for him, if they were here under different circumstances. If her life had not been flung from one end to the other.

And now, as she pretended to listen to the meek, silly young man read the dreadfully boring *Fordyce's Sermons* she could not help but worry. As she had succinctly overheard through the walls of the study and sitting room, the elder Mr. Collins had ordered her aunt and uncle to vacate Longbourn this very day.

Maria, their maid, had been dispatched to pack their things for them to leave after their mid-day meal. Not even Mrs. Bennet's overexcited pleadings and cries had convinced the miserly old man to allow her brother to stay.

Elizabeth let out a mournful sigh, remembering a time when Mama would do the same to Papa--he refusing to do something that she had asked, allowing herself to be worked up, before agreeing or presenting her with something better than what she had expected.

Her excited shrieks would fill the entire house, a ritual that used to annoy Elizabeth, but now she wished for it, more than anything in the world.

"Something the matter, Miss Bennet?"

Elizabeth was jerked out of her musings with the question, asked by the elder Mr. Collins, in a tone dripping with insincerity.

Elizabeth gave him a smile that matched his own attitude, and replied in an equal tone, "Not at all Mr. Collins. However, *Miss Bennet* is getting a bit restless. I beg your leave to dress for a walk. Miss Bennet needs to exercise her ankle."

The elder Mr. Collins shrugged his shoulders and focused on the wall behind her, and so Elizabeth took that for permission, and got up, nearly dragging Jane with her. She had to leave this house, those people, else she did not know what she would do or say.

After assuring her Aunt Gardner that she would return before their mid-day meal, Elizabeth and Jane set off into the very woods that had upturned their lives. Elizabeth closed her eyes and inhaled deeply, breathing in the scents of the woods she'd traversed her entire life.

It was a particularly beautiful fall day, and Elizabeth enjoyed the variety of colors that surrounded them. Jane walked steadily beside her, leaning heavily on her cane. Once Jane's breathing changed, she led them to a large rock for Jane to lean upon and rest.

"How are you feeling, Lizzie?"

Elizabeth turned to her sister, not even managing a smile for the one that Jane bestowed upon her, even more frequently since the accident.

"I'm worried, Jane. That is all. There is a reason we never heard much from this cousin, or his son for that matter. He treated Papa abominably, simply because Papa stood to inherit Longbourn, dared to marry Mama, or any woman for that matter, and *try* to conceive heirs. And I most certainly do not like how both dismissed your pain and what you have suffered! Even if they are to inherit--that does not mean they have a right to treat us or you like that! Papa is not dead yet!" she finished angrily.

Jane stood upright, and then leaned into Elizabeth with a soft sigh.

"I can only hope and pray, Lizzie, that Papa will wake up. That everything will be resolved for our own good, in the end. That is all we can do, Lizzie."

Elizabeth pressed a kiss into her sister's hair, desperately hoping that she would be correct, and that it would all work out to the betterment of their Mama and sisters. But that would not change what had happened--perhaps with Papa, but not with Jane.

Elizabeth hesitated for a moment, before saying softly,

"I-I wish that I had been in that carriage with Papa, Jane."

Jane tightened her grip around Elizabeth, wishing she could say what she wanted, without hurting her sister, without acknowledging her own hurt herself.

"Don't wish that, Lizzie. Things happen, because they are meant to. And there is nothing we can do about it. We can only choose how we handle the adversities that life, and, well *God,* " she added cheekily, hoping it would cause her sister to laugh, "brings to our paths."

*****

Elizabeth and Jane walked for another ten minutes or so, until Elizabeth noticed that Jane was leaning more heavily on her cane, her breath coming out in short gasps. They went back, and Elizabeth went to help her sister into the house, when Jane waved her off.

"No, Lizzie, Mary can help me into the house. I'll sit on the divan, and do some reading. I know that is your favorite walk. Go. I am a poor companion for it now, if I ever was."

Elizabeth smiled gratefully at her sister. It *was* her favorite walk, one she had not taken in many weeks--at first, out of fear that it would remind her too much of what had happened, then, because it became a symbol of everything she now held over her elder sister.

"Yes, Jane, I shall--."

"No, you shall not."

Elizabeth frowned as she turned and faced the elder Mr. Collins, his voice oily-smooth and indulgent in the knowledge that he now held her fate within his hands. She held her temper in check, and smoothed her face of all disgust or anger.

"Mr. Collins?" she questioned quietly.

He studied her with a piercing gaze, intent on reminding her of her place, a fact she was not likely to forget as she listened to the clock tick, as her wait grew longer and longer. Finally, he deigned to answer her.

"Miss Bennet, it is not appropriate for a young woman of your--" here his mouth curled as though he tasted something particularly unpleasant-- " *stature* to walk in the woods alone. As you are well aware, one might not know what could happen. If Cousin Bennet had been alone in those woods, who knows how long it would have taken him to be found, and what may have happened to him."

He finished his point with a sordid smile, as though he wished to elaborate.

"I thank you, sir, for your concern of my safety," she retorted icily, "although I would wish that you would address me properly, as Miss Elizabeth. Miss Bennet, as you see," she said, gesturing to a somber Jane behind her on the divan, "is seated right behind myself."

The elder Mr. Collins said nothing but strode out of the room, and yelled "William!"
Elizabeth frowned, not knowing why he was calling his son, although noting that it was the first time that she had heard him refer to him by name.

He turned to her saying abruptly, "You are now a member of my household, *Miss Bennet*. You will behave accordingly, and that starts by being escorted when you are not within this house. My heir will escort you on this walk."

The younger Mr. Collins, although she had surmised from their second meeting that he was a fool, she had not paid much attention to due to the more present threat that was his father, arrived looking shamelessly out of breath.

Had he *ran* down the stairs? Elizabeth glanced over to the elder Mr. Collins, noting how his face darkened even as he looked over his own son.

"You will escort Miss Bennet on her walk. Go."

The breathless Mr. Collins gave her what could only be loosely described as a grin, and offered his arm. Taking it gingerly, Elizabeth wondered what she had gotten herself into.

*****

Elizabeth sat between Jane and Mary, her eyes focused on the few slices of pheasant that she had mindlessly cut into small, bite sized pieces. She did not feel like eating, her stomach rolling as she tried to force a small piece down her throat. Immediately after her walk with the younger Mr. Collins, she had tried to go directly to his father, who had ensconced himself in her Papa's study.

He had not wanted to hear what she had to say, and had ordered her from the study. She did not know what to do, or who to go to. Mama surely would not be of much help, as they were both under the same rule.

The table was silent, not even Lydia and Kitty doing their usual giggling and whispering among themselves, when they were not fighting that very instant. Beside Jane, Mama was glaring mutinously at her own plate, having been supplanted by the younger Mr. Collins, who chewed noisily, making small hums of pleasure at the rich food.

Elizabeth shuddered, as she felt his eyes upon her. She glanced away at the elder Mr. Collins, who ate very little, and focused more on his wine glass, his eyes already growing bloodshot.

Draining the rest of his glass, the elder Mr. Collins brusquely motioned for Mr. Hill to refill his glass, and then abruptly addressed those seated,

"I suppose now that the *Gardner's*,"--he said the name as particularly repugnant word-- "are gone, we can discuss the changes that I am going to implement in this household."

It was Elizabeth's turn to curl her lip.
"And what sort of changes would you be making, sir?" she asked boldly, looking him straight in the eye, refusing to

back down from his tone.

"Didn't my heir inform you, Miss Bennet?"

He watched with satisfaction as her face went white with barely subdued rage. She kept her tongue, though. Although it was too little, too late for that sort of thing. She had already opened the floodgates. Well, it would not be happening again. Not unless she wanted her twit of a mother, cripple elder sister, and silly, nitwitted younger sisters to be able to live in *his* estate.

He had waited over twenty years to have his due, and he wasn't going to let some female upstart gain threshold over him. His heir, useless as he was, would need to be taught how to handle her. Keeping her burdened with his child, year after year, would be an excellent start.

First, the old fool upstairs would have to pass on from this world, and then their plan could move forward. If it came to pass that the old man was taking too long to pass, he could *help* him.

It would even be seen as a mercy, for Thomas Bennet was not truly alive in any sense. A mummer's life.

 If he did not naturally pass within the time it took to *train* a wife, he would explore alternate means of gaining his due.

However, there were still things he could do, as the *defacto* head of household. And it seemed that Miss Bennet would need the extra time in order to teach her her place. It seemed the walk with his heir had done absolutely nothing but raise her ire. He could not blame her, for his heir was foolish, but in a way that could be manipulated and used for his own good. In time, she would realize, no matter how foolish, it was not her place to question, but obey. Not if she wanted her family to survive.

Gesturing for his wine glass to be filled again, he tipped it back with the ease of a man who had been drinking to the excess, for many years. A coughing fit overtook him, and he hastily withdrew his handkerchief from his pocket, to collect the excess phlegm.

Afterwards, he barked at his heir to get him his pipe, and some tobacco. The foolish boy did so, the only useful thing he was able to do--obey a direct order.

With his pipe lit, and smoke filling his lungs, he exhaled a pleasure filled sigh, and gave Miss Bennet a smile. A genuine, pleasure filled smile.

Chapter Six

A short time later.......

It was still quite dark, but Jane saw no need to wait any longer. Her ankle was burning, and she could not sleep. The sun would be up in an hour, generally when she and Kitty started their work. Jane sat up and swung her legs, with some difficulty, to the edge of the bed. Grabbing blindly for her cane, she helped herself up with a small wince, and moved to light the candle. The light illuminated them in a soft glow. Kitty was still asleep, her face serene and calm. There were no worries when one was asleep, nothing to do but dream.

With some difficulty, Jane went to her gowns and laid out a simple morning dress and wrap on the bed, before quickly undressing in front of the small bowl of water. She swiftly gave herself a quick wash and splashed cool water on her face, securing her long blond hair into a simple bun. Hearing movement from the bed, she saw that Kitty was awake.

"You don't have to get up for a while yet, Kitty." she said, as she watched Kitty rub the sleep from her eyes.

"It's all right, Jane. This is more sleep than what I get with Lyddie. Lyddie likes to kick, and is always grabbing the covers from me. Poor Mary!"

Her eyes lit up with a mischief that Jane had not seen in a long while. Of course, even that dimmed at her next sentence.

"It is a good thing Mr. Collins did not put her with--." Kitty trailed off, unsure how to proceed. With great difficulty and pain, Jane limped her way to the bed, without her cane, and sat next to Kitty, feeling quite silly in her undergarments. She pulled her arms around Kitty, laying her head on her breast. Kitty pulled away after a minute or so, hopping to the end of the bed where her gown was, and picking it up.

"Come Jane! Put your gown on, and I shall do your hair better. Lyddie taught me a style that I think would become you very well."

Smiling, Jane allowed her sister to do so, and then returned the favor. In some ways, Jane was glad that she and Kitty were now sharing a space. She was seeing a side in her second youngest sister that she perhaps never would have seen, being that she and Lizzie were so close. Yet, Lizzie was her sister, her best friend, and it was not the same.

Jane ached for her sister. Lizzie was all alone, and there was nothing that any of them could do about it. She would marry Mr. Collins, and they would all be able to stay at Longbourn. Perhaps, in a few years, Lizzie would be able to convince the elder Mr. Collins that Lydia, Kitty, and Mary would be better served going to live with their Aunt and Uncle Gardner, but Jane would stay. Always.

She knew that no matter how she looked, she was now un-eligible for marriage. No man, who would have taken her with her dowry and looks before the accident, would take her with the added problem of her ankle and cane.

Perhaps this was God's will. God's gift to her. She had been sitting right next to her papa when the accident occurred, yet she received relatively inconsequential injuries compared to his. If she had gone the same way he had, her Lizzie would be going through this ordeal alone. Would be dealing with both the Mr. Collins' alone, and Mama.

Jane knew Lizzie was strong and stubborn, but the Bennet household was not the same.

Jane remembered, ever since they had come through womanhood together, gone to the same assemblies, danced with young, handsome men, and fussed over their gowns, that they had an idea of how their lives would turn out.

Lizzie had always teased her under the coverlet, that a wealthy young man would suddenly appear at the assembly, fall passionately in love with her, and marry her on the spot. Lizzie would be the maiden aunt to their many children, and they would live happily together.

That was not to be, not anymore, and Jane would make the best of it. She would take care of her sisters in any way she could, and that would now be her purpose. She would deal with Mama, and work upon the Collinses in order to give them their best chance.

Jane helped Kitty arrange her hair, although she was wildly out of practice due to both she and Lizzie's preference for simple hair styles. Her fingers ached with all the braiding she had been doing recently.

The sun was now up, and she and Kitty started their day, making their way to the small room that their Papa had been moved to.

Mr. Hill had been in charge of Papa's care, washing and feed him through a tube that the apothecary had sent for. The elder Mr. Collins had insisted that Jane and her new bedmate, Kitty, take on some of the responsibility for their father. Although he was not quite so shocking as to insist that Kitty and Jane bathe their father, they were now responsible for feeding him, and turning his body so he did not develop sores.

Kitty went downstairs to get their Papa's food ready, a thin gruel made of vegetables, meat, and gravy.

Jane was left alone with him. As she often felt Lizzie do so in the days after her accident, she laid a cool hand on Papa's forehead. His body was warm, and she dreaded the day that he would grow cool under her touch. Her hand trailed down to touch his forehead and lips, caress his beard that was just starting to grow in. Mr. Hill would need to shave him later tonight, after his wash. Smoothing over the skin of his neck and cheeks, she saw that he was getting thinner and thinner, despite their best efforts.

The elder Mr. Collins claimed that their papa did not need as much food, when he was not contributing anything to the household, yet Jane and Mrs. Hill found ways to sneak more and more food into him--using some of the scraps that might normally go to the pigs, and so on.

Every day, Jane's body tightened with tension whenever they went into Papa's room to ready him for the day, hoping and praying that this would not be the day that she found him dead. From then on, it would be a four or five months or so before Lizzie and Mr. Collins could properly wed, perhaps even before, due to the special circumstances that they were in. Most people, from around Meryton and even London, would perhaps cluck their tongues over it for a year or so, and then happily agree that it was for the best.

It would come to that, one day soon, and Jane hoped she had the strength to hold herself up, as well as Lizzie.

Their morning meal would not be due to start for another three hours, so Jane and Kitty walked to their greenhouse, a short distance from their home, to tend to the plants.

Jane could still hear all the goings on within the kitchen, and it seemed that Lydia was not adjusting to her new duties.

As Jane and Kitty had to take care of their father, feeding him thrice a day and the like, so Mary and Lydia had to help Mrs. Hill with the preparation of meals. Jane thought Mrs. Bennet would have died of shame if it had not meant that she could not screech in the face of the elder Mr. Collins.

An hour or so later, Kitty and Jane headed inside to change their shoes for a light walk about the estate. Jane was determined to get over the pain of her ankle, sooner, rather than later, as well as the added opportunity that it gave her to escape the house. Kitty retrieved her boots, and on their walk they went.

Kitty skipped gaily ahead of Jane, who has glad to see her happy. Once separated from Lydia, Kitty had become reserved and quiet, almost instantly. Jane had been worried, afraid that Kitty would hate that she was stuck with her, her crippled elder sister who needed help to dressing herself, and the like.

She knew that Mr. Collins had only paired them together

because it was a way to separate Lydia and Kitty, both of whom spent their days alternately spending quality time gossiping and doing lacework, or otherwise fighting over the silliest of things. Where Papa shut himself in his library and Mama took Lyddie's side, Mr. Collins, neither of them, stood for it.

And thus, there they were. Pairing a silly girl with a cripple, and an even sillier girl with a moralising force.

Their walk ended, and so their morning meal began. Their seating, of course, was regimented to Mr. Collins' choice, and it had caused no small amount of grief. Mama still ground her teeth whenever they sat to a meal. Jane smiled sadly as she finally saw Lizzie again, for the first time today.

Lizzie sat above her, yet they were still together, so Jane did not much care for their seating. Both Mr. Collins joined them, the younger Mr. Collins greeting his father obsequiously. Receiving a grunt in return from his father, Mr. Collins focused his attention on Elizabeth.

"And how are you this beautiful morning, my dear Miss Bennet?" he asked her in an oily voice that Jane supposed was meant to be affectionate.

Jane watched as Lizzie paused for a brief moment, as she had been pouring herself some water from the decanter in front of her, her hand shaking slightly. Jane gently took the decanter from her, pouring the water for her.

Lizzie flashed her a grateful smile, as the elder Mr. Collins cleared his throat in clear warning.

As Lizzie turned to Mr. Collins, Jane could see the hint of strain in her smile, the tired wariness in her eyes.

"Yes, of course, Mr. Collins it is a lovely day. I am well." she said, and then hesitantly continued on. "I saw that Jane and Kitty took a walk this morning."
The younger Mr. Collins smiled again. The elder Mr. Collins looked at his heir, with interest in what he was about to reply to her obvious query.

"Yes, I imagine so my dear, but Miss Jane *must* exercise her leg for the betterment of her health. You, however, are too busy to do such things. Perhaps later, in this coming Spring, you shall have much time for such frivolities." he said, referencing the lessons she now received in the morning before their meal, and afterwards.

Jane forced herself to calm as she glanced at the smirk that briefly touched the elder Mr. Collins' lips. Forcing herself to change the subject, she turned to Mary to compliment her on the preserves she and Lydia had helped Mrs. Hill make the previous days. Beside her, Lizzie relaxed minutely as

Lydia began to complain of all the work it took to make her favorite preserves, her eyes darting nervously to the head of the table, although in a much quieter voice than she would have if it had been only six months previous.

Jane slid her hand in Lizzie's lap, finding her fingers. They would always have each other, no matter what.

*****

"Jane, my dear, come and sit next to your mama!" Mama brightly patted the seat next to her, encouragingly.

Jane sat next to her, somewhat resigned, as Mama had taken to bemoaning their fates, in a much quieter voice, though, to Jane near daily. She had just returned, her and Kitty from turning Papa, and she was tired. Much too tired to deal with Mama as she had to. As uncharitable as it was, Jane was glad that this was the only part of the day that she and Mama spent any real time together.

The elder Mr. Collins insisted on the Bennet women being separated for the majority of the day, for the betterment of their general health and the Longbourn estate, especially keeping Elizabeth away from them. Jane knew that he thought it would break them, break her.

She would see to it that it would not, and they, the Bennet

family would go through this. Any child that Mr. Collins and Lizzie may have would bear the name "Collins", but Jane would give her life so that the child would grow to be a Bennet.

"Jane!"

Jane jerked out of her thoughts guiltily, as it was Lydia who was now demanding her attention.

"Yes, Lyddie?"

Lydia spoke at full speed, especially now that they were left to their own company.

"Tonight in our room, Mary and I are going to rip Mary's bonnets to shreds. They're frightfully dull, even if for half mourning, and I shall also have to show you a new hairstyle that becomes her a lot more than the dull bun she keeps it in! Do you have any more ribbon? I'll trade you my green slippers for any scraps you may have."

Jane laughed as she said,

"They were mine before, but yes, Lyddie. I have some ribbon in my room from when Lizzie--."

Beside her, Mama heaved a great sigh. Jane continued on, as though nothing had happened.

While Mama and Lizzie had not been as close as they could have been, before the accident, their relationship had been strained further, afterwards.

Although Mama had not been quiet about it, to Jane, to anyone who was not named "Collins", it was easy to see in her attitude.

Jane wanted to shake her, slap some sense into her to see the sense of how she was behaving--how it affected everyone else in the household. Especially Lizzie.

*****

Jane sat upright next to Lizzie, hardly comprehending what she was hearing. After their evening meal was finished, the elder Mr. Collins ushered them all into their parlour. Lizzie had stayed behind her, as always to make sure that she did not need any help.

Jane, not for the first time since her accident, had thought rather uncharitably that she did not want any help. It had only been weeks since the accident, and Jane was simply tired of the pity. Of being catered to, of being asked about her feelings, of being treated like an invalid.

She settled down next to Lizzie, and gave the elder Mr. Collins her full attention.

"I shall be brief." he said, his voice oily and condescending as it generally was when he addressed them; he was enjoying every single word. They were the glasses of red wine he had guzzled down at dinner.

"Mr. Bennet and I were not on the best of terms, as I am sure he informed you all---."

"He certainly did!" Mama exclaimed, jumping to her feet. "He explained to me what a disgraceful---!"

The elder Mr. Collins cut her off with a high and tight voice, a dangerous edge to his words.

"Calm yourself, Mrs. Bennet. I am only going to say this once. I am in charge now. Your husband is not dead, yet he may as well be. You know this. We all know this. It is only a matter of time before he will be dead and buried in the ground. When that happens, you shall all be at my mercy. I know well of what portions you all shall bring to any such marriages you may make."

The tone of his voice concluded that he thought that this was a rather ludicrous, if necessary statement to make. He turned to her sister Lizzie then,

"Miss Bennet, tell us, what portion shall you bring to your marriage to my heir?"

Jane withheld a wince, wanting to be strong for Lizzie, for herself. She was no longer Miss Bennet. Not to this man, not to her friends and neighbors.

He was merely putting a voice to all the thoughts that went through everyone's minds once they heard about the terrible, terrible accident, and what had happened to Jane. Mama sat ramrod straight at the news, and looked as though she desperately wished to protest. Her face slowly turned a deeper and deeper red, as though the words she had to keep within were physically painful.

Moments passed, and the younger Mr. Collins said in a faux soothing voice, "My dear, my gracious father asked you a question. Answer him. Naturally, I do not judge you for your father's actions, and inattention to the finances of Longbourn. Such things were none of your concern. We shall have to discuss it after your father's death, but such things---."

His own father cut him off, already bored by the proceedings. The younger Mr. Collins sat back in his chair, quietly defeated. His father turned to Lizzie again.

"Miss Bennet?"

Jane felt Lizzie take a deep breath, and then answered in a low, slightly trembling voice. Jane had never heard her speak in such a tone. Lizzie had always been a self assured, confident young woman, always ready to make an opposing point or defending a dear friend.

"I will bring a sum of one thousand pounds, on the event of my marriage to Mr. Collins," she paused, before continuing with, "after my papa's death."

The elder Mr. Collins smiled malevolently at Lizzie, as though she were a young child performing a dictation of the alphabet or numbers for her mother for the very first time.

"That's right." he said, his voice dripping with false sincerity. He addressed the rest of them. "This marriage will not take place for some time, so before that we shall get this household in order. Your daughters," he said, specifically addressing a silently fuming Mrs. Bennet, "are out of control. I am speaking of the two youngest ones."

Lydia and Kitty squawked in outrage at being spoken as thus, yet were quelled by the attention of his gaze on them. "Their behavior reflects badly on this home, and I will not allow it. As for the other two--" his gaze resting on Jane and Mary, "they shall prove that they are the worth the pounds it takes to feed them. To that end, there shall be changes in accommodation."

He studied them for a few moments before saying "Miss Jane and Miss Kitty shall the room that Miss Kitty and Miss Lydia share. Miss Lydia will move into Miss Mary's room, while Miss Bennet will stay where she is. It is not negotiable." he said harshly, at Mrs. Bennet's protest.

"Miss Jane and Miss Kitty will take over the care of their father. He is taking too much time away from Mr. Hill's duties at the farm. The two others will help Mrs. Hill in the kitchen before breakfast.

I am sure we can find some things for you to do, Mrs. Bennet that do not include bankrupting the estate."
he said, referring to Mrs. Bennet's rather limited and uninformed performance as the Mistress of Longbourn, at least in the matters of finance and savings.

"Each and every one of you shall earn your place in this household. You are the ones who bring nothing but debts, and all of you would do well to remember such a thing. The only reason you and your daughters have a place here are because of the simple fact that your daughter will be marrying my heir. And that mercy does not extend far."

Jane did not know where to look, from the elder Mr. Collins, his face impassive yet shining with satisfaction, to her Mama, who had forgone her usual shrieks, directed Mary to retrieve her smelling salts, to Lydia and Kitty who were hysterically protesting the restrictions that were now placed upon them. Her gaze swung to her sister Elizabeth. Lizzie looked down to *her lap, her fingers going from tightly clasped within each other, to playing with the fabric of her gown.*

None of this was news to her. Lizzie knew before everyone else, exactly how their lives would be going forward from this day.

Chapter Seven

Start of Canon Pride and Prejudice.......

Elizabeth smoothed down her gown, trying to keep her nerves steady as Mrs. Bennet jerkily fixed her hair into an elegant and simple updo. She winced, drawing her shoulders in as she was stabbed with a pin once again. Beside her, Jane reached to touch her mama's shoulder, already dressed for the coming assembly. Mrs. Bennet turned to Jane.

"Mama, would you like a glass of port? Mr. Hill put a few bottles of Papa's port in my and Kitty's room, in case I had need of it during the night."

When the Collins had arrived, Jane's use of laudanum had been curtailed, citing the price and knowledge that use of it would not return her ankle to its natural state.

Mrs. Bennet nodded gratefully, and Elizabeth could not help but embrace her mama. The woman that was her mama would have been flittering up and down the stairs for the whole of a full three days before the assembly would occur, making sure that her girls were arrayed in the finest garments their money could buy, simply for the fact that a wealthy, honorable gentleman was to be their new neighbor.

A possible match for one of her girls. For Jane, the loveliest of all the Bennet sisters. And now that would never come to pass.

"Mama," Elizabeth could not help but say, "everything shall all come to pass it as it should. We need not worry ourselves with situations we cannot change." Kitty entered the room, bearing the small glass of port that Mrs. Bennet swiftly drained in a single turn. Elizabeth held back a wince, as her mama began to gain more and more of a tolerance for such a drink--like the elder Mr. Collins.

"Of course, Lizzie, I do not blame you, nor dear Jane! Oh how I wish your father had not taken my dear girl in that carriage! We would not be on the verge of starving in the hedgerows!" she said, grasping the hands of an uncomfortable looking Jane.

Elizabeth tried to soothe Mrs. Bennet--"Mama, we shall not starve--"

Mrs. Bennet continued on, "Of course that perfidious Mr. Collins shall marry you when your father is cold in his grave, but that man is just like his father! A miserly fool who shall turn the rest of us out, mark my words!"

The hard thing with her mama was that it were as though

everything had happened only the day before. Mrs. Bennet had not grieved, but remained in a constant state of newfound fears. However, they were not new, and had even lessened somewhat. Mrs. Bennet had turned into a more subdued version of herself, due to outward influences, but ever so often, her true self returned.

Elizabeth was tired of it. She already had to be strong in front of their neighbors and society, and then within her own home--with her mother, her younger sisters, and Mr. Collins. The only person who had an inkling of her true feelings was her dear Jane. And she had made Jane promise never to tell a soul.

"My dear, are you ready?" Mr. Collins asked anxiously from the bottom of the staircase.

Elizabeth held in a shudder, but just barely. If there ever was a man that could make her skin crawl, Elizabeth was sure none could do such a job as Mr. William Collins. She was only grateful, as terrible as it sounded, that his father was gone--dead for close to nine months now.

Mr. Collins had found his father dead shortly before Christmas, in his bed.

He had not been in her papa's study, when she had gone to meet him at their usual time in the morning before their morning meal.

She had waited and waited, sitting ramrod straight in her chair across from the master of the house, her eyes fixed forward. Waiting for the elder Mr. Collins, whilst praying every morning and night that his cough would grow weaker and weaker, until one day, he just did not cough anymore.

He had been dead, died in his sleep, and Elizabeth was glad. As bad as Mr. Collins was, he was nothing to his father. In many respects, her torment had been abated with the death of the elder Mr. Collins, and that was not something Mr. Collins could take from her. Elizabeth could have felt a smidgen of sympathy for him. To be raised by such a man.

However, any modicum of sympathy she had was gone once he opened his mouth, as always. And she would never forgive nor forget what he had said about Jane upon their first meeting.

Brushing a kiss on her sister Lydia's forehead, she promised her that she would tell her everything about the the gowns of their new neighbors, the Bingleys, who were said to be attending the assembly tonight. Going down the staircase, she took the proffered arm of Mr. Collins as he led her out of Longbourn to attend Meryton's local assembly. Glancing back, she returned her sister Kitty's smile with one of her own. She, Jane, Mr. Collins, Mama, and Mary were going to the assembly rooms in Meryton for the local ball.

Charlotte Lucas, her dear friend, had to see her and her sisters with the news.

*****

"My dear Miss Bennet, your dear friend Miss Lucas is awaiting you in the parlour." Mr. Collins bowed over Elizabeth's hand, gesturing grandly to her friend Charlotte who was a mere ten feet away. To keep appearances, Elizabeth bobbed a short curtsy and went to her friend. Mr. Collins left, finally.

"Shall I pour the tea?" Charlotte asked archly, as her hands moved to do so already.

"Yes, thank you Charlotte." Elizabeth accepted the offered cup of tea, and sipped it slowly, ignoring the slightly bitter taste.

The hot liquid settled the deep, sinking feeling she felt every time Mr. Collins was near. "So what news do you bring for us today?"

Charlotte offered her friend a knowing smile. "Well, as it happens," she started playfully, "I do have some news. I am surprised your mother has not heard of it yet." she chided gently.

Elizabeth smiled uneasily. Although Charlotte was much more aware of the turmoil that the Bennet family had gone through, were still going through, there were many, many things that Charlotte was unaware of, would not understand. Charlotte was so practical and unbending. Nothing ever took her by surprise, or startled her.

Elizabeth could see now, telling her friend all that had happened to them, in every excruciating detail, and Charlotte would point out the good that had come from something so horrifying as what had happened. And some good had come.

Lydia and Kitty had been forced to grow up quickly, and had been forced to give up their adulation of the officers in their fine red coats. Mary had been pulled from her own world of practicing the pianoforte incessantly, and of her constant, and unnecessary moralizing.

In the months that Elizabeth had been separated from her sisters, Jane had grown close and mothered the three of them in ways that their own mother could not.

After the elder Mr. Collins died, and some terse discussions followed in Jane and Kitty's room, they had gotten their grievances out, and accepted Elizabeth as their sister--their true sister. It was no longer them against Elizabeth, as Lydia, Kitty, and Mary had felt even before the accident. They truly were sisters in every sense of the word.

All of that was due to the very man who thought he could destroy them.

"Well, you know Mama has no time for such things anymore, Charlotte. But tell me the news!" she said excitedly. Although much more reasoned and mature, Kitty and Lydia, and even Mary were still only young girls. Being inside the house, no longer being allowed to consort with the officers, no longer able to bang on the piano at all hours, was stifling for them. Diversion was needed.

Charlotte obliged her. "A Mr. Bingley has arrived from London, to lease the Netherfield estate. He visited my father some weeks ago, right before settling the lease. I believe he is returning for the next assembly, with some guests."

"Is he married?" Elizabeth inquired, smiling archly at her insinuation.

Charlotte returned her smile with a demure one of her own. "I believe not. My father was quite knowledgeable on that score." she replied, her smile turning more sedate and fixed as she ended her sentence. Lizzie reached for Charlotte's hand, a nondescript expression fixed firmly on her face. Charlotte allowed her to take it, but only briefly. Charlotte Lucas was not built to entertain any form of pity, especially not from others.

Elizabeth took another sip of tea, as Charlotte continued her exposition. "No matter what you may hear from Mrs. Long or the Goulding's, Lizzie, I promise you that Mr. Bingley is not arriving with any more than his two sisters, the husband of his elder sister, and a friend."

Charlotte swiftly added a spoonful of sugar to Elizabeth's tea, and stirred gently before continuing, " I am sure you will hear of it when they come to visit Mrs. Bennet. Maria had gone to visit Mrs. Long's youngest daughter, with Mother, shortly after my Father called on Mr. Bingley. According to Mrs. Long, and her daughter, Mr. Bingley shall be bringing a dozen ladies and seven gentlemen. I imagine that tidbit had made its way throughout every parlour in Meryton."
Elizabeth could do nothing but smile at her dear friend, who had continually done her best to bring some happiness into Elizabeth's life since everything had happened. Elizabeth made a mental note to speak to Mr. Collins about calling on Mr. Bingley before he went to Town, and was immediately glad that she did not have to go with him. Watching his interactions with their own neighbors was humiliating enough--especially when she was constantly faced with the knowledge that she would have to marry this man.

It was painted on the face of every person Elizabeth came into contact with. The Bennet girl, not the eldest one, that was going to marry a fool to save her family from starving in the hedgerows. A pity about the eldest, God bless the father, but wasn't it wonderful that such a man would fulfill his Christian duty?

Elizabeth felt her smile slip, and endeavored to think of happier things. "I shall have to tell Mama, Mrs. Goulding often visits Friday mornings, and I think Mama shall enjoy being proven correct when the assembly comes."

"Indeed she shall." Charlotte agreed

*****

Fitzwilliam could not say that he utterly despised and loathed any form of a dance, but his natural reticence did not help his mood, especially when one factored in the stares and whispers of the townspeople. The ladies covertly studied Charles and himself, their whispers interspersed with coquettish smiles and hushed giggles. Their mamas did little to dissuade them, however public they were behaving.

 A pair of dark eyes met his, startling him from his cynical thoughts. *Georgiana.* His sister's wan eyes, and quiet, stilted manner invaded his mind. Fitzwilliam, just in time, stopped his lip from curling into a dark frown. The lady in question had already looked away, turning her head to her companion--who was quite easily the most beautiful woman in the room, although dressed sedately for her age and beauty.

He mentally shook his head, trying to forget those dark eyes, and focus on the matter at hand. This damned assembly. Although he cared not one whit on whether or not they liked or disliked him, it was for Charles that he was here. Let them say what they wished about him or his character; it was of little import to anyone but themselves.

He could feel their eyes following him, as he, Charles, Caroline, Louisa, and Hurst made their way to the squire, Sir William Lucas. Fitzwilliam inwardly sighed, wishing to get this farce over. The sooner he settled Charles, the sooner he could leave for Pemberley, and for his *sister*. His Georgiana. And forget those dark eyes, although it was quite possibly that her mama would be hauling her forward the moment their introductions were done.

Fitzwilliam heard his name, jerking him out of his thoughts. He smoothed his face into a somewhat pleasant expression, and sketched a short bow at Sir William. "I apologize sir, I was momentarily distracted."

The red faced, rotund man returned his bow with a large flourish, and then eagerly responded with "Of course, of course Mr. Darcy. I simply stated that---."

This time, both Mr. Darcy and Sir William's attention was diverted from one another, and their own party, by the added presence of a simply, almost clerically inspired garb of a young, heavyset man. Fitzwilliam studied the man, who was only slightly shorter than himself, as he spoke, his voice taking on an excitable quality--this man was clearly eager to be introduced to Fitzwilliam, and the rest of his party.

Unfortunately, Sir William seemed to be used to such vulgar and ungentlemanly displays of manners, that he tolerated, nay encouraged it for several moments. This in turn led the unknown gentleman to expose himself to Fitzwilliam and his party.

Before Sir William could introduce the gentleman to Fitzwilliam or anyone else, the man had taken the task to himself. Bowing for a period of time that could only be construed as a token of his reverence for his family name, the man eagerly introduced himself.

"Mr. Darcy,"--the man bowed to Charles and Mr. Hurst, although it was nearly not so low as his own--"I am Mr. Collins, of Longbourn Manor." This was said with a half mixture of authority and uncertainty, as though he were afraid that Fitzwilliam nor Charles were aware of their new neighbor, and head of one of the most socially *prominent* families of Meryton.

"I believe I have already met your friend and host, Mr. Darcy. You, however, were in Town, I believe he said. Along with his dear, lovely sisters." This last remark was delivered to Caroline and Louisa with a magnanimous smile, whom Fitzwilliam was sure did not appreciate the sentiment delivered to them by the owner of a small estate in Meryton.

However, the name of the estate did sound familiar. The name of the owner, did not. Shortly before Fitzwilliam left London, he had received a very blotted letter from Charles, speaking of their neighbors, and his visit with the master.

Fitzwilliam uncharacteristically had not been able to read much of the letter, so he was unaware of the story Charles had wished to tell, but he was now having an inkling of what Charles had been trying to tell him. Something told him it would not be the last of it.

Fitzwilliam watched in awe and shock, as Mr. Collins of Longbourn Manor, then gave a short bow and a half murmured apology and gave short, quick strides across the room to speak to a matronly woman.

Caroline and Louisa gave inelegant snorts, and whispered among themselves, cuttingly. Mr. Hurst simply grumbled under his breath--Fitzwilliam knew he was simply biding his time until he was able to have his wine glass filled, again and again. As Fitzwilliam was in no mood to do so, Charles accepted the booming apologies of Sir William, graciously as always.

Skittering back to Charles and himself, Mr. Collins gave a few quiet heaves before saying, "My apologies, Mr. Darcy, Mr. Bingley--" Beside Fitzwilliam, Caroline nudged her sister, and both gave Mr. Collins a deep curtsey, whose eyes widened in awe at the implication they were giving him.

Bowing even lower to them, he turned to the matronly woman--who had now joined them with three other ladies, each of them somberly dressed. They were in the latter stages of mourning, he noted.

"If I might introduce you ladies and gentlemen to my fair cousins--" Fitzwilliam, who was now dreading the implication of any introduction to female relatives from a man as foolish as Mr. Collins was, was shocked to see the *her*.

The woman from the assembled crowd who had looked away from him. Her eyes were a deep, rich brown, not blue as Georgiana's were, but they held a familiar peculiarity in them that was shared by both ladies.

Mr. Collins gave an oily smile in the direction of Caroline and Louisa, who returned their smiles with a knowing glint, and began the introductions. The matronly woman, who bore a passing resemblance to the fair haired beauty, was Mrs. Bennet.

She gave a somewhat terse curtsey, which may have been explained by the introduction of the fair haired beauty--Miss Bennet. The Miss Bennet who used both of her hands on the top of her black and gold cane to give a short, yet startlingly graceful curtsey.

Fitzwilliam had glanced over to Charles, whose face was frozen in a charming smile as his eyes traveled down the length of Miss Jane Bennet's gown, to her cane.

He would bet every pound he possessed that Charles had been about to ask Miss Jane Bennet, the most beautiful woman in the room, to dance until he saw the disability that prevented her from that--as was his usual practice with the beautiful, sweet women that he fell in love with at every ball they attended previous.

Fitzwilliam felt pity flash through him as he, Mr. Hurst, and Charles bowed to her. He did not dare to look at Charles, and was loath to imagine the thoughts and expressions of Caroline and Louisa. And then it was on to the next introduction--the woman in the crowd.

"This is my fair cousin, Miss Elizabeth." Mr. Collins said with a flourish, an excitable nature to this voice came stronger and stronger with each and every word that left his lips.

Miss Elizabeth gave the five of them a curtsey, her dark eyes shining with intelligence and mirth as she greeted Louisa and Caroline,

"How do you find Meryton to your liking, Miss Bingley? Mrs. Hurst?" she asked, as she studied Louisa and Caroline, who were arrayed in the latest fashions London had to offer.

"I imagine it is somewhat more quiet and sedate than you both are used to? I felt quite the opposite the first time I visited London."

Mr. Collins had stepped forward then, a furrow worked deep into his brow, as he tried to decipher from the glittering smile that Caroline produced towards Miss Elizabeth was kindly meant or otherwise.

"I do not imagine that my dear cousin meant any offense, Miss Bingley." he stammered, his gaze going to and fro from Caroline, to Miss Elizabeth.

Caroline smiled graciously at Mr. Collins, before answering sweetly, "We have not been in Meryton long, Miss Eliza, but my sister and I fully support our brother in leasing the loveliest estate in all of Meryton. We hope very dearly that he shall purchase it as soon as it is available."
Fitzwilliam watched in satisfaction as Miss Elizabeth recognized the intent of Caroline's rejoinder, dismissed it with a knowing smile, and another curtsey.

There was another sister--a Miss Mary Bennet—with
the same dark brown hair and eyes as her sister Elizabeth.
Although she was somewhat plainer than her elder sisters,
she had the same pleasing figure and did not seem to
inundate herself (nor her sisters) with the same unnecessary
fripperies that Caroline and Louisa favored.

There was an awkward pause, as Mr. Collins simply waited
to be acknowledged further, and it seemed that his cousins
were following his lead--until Miss Elizabeth spoke to her
cousin.

"Mr. Collins," she said, her voice smooth and modulated,
"Perhaps we might go to the seating arrangements across
the hall."

An apologetic edge crept into her voice--"Jane's ankle is
bothering her, and I am sure, Mr. Bingley has to introduce
his guests to other families in Meryton."

Mr. Collins gasped loudly, before bowing even deeper than
before--and turned to Charles, Mr. Hurst, and himself. "I
truly must apologize my dear sirs. As my dear cousin
reminds me, and indeed my own exalted father, were he still
here, God willing, would have reminded me, we are
gathered together in a social situation, and I am sure
there are many other, worthy and admirable guests for you
to meet. I hope we shall meet again, perhaps within the

confines of my estate, Longbourn?"

Fitzwilliam turned to Charles in answer, as he was his host, and watched as Charles gave a surprised, yet fumbling answer in the positive, while Louisa, Caroline, and Mr. Hurst simply acted as voyeurs in the exchange between the masters.

As the Bennet-Collins family eventually drifted away, more and more families began to come forward--pushing their daughters to the front of the pack to be introduced to Charles and himself.

Seeing this, Fitzwilliam immediately bowed out to Sir William, and began to take a turn about the room--watching as Charles was introduced to all sorts of manner of ladies. Most were pretty--although none had reached the beauty of Miss Jane Bennet--and had what he could only charitably describe as eager manners.

Caroline would cautiously berate him later for abandoning her to the hordes of townspeople, but he found that he would not spare another moment's thought on it.

He could still hear them, Fitzwilliam thought as he crossed the room to pour himself a small cup of punch. The shocked and scandalized whispers of Charles' new neighbors, of his proud and arrogant behavior, the most abominable man in the room! No matter if he had ten thousand pounds or not! Fitzwilliam gave a short smile of grim satisfaction, as his cup reached his lips, and he took a small sip.

Chapter Eight

Netherfield Estate, after the Assembly

Caroline Bingley languidly walked the length of the drawing room, before stopping by her sister, and settling next to her on the sofa. Mr. Darcy sat upright in a single armchair next to the fire, while Charles stood, absentmindedly rearranging the coals with the long, iron poker. Louisa's husband, Mr. Hurst was already stretched out on the other sofa, sound asleep, his glass of port settled precariously by his feet. Although knowing the oafish drunk, the last thing in the world he would do was knock over a full glass of alcohol.

 Caroline studied Mr. Darcy closely for a few minutes, glad to see that his face was no longer closed off and more relaxed than it had been at the horrid Assembly of the backwards town that her brother had decreed would be his estate.

Mr. Darcy had only arrived late the night before, so she had little time to speak to him, nor learn his habits. Caroline had insured that Charles would keep London's hours while they were residing in Netherfield, a feat that was not entirely difficult as her brother was not an early riser at all, but she did not know whether or not Mr. Darcy did so on his estate,

Pemberley.

Although in the few years that she had known him, he had
spent a significant amount of time in Town with her brother,
leaving only to attend to his sister, dear Georgiana, while
she was at school and on holiday, as well as returning to his
grand estate to oversee the yearly harvest.

Seeing Mr. Darcy arising to pour himself a glass of brandy,
Caroline readily stood and trailed after him, intent on
fortifying herself with a small glass of the wine that was
seated among the brandy and port bottles. Watching Mr.
Darcy return to his chair, glass in hand, she sipped at her
wine, before deciding she was ready to speak. To tease.

"So, Mr. Darcy, how did you enjoy the little country ball? We
shall not bother to ask Charles, I think, we all know how
well his evening turned out." she said impishly, referring to
the meeting of the eldest Bennet girl, Jane.

"And let me inform you, Mr. Darcy, that you had the great
privilege of meeting the great Hertfordshire beauties, the
Bennet girls. As well as the master of one of the most
prominent families in the Hertfordshire-Meryton area, Mr.
Collins."

Mr. Darcy turned to her, with an expression that said he was
not impressed with anything that had occurred that evening,

and stated absentmindedly,

"I saw very little beauty, and even less intelligence, Caroline. This town is rather full of vulgarity and gossip, so by my reckoning, the most prominent family must be the one who is able to spread the gossip first, and in that the Bennet family is beaten. I would say the Lucas family out lengthens them by more than a breadth. Although their deficiency in that area is more than made up for in the fact that I am sure the master of Longbourn creates as much gossip as there is to disperse to the townspeople."

Caroline gave a high titter, that ended in a sharp, ugly laugh, adding to her agreement of the estimable Mr. Darcy's statement, with Louisa echoing her, with a "Hear, hear, Mr. Darcy! I quite agree.", remembering the way the Bennet chit, Miss Eliza had spoken to her.

Charles, of course, had to defend the virtues of his new pets, the Bennets, "Come Darcy, there were several pretty girls at the ball, especially the eldest Miss Bennets! Even the youngest one, Miss Mary, does not fade into the background of her sisters. And they were indeed pleasant and well mannered girls. It is hardly their fault that Mr. Collins is now their head of household. Especially when you take into account what has happened to their family, their father. It is a significant upheaval, Caroline, and the Bennet ladies bear it remarkably well."

At this, Caroline watched as Mr. Darcy glanced inquiringly at Charles, confusion and interest evident in his face.

"Charles, did you not tell Mr. Darcy of the infamous Bennet's, and your visit with the ever loquacious, Mr. Collins?" Caroline inquired.
Charles looked back to Mr. Darcy, "I sent you a letter telling you of my visit, did you not receive it?"

Caroline watched with pleasure as Mr. Darcy gave a low laugh, his eyes filled with mirth as he acknowledged, "Yes, I did but could not read one jot of it. I thought I could read your handwriting tolerably well, but you must have been in a hurry when you wrote it--or in a carriage."

Charles flushed a dull red, as Caroline and Louisa crowed their agreement, for Charles' handwriting really was not fit for the master of an estate. Only for a few minutes, for Caroline had to catch Mr. Darcy up on the local gossip.

"Well, Mr. Darcy," Caroline began, "this is probably the most exciting thing to happen in Meryton, you must understand. I have been informed of it by almost every neighbor who called on Netherfield in the past fortnight. Apparently sometime last year or so, the eldest Miss Bennet and her father were involved in a carriage accident, on her birthday, how intolerable!" she added with an exclamation of sympathy,

"Mr. Bennet is currently in a coma from the accident and is being cared for in his home. The current Master of Longbourn, Mr. Collins arrived with his father some weeks after the accident. His father passed this last Yule, but not before implementing some much needed improvements to that family!" Caroline said triumphantly.

Charles studied her cautiously, "To what are you implying, dear sister of mine?" The Bennets seemed like a perfectly respectable family that had gone through a great deal of adversity in the past year, yet held together admirably. Caroline gave her brother an indecipherable smile.

"I understand, dear Charles. despite their foolishly behaved cousin, they seem to be the model of propriety. But, as I have been informed by several of our new neighbors, that propriety came after their father's accident. The mother was apparently a shrieking mama who delighted in informing her neighbors that her eldest daughter would make a match with a wealthy man, solely due to her beauty and want to better her family. The two youngest girls--a Miss Lydia and Miss Kitty--were shameless hoydens that flirted with anything contained within a red coat. At fourteen and fifteen, that!" Caroline added with a shocked tone.

"And Miss Eliza--well, it does not seem that the accident, nor subsequent change in the head of household has changed her temper very much." Caroline stated rather contemptuously, "Even from our brief meeting, it seems Miss Eliza has not quite learned to temper her tongue. It speaks of a conceited independence, truth be told."

Mr. Darcy looked away in disinterest, Caroline noted in satisfaction. Perhaps she could channel his disinterest in the local populace into convincing Charles to purchase an estate closer to Pemberley? However, Charles still could note hold his tongue, as he tried to defend the Bennets once again. "Oh dear Lord, Charles, one is allowed to feel sorry for them, of course!" Caroline tempered her previous words, with a soothing tone. "However, I feel that the issue of the Bennets past conduct is something that Mr. Darcy should hear from his friends, not from a local busy body who would then spread his reaction throughout the town! Think of how Mr. Darcy and the Bennets would feel!"

Charles turned his head to his hands, "Of course, Caroline. But I hardly think it is appropriate conversation to begin with! The worst that one can accuse the Bennets of being was having a permissive father! Therefore, how they behaved in society before we arrived in Meryton has nothing to do with us. Beyond that, I think they have shown to have a great spirit during troubled times. Especially Miss Bennet--."

Caroline could not contain herself at that, nor could Louisa, as they each exchanged smirks and knowing looks.

"Poor, dear Jane Bennet. So lovely, it is such a pity she shall not be wed. I should hate to have something as awful as that happen to my person." she gave a faux shudder, her eyes gleaming in satisfaction as Charles turned his head away from her, and back to the coals.

Louisa tittered, as she turned to Caroline, "Sister dear, you forgot the news between Miss Eliza and Mr. Collins!" Caroline's eyes lit up as she returned Louisa's titter with one of her own, before turning to Mr. Darcy, who had gone back to studying his hands with a serious mien dominating his features.

"I quite forgot to say, Mr. Darcy. The Bennet's estate is entailed upon Mr. Collins, however, as I stated before, their father has not yet passed on. Once he does, Longbourn will become the possession of Mr. Collins, and he shall be able turn the Bennets out as soon as he wishes. As I understand it, the Bennet girls will receive equal portions from their mother's dowry, which was about five thousand pounds. That is," Caroline stated with a small smile, "unless Miss Eliza does not marry Mr. Collins. Everyone in Meryton speaks of their de facto engagement. Once Mr. Bennet passes on, Mr. Collins and Miss Eliza shall be engaged, and marry once the time for mourning has passed. Perhaps even sooner, as I have been informed by Lady Lucas that no one would look down on Miss Eliza for marrying so soon after her father's death, to secure her sister's futures."

Mr. Darcy simply noted drolly, "How very kind of them."

Caroline and Louisa both tittered, agreeing with him. Beside them, Mr. Hurst abruptly woke up with a loud snort, muttering unintelligibly, as he picked up his glass, and tried to stand up. Caroline glanced at her sister with a look of barely disguised disgust; Louisa had no such qualms, as she went to ring the bell for a footman to assist Mr. Hurst to his rooms.

It was decided, then, that they would all retire for the night. Caroline followed her sister to her own set of rooms, settling herself at the vanity.

"Sister, what do you think of inviting the two eldest Bennets for a dinner in a week or so?"

Louisa glanced back at Caroline absently, as she removed her jewelry, "How so, Caroline?" Caroline gave herself a quick spritz of the perfume resting in front of her, inhaling the lovely fragrance.

"Well, they are the closest thing we have to a prominent family in this backwater town. It is either they or that old maid, Charlotte Lucas. At least Jane Bennet is a lovely, sweet girl, unlike Miss Eliza."

"Poor dear," Louisa tutted, as she rung the bell for her maid to help her undress. Caroline swiftly locked her sister's jewelry in her box, before the maid should come. God knew what servants would try, if they thought they could get away with it, or the opportunity. It was best not to even give them the chance, as Caroline did not wish to constantly interview and hire new staff.

"We are in agreement then?" she asked. As Louisa nodded absently, Caroline spoke her thoughts aloud "Yes, well we may do so any time within the next week, really. I think Charles and Mr. Darcy have been invited to dine with the officers sometime afterwards, but it does not matter which day that shall come to pass."
Caroline thoughtfully fingered her own jewelry, as she went through the positives and negatives on such and such day, as when to invite the Bennet chits. Perhaps a day when Charles and Mr. Darcy were out shooting with Mr. Hurst, or dining with the officers, as Caroline and Louisa would have nothing else to do. Or perhaps with Charles and Mr. Darcy there......... Caroline murmured "good night" to her sister, as she made her way to her own room, ready for bed.

*****

Coming back from the assembly was no more exciting than going towards the assembly. At least not in the Bennet ladies eyes. Mrs. Bennet was silently pouting in the wake of their introduction to the charming, handsome, and very wealthy Mr. Bingley, and his guest, Mr. Darcy. Mary had no opinion, one way or another, as her habits during assemblies had not changed--however this time, she had Jane to accompany her at all times, as she sat, watching others dance.

Jane was silent, neither her manner nor her actions betraying what she felt inside. Elizabeth could do nothing but hold her sister's hand, as always. Jane squeezed it gratefully, betraying how she felt in that single moment.

Mr. Collins was ecstatic, Elizabeth could tell, although he had not yet said a word. His first introduction with Mr. Bingley had been startlingly brief, as Mr. Bingley had been on his way back to Town, and had graciously extended him a few moment's time of conversation.

As the Bennet-Collins family removed themselves from their carriage, and entered Longbourn, Elizabeth made a move to go with Jane into the parlor. While it was very late, they all knew that Kitty and Lydia would still be waiting for them, anxiously awaiting their review of the night's assembly.

 Mr. Collins called after her, "My dear!" Elizabeth stopped and turned. Dipping into a slight curtsey, she nodded to Mr. Collins, "Yes, sir?" she said.

Mr. Collins granted her a condescending smile, "I understand that you are eager to enjoy a visit with your sisters, before going to bed, but I feel that we should speak of your conduct tonight."

At Mr. Collins's words, Jane had silently went back to her sister's side, offering herself as support.

"Now run along, Miss Bennet." Mr. Collins said condescendingly to Jane. "Miss Lizzie and I have some things to discuss." Elizabeth gave her sister an encouraging smile, a smile she knew that Jane would be able to see through within an instant, and briefly, their hands touched. Jane gripped her fingers hard, and then let go, giving a nod to Mr. Collins, she joined her mother and sisters in the parlor.

Mr. Collins and Elizabeth were now alone in the front hall of Longbourn. Elizabeth brought her hands to herself, as she tried to settle the uneasiness she felt.

At the very least, when his father had been alive, there had been some distance between them, as father and son spent several hours enclosed in her Papa's study, leaving the Bennet women to their new duties. Now it was only she and Mr. Collins, propriety holding what little distance remained. For now.

Elizabeth furrowed her brow in confusion, although she was sure she knew exactly what Mr. Collins was speaking of.

"To what do you refer, Mr. Collins?" Mr. Collins gave an exaggerated sigh, as he motioned for her come closer to him.

Elizabeth obliged.

"Sir?" she questioned.

"My dear, I understand that you have moved within limited society while here in Meryton, and have not had the advantages that I have had during my studies with the cleric in London. I understand," he said in an affable tone, licking his lips noisily, as he eyed her, "but you must learn to hold your tongue, my dear. I enjoy your spirited and witty conversation within the comfort of our home, as did our dear Father, however, when it comes to our neighbors, I will not brook any hint of it. The Bingley's are now one of the more important families here in Meryton, despite their unfortunate root in trade, and as such you need to speak to them with every affability required. Am I understood, my dear?"

Elizabeth swallowed lowly, before nodding her head. "Of course, Mr. Collins. I shall endeavor to do so in the future." Mr. Collins' hand went to stroke her cheek-- Elizabeth stepped backwards in avoidance, her back brushing the front entrance into Longbourn.

Mr. Collins," she said, a hint of uncertainty creeping into her tone, "that is most improper." Mr. Collins countered her step backwards, with a forward step of his own. The space between them was becoming compressed, and, Elizabeth thought as she inhaled a shallow, ragged breath, there was nowhere else for her to go.

Silence descended, as Elizabeth fought the urge to flee, and Mr. Collins did as he wish--trailing a single finger down her cheek. He smiled as she tightened her jaw in an attempt to keep her flesh from reacting to his touch.

"Mr. Collins," she tried to protest quietly, not wanting her Mama or sisters to hear, but found herself unable to say another word. Mr. Collins gave her another one of his grins, before shushing her, and moving closer to her, encroaching the distance between them. Elizabeth could do nothing, would do nothing.

A sound was heard behind Mr. Collins, a feminine gasp, and all Elizabeth saw was a flash of Lydia's ribbons on her new bonnet, trailing around the corner.

Chapter Nine

Sir William Lucas' party.....

Elizabeth glanced around the room, her eyes lighting up in pleasure as her gaze fell upon her dearest friend, Charlotte Lucas. Charlotte gave her a short wave and a smile, and motioned for her to come over. Elizabeth hesitated, and then turned to Mr. Collins who was still greeting Sir William with all the affability and condescension he could muster.

"Mr. Collins," she said softly, for her arm still smarted from where he had grabbed her from the carriage, when she had attempted to depart from their carriage without his assistance, still shaken by the night of the assembly. Every day, she realized with growing despondency, he became more and more like his father."Jane, Mary, and I shall go over to Charlotte. We do not wish to intrude upon your conversation with Sir William."

Mr. Collins beamed, for the first time giving her a short bow, as he said in an excitable tone, "Of course my dear cousin, how very gracious of you indeed! Yes, it is indeed very gracious of Sir William to invite our dear family to his beloved home," Mr. Collins gave a lower bow to Sir William, as he continued on, "granting us the pleasure of his and his family's delightful company!"

Elizabeth, Jane, and Mary gave Mr. Collins and Sir William curtseys, and left them alone, to Charlotte.

"Charlotte!" Elizabeth greeted, embracing her friend with a gentle hug and a short kiss. Beside her, Jane settled into a chair with Mary, letting out a small hiss of pain as she did so. Elizabeth glanced worriedly at her sister. Jane's return to Meryton society had not served her injury well, despite all the time she had spent walking with Kitty, and sitting down at assemblies. Elizabeth could do nothing but attribute the pain to the distress that now permeated their lives.

"Shall we take a turn about the room?" Charlotte asked cheekily, as a smiling Mr. Bingley bowed to a seated Jane. Elizabeth took her friend's hand, and joined her in walking a short distance, both of them still able to observe the conversation between Jane and Mr. Bingley.

"What do you think of them?" Elizabeth inquired of her friend, as she watched Mr. Bingley out of the corner of her eye, with the rest of her attention focused on Mr. Collins, who was still on the other side of the room, speaking to Sir William in rather animated language and movement.

Charlotte arched a brow, "What do you think of them, Lizzie?" Elizabeth studied her friend a few moments, in confusion.

"You cannot be serious, Charlotte!" she exclaimed in

surprise, reading the answer plainly on her friend's face.

Charlotte gave an elegant shrug, glancing back at a primly seated Jane, and the retreating back of Mr. Charles Bingley, as he went to rejoin his proud friend, Mr. Darcy, who seemed to be looking at her a great deal. Elizabeth could not imagine why.

After their introduction at the previous assembly, Mr. Darcy had stalked away from any further introductions by Sir William, and had spent the majority of the evening walking here from there to pour himself some more punch, and standing alone.

 Only Miss Bingley and Charles Bingley had attempted any sort of conversation, beyond a few brave souls who thought they could have a look behind the mask of the great Mr. Darcy of Pemberley, in order to win him over for their daughters.

After that night, it was decided that Mr. Charles Bingley was the most amiable, handsomest man who had ever come to live in Meryton, while his friend, Mr. Darcy was universally disliked by the populace. Not even close to the handsome Mr. Bingley in looks and spirit, and they could not wait until he left Meryton and returned to his home in Derbyshire.

Elizabeth let out a soft cough, putting her hand over her

mouth in disguise of her lips narrowing into a straight line as she considered Mr. Bingley. Although it was no longer a surprise, nor a shock to her senses--nor Jane's, she supposed--she found that she could not forget Mr. Bingley's reaction, nor his subsequent conversation with his friend, to Jane's injury

"Lizzie?"

Elizabeth was thrown out of her thoughts by Charlotte's careful, questioning tone. "Yes, Charlotte, I am sorry. My mind was elsewhere."

Charlotte gave her one of her indecipherable smiles, before saying, "I was just saying that I was quite serious about what I said earlier--about Jane and Mr. Bingley."

Elizabeth scoffed quietly, glancing back at Mr. Bingley and Mr. Darcy who were still in conversation, "Charlotte, he is simply being polite to Jane, after he and his friend spoke of what a shame it was that the most handsome woman in the room was lame, within her hearing!" Charlotte opened her mouth to retort, and Elizabeth gave her no opportunity, "And that was after his dear friend teased him about not being able to fall for the most beautiful woman in the room!"

Charlotte's eyes shifted towards a serene looking Jane, who was now speaking softly with Mary. Mr. Bingley and Mr.

Darcy were still across the room, speaking to each other, yet Charlotte noticed their gazes often betrayed to their direction.

"Speak sensibly, Lizzie. As you are well aware, the majority of the neighbors greet Jane kindly to her face, retreat to other, pretty young ladies who are able to dance, and then gossip about her misfortunes behind their port bottles and embroidered screens. There is no earthly reason why Mr. Bingley cannot and does not join them in their behavior, except for the fact that he likes her. May even love her, as time goes on."

Elizabeth looked at her friend in shock. "Why not, Lizzie? Jane simply has to walk with a cane, and contrary to the expectations of our neighbors, it is not the end of a woman's prospects, especially with a woman as beautiful as Jane. There are a few gentlemen who would overlook such a thing, and it appears Mr. Bingley is one of those gentlemen." she finished cheekily.

"You are speaking as though Jane shares his feelings, if he has any at all, Charlotte." Elizabeth reminded her friend steadily. "Jane heard him, Charlotte. It hurt her feelings. We already have to deal with Mama--."

Elizabeth cut herself off, aware of what she was about to expose. There were some things, she learned, that she did not want her dearest friend to realize. Charlotte was one of the few who had not changed her behavior or address towards the Bennet family, and Elizabeth would do all that she could to preserve that.

"Well, I am simply saying that it would do Jane well to know that she is not on the shelf yet. She should move fast, encourage Mr. Bingley's interest, and leave him in no doubt of her own."

"And, pray tell, do you know that she is interested in the man who insulted her, Charlotte?" Elizabeth queried, not knowing where Charlotte received half of the thoughts that came out of her head.

Charlotte glanced back at Jane, before turning to her friend.

"Lizzie, I do not pretend to know Jane's heart, but what I do know is that she has not so much as looked twice at another gentleman since her brief courtship, when she was your sister Lydia's age, and yet there she is returning Mr. Bingley's looks."

Giving her friend a sly wink, Charlotte glided across the room to the pianoforte, offering to turn the pages for anyone who wished to play. As Mary settled at the piano, Elizabeth tried to join Jane at her seat, as there were a few couples lining up to dance, but Mr. Collins reached her first.

He bowed over her hand, before gesturing to the lined up couples, "My fair cousin, would you do me the honor?"

Elizabeth glanced anxiously back at Jane, who was smiling at her in shared sympathy, before stammering, "Y-yes of course, Mr. Collins. I--." Ignoring the rest of her answer, Mr. Collins offered her his arm, and they both moved to line up with the other dancers.

"My dear, I had hoped to apologize for my behavior earlier." Mr. Collins began sensibly.
Elizabeth forced a smile, silently reminding herself that *he was not his father, that his father was dead*, before replying, "I thank you, Mr. Collins." There, that should do.

Mr. Collins continued on, "Although I understand that you ladies have a natural delicacy and propensity towards requiring an almost constant correction, as my dear father learned from his father, I am not proud to say that I lost my temper, and in front of Sir William's home!"

Mr. Collins shuddered, and then cast his eyes about the room furtively, as though the inhabitants were eavesdropping upon every word.

Elizabeth willed her face to be taut, to not betray her feelings, as Mr. Collins granted her another condescending smile, "Do not worry, my fair cousin. We shall have plenty of time, the both of us, to correct our faults in the privacy of our home! I am heartily sorry, and indeed, I promise to never correct you in public, my fair cousin!"

The dance moved swiftly, and for that Elizabeth was grateful. Ever since the night of the assembly, Elizabeth had tried her best to not be alone with Mr. Collins, and in that endeavor her sisters and Mrs. Bennet had obliged.

She knew it was a false hope, as being the head of household, all Mr. Collins had to do was request a private audience with her in her papa's study, but so far he had held off.
The distance between them was slowly declining, and nothing would stop it. Indeed, her father's death would only settle it once and for all.

*****

A letter addressed to a Miss Jane Bennet, from Netherfield Hall, had been brought to the Bennet-Collins family while they attended to their morning duties. This morning, Elizabeth had slipped away from the parlour, where she was supposed to be attending to her needlepoint, and had joined Jane and Kitty in their daily care of Mr. Bennet.

Any letters or notes, of course, were under strict instructions to go through Mr. Collins first, as he did the same with their letters to and from the Gardner's, so Mrs. Hill had brought the letter to Mr. Collins in his study, and it was he who had read it aloud to the assembled party during their morning meal.

Elizabeth and Jane had been invited to dine with Mrs. Louisa Hurst, and Caroline Bingley. Elizabeth remained stony still and silent, as Mr. Collins read the letter. It was addressed to Jane, yet meant for Elizabeth, the true Miss Bennet, no matter what Charlotte implied.

Beside Elizabeth, Lydia and Kitty shifted in their seats uncomfortably. Ever since the elder Mr. Collins had taken them out of society, they had sorely been deprived of company. Before, Lydia and Kitty had spent their days chasing after the officers in Meryton, begging money off of their elder sisters in shopping for various fripperies they did not need, nor earn. Now their days were filled with making jellies and jams, taking care of their father, and enjoying the company of their sisters.

That enjoyment was hard won, yet in moments like this, Elizabeth ached for her sisters. The only reason she had not voiced more opposition towards their introduction to society at such a young age, had been that she had found it very unfair on the younger sisters to not have their share of society and amusements, simply because they were too poor to merit a match. They were social girls, and they needed the society of others.

Finally finished reading the letter, Mr. Collins surveyed Jane and Elizabeth from the head of the table. He was excited, Elizabeth realized, as he licked a bit of jam from his bottom lip.

An invitation to dine with the sisters of the most eligible man in Meryton, was a great boon. Especially since the invitation stated that it would be a private audience, not a neighborhood tête–à–tête or tea. They were merely extensions of his prestige, his status in such a town.

At the end of the table, Mama had set her cutlery down with such force, and knocked over her tall glass, spreading water all over the table. Lydia flounced up out of her seat, and almost skipped to the kitchen, glad to be out of the presence of Mr. Collins for even a few brief moments, as she returned seconds later with a rag.

Mrs. Bennet looked mutely ahead at Mr. Collins. As Lydia mopped up the mess, the both of them, Mrs. Bennet and Mr. Collins engaged in a staring bout, as Mr. Collins waited for her to say something. At length, Mrs. Bennet seemed to give up, and apologized stiffly.

Mr. Collins seemed satisfied with her apology, and returned to the matter of the letter from Netherfield,

"Well my fair cousins, I shall happily allow you both to go
and meet our new neighbors on a more intimate note.
However," and at this, his voice turned stern, which belied
the natural intonation that his voice carried, which
reminded Elizabeth, often, of a young man pleading to be
noticed. "I must stress the importance of the both of you to
be on your best, honorable behavior while visiting the
Bingley household. As I have already spoken to Miss Lizzie
about this previously,--"

Elizabeth felt her stomach turn in remembrance of his
words, "I shall turn my attention to you, Miss Jane."

He peered at her over the letter, giving her a condescending
smile, as though her intelligence and capacity for
understanding and knowledge of appropriate behaviors had
somehow been damaged in the accident, instead of her
ankle.
"As my father often worried, I too worry that being in
society is rather damaging to your health. Today will be an
excellent test of that, as I shall inquire after the both of you
at the next assembly or neighborhood tea that Mr. Bingley
and his sisters attend. However, despite this, I caution you to
be on your best behavior, and display yourself as a lady
benefiting your situation in life. As it is, no true gentleman
or lady have ever been adverse to those who display truly
humble behavior in their speech and actions. It was very
good of Miss Bingley and Mrs. Hurst to invite you to dine in

their home, and I expect you to be very grateful for the opportunity. As my own excellent father said often, those who are not truly appreciative of the situation in life and opportunities that God has granted them, do not tend to keep their standards of living very long."

He finished the speech with a sordid smile masquerading as an affectionate gesture, while Elizabeth's eyes widened in disgust and dismay at the implications of his words. Beside her, Jane expressed her assent, "Of course, Mr. Collins. I thank you for your advice. May Elizabeth and I be excused, to get ready for the visit?"

Mr. Collins gave them an enthusiastic reply, informing them that he would have Mr. Hill go down to the farm and retrieve the horses, for the carriage. Jane and Elizabeth slowly made their way up the stairs, listening to the excited chatter of Lydia, Mary, and Kitty as they rushed passed them in an attempt to reach Elizabeth and Jane's rooms, respectively, and select the ensemble that they wished their sisters to wear to such a visit.

By the time Jane and Elizabeth reached Elizabeth's room, which was the largest of the sister's space, Kitty already had an armful of Jane's gowns spread along the bed, Mary had flung the closet door open and was selecting from Elizabeth's gowns, while Lydia had gone into the room she shared with Mary to select bonnets from her own personal assortment.

Somewhere along the confusion, as Lydia, Kitty, and Mary squabbled over who would wear what bonnet with what gown, Mrs. Bennet came into the room, looking forlorn and tired. At a glance from Elizabeth,

 Mary went to her mama, holding her. Mama began to cry into Mary's shoulder, prompting Lydia to run into her mama's room for her smelling salts.

"Come Mama, sit in the chair and rest a while." Lydia said soothingly, as Mrs. Bennet let Mary go, and allowed her youngest daughter to bring her to the chair.

 She collapsed into the chair, inhaling deeply. Lydia had always been Mama's favorite, next to Jane, and on the days she could not stand to look at Jane, Lydia was there to comfort and console her---glad to escape the kitchen, at the very least.

Elizabeth looked away, studiously trying to give her sister the time she needed to comport herself away from her prying eyes.

Jane was--. Here, Elizabeth paused in thought, searching her mind, reflecting on all that had occurred, as she tried to accurately convey all that Jane had accomplished, how she had transformed herself in the wake of the tragedy that befell their lives.

In the end, all Elizabeth could affirm was that Jane was *strong*. It did not seem to be the case, her dear, sweet sister Jane, whose shy smiles and open and easy countenance was enjoyed by every person who had the pleasure of meeting her, including the unworthy.

They would survive this, Elizabeth mused, as she presented herself to her awaiting sisters. Jane wouldn't let her alone, and nor would she let Jane alone.

*****

Leaving a gentle kiss on her Papa's forehead, Jane and Elizabeth walked down the stairs to the foyer, where Mr. Collins was awaiting them.

"I should like to speak to Miss Lizzie in private, if you would wait in the carriage, Miss Bennet." he said, in a tone that clearly stated Jane had no choice. Jane turned to her sister, waiting for her slight nod, before she continued to walk outside, to the awaiting carriage. Mr. Hill helped her into the carriage, and there she waited for Lizzie to come out with Mr. Collins.

A few minutes later, she did, escorted by Mr. Collins, and looking very grim. As Mr. Collins gave Mr. Hill a nod to drive away, Jane asked her sister, "What did Mr.

Collins want, Lizzie?"

Elizabeth responded flatly, "Simply to remind me that I have an obligation to him, as the future Mistress of Longbourn to display the appropriate behavior, or steps would be taken to correct my behavior." She looked out the window, at length, before turning to her sister with sad eyes, "In the end, Jane we may need to go to Aunt and Uncle Gardner."

Jane gripped her sister's hand tightly. "Lizzie, at this point not even Mama would blame you for refusing to marry him."

Jane started, referring to the few pounds and shillings they had been able to tuck away, here and there from Mama's pin money, and the small amounts they each received monthly, "We at least will have the money to leave when--"

"When Papa dies." Elizabeth said flatly.

A long silence reigned.

"If anything," Jane ventured when Longbourn was out of their sights, "it would be lovely to see Netherfield again, Lizzie. I remember Mama toured it several years ago, I believe I was twelve or thirteen years old. Do you remember? Mama lamented that it was not closer to our farm, so that we would not be able to use the horses more often, than we would at Longbourn. So said she."

Jane laughed softly.

Elizabeth gave her sister a knowing look, an acknowledgement of the position they found themselves in. Although she had not spoken to Miss Bingley or Mrs. Hurst after their first introduction, beyond a polite greeting at Sir William's, she understood what character of ladies they were.

While she at least had some experience with them, Jane had barely warranted a polite greeting on both occasions they had to give them, yet she had warranted undisguised curiosity and looks from across the room. Not conversation.

Elizabeth sighed into her sister's shoulder for a moment. It was going to be a long evening.

Chapter Ten

Elizabeth and Jane had been let into Netherfield by a grim butler, who in turn, led them to an empty parlour where a tea service was already laid out. The man bowed before stating,

"My apologies, Miss Bennet, Miss Elizabeth," with a nod to each respective lady, "I shall inform Mrs. Hurst and Miss Bingley that you have arrived. Do make yourselves comfortable." With another bow, the man was gone, away to inform their delightful hosts that their guests were, presumably, early.

Elizabeth turned to her sister, turning a critical eye over her light blue gown, making sure she was in order before allowing her sister to sit down. She simply sat on the couch next to Jane, uncaring of any wrinkles that may or may not have found their way onto her gown.

None of it mattered anymore. despite what she had said to Jane in the carriage on the way over, she did not know if she had the strength to refuse Mr. Collins. Perhaps if her father had still been alive and well, if she had not been separated and secluded from her sisters and mama almostimmediately after her Aunt and Uncle Gardner had left, being forced out by the elder Mr. Collins.

Once again, she thanked God for the death of the elder Mr. Collins, who implemented the new reign under which the Bennet women now lived. His son would never be what he was, Elizabeth though drolly, but he certainly was doing his best. And that was enough. More than enough.

A noise was heard and Elizabeth mentally shook herself from her thoughts, as the door opened and in swept Louisa Hurst and Caroline Bingley. Both stood out in Meryton, their dark and ostentatious gowns contrasting wonderfully with the simple, light colors that the denizens of Meryton favored.

Or, rather, were able to afford. If their lives had been unaltered, Mama would most certainly be badgering Papa or Uncle Gardner about the new style of lace on Mrs. Hurst's gown, Elizabeth decided, as she offered Jane her arm. Once they were both up, Elizabeth and Jane gave a graceful curtsey to their hosts, and thanked them both for inviting them over to their great estate.

"Of course not, my dear Miss Bennet, Miss Elizabeth. It is a great honor to have you in our home. I hope we shall become great friends." Miss Bingley gestured for them to sit down, and poured the tea. There were a few moments of silence, as the tea was poured, sugar and milk added, and then conversation was had.

"How was your journey here, Miss Bennet? Miss Eliza? It has been quite wet these past few days, and it would be such a shame if your carriage was not able to go through the mud, if it rains again later today. Would your family be able to send another carriage, or should I inform our stablemaster to be aware of such a possibility?"

That last sentence, delivered with as a cloying smile as one could expect from a woman who wished to be as far away from her current location as Caroline Bingley wished. Elizabeth tilted her head, studying Miss Bingley. No, Netherfield Park was not Pemberley, for the simple reason that she was not Mrs. Fitzwilliam Darcy, and it seemed Miss Bingley had yet to get over that little tidbit.

Jane answered graciously for the both of them, "That would be lovely, Miss Bingley. It is very kind of you to offer such a service." Elizabeth waited for her sister to finish speaking, before a mischievous smile spread
across her face.

"Yes, indeed, Miss Bingley. It is very kind of you to make such an offer. I only hope that the weather does not turn, as it frequently does, to the point to where your own carriage will not traverse through the mud. Then we shall have to trespass on the hospitality of your brother for a few days until the roads dry."

Calmly and with ample satisfaction, Elizabeth watched as Miss Bingley's face went suddenly blank for a few moments, as she realized the implications of Elizabeth's words.

"Yes, indeed, we should hope not." Miss Bingley said tightly. Mrs. Hurst who seemed to have slightly better manners than her sister, quickly replied, "Of course, my dear Miss Bennet, Miss Eliza, we should be glad to host you if the occasion should arise."

Elizabeth gave Mrs. Hurst a benevolent assent with a small nod in her direction, "Of course, Mrs. Hurst. I know that Mr. Collins is hoping to invite your party into Longbourn sometime in the near future, so you have my assurances that should such a thing ever happen, we should be happy to host you and your party, as well." Elizabeth gave Miss Bingley a sweet, sincere smile, her eyes dancing with mischief, as Miss Bingley considered her neighbor's words.

Jane's hand slipped into Elizabeth's, as she watched Miss Bingley go grey for a brief moment, at the indication that she may have to stay more than an evening in the company of Mr. Collins and the Bennet family. Of course, she recovered herself fairly quickly, as the questions then turned to their father, and the accident. An attempt to glean any information that no one else knew, Elizabeth realized.

"Oh my dears, I apologize most heartily!" Miss Bingley

started. "I understand what a devastating topic it must be, but I should feel ill of myself if I did not ask after him--and you! dear Jane--" was said as an aside when Jane's gaze betrayed to the black and gold cane laid out beside her, "as the neighbors have all informed myself and Louisa as to his condition. However, I would wish to inquire after him personally. How is your father?"

Jane startled next to Elizabeth, putting her tea cup into her saucer with a bit more force than required. Her hand startled for a moment, as she watched the satisfied gleam within Miss Bingley's eyes, and the well hidden, but unabashed curiosity in Mrs. Hurst's.

Elizabeth smiled thinly, glad that Jane was with her, and that Jane was not alone with these harpies. Glad that she had someone to hold onto, to not face this alone. Caroline Bingley and Louisa Hurst were not Mr. Collins, nor his father. She was not afraid of them.

In all honesty, now that she was here, she welcomed the opportunity to *breathe* for an afternoon, to be her natural self--a connoisseur of human folly, as her papa had once remarked--and realized that Miss Bingley and Mrs. Hurst, if asked, could hardly testify to Elizabeth's impertinence, unless they wished to be faced with their own.

 Swallowing a lump within her throat, she asked, a bit more pointed and sharp in her tone than she expected, "What is it that you wish to know, Miss Bingley?"

Miss Bingley spread her hands out in appeasement, aware that she had touched a nerve with Elizabeth, as she stated, "I simply wished to ask after his condition, as a neighbor and friend, Miss Eliza. I know I should dislike it excessively if such a thing had happened to my father." Mrs. Hurst simply looked, back and forth from her sister to Elizabeth, as though they were a sporting match.

Jane spoke beside her, always the voice of reason and compassion. "Our father is still in a coma, Miss Bingley. The doctors do not believe that he will wake up, but of course our family prays for that moment, every single morning and night. Thank you for inquiring after him, our mother shall be comforted that we have such caring neighbors."

Miss Bingley accepted Jane's kind words, and then there was an awkward pause, as no one said anything. Elizabeth waited, her breath caught in her throat, for them to ask more questions. Everywhere they went, they were asked, or it was talked about. And each time she answered, her breath never was released, nor did her belly seem to untangle itself from the many knots it formed.

Mrs. Hurst seemed to take the plunge, as she asked "How is your family taking such news, Miss Bennet?" Miss Bingley added on to her sister's question, stating

"I understand you have three younger sisters, is that correct? Two of them, I was informed by Sir William, I believe, were out last year, but your new guardian, Mr. Collins recalled them from Society? And I believe he is your cousin, or so I have been informed" she stated, her head tilting in apparent disbelief and confusion.

Elizabeth opened her mouth to respond, and Jane must have seen the harshness of the reply before it left her lips, as she smoothly spoke over Elizabeth, before Elizabeth could formulate her words.

"Yes, Miss Bingley, you are correct. After our accident, my Aunt and Uncle Gardner came to stay with us a few days, in order to sort things out and inform the heirs of our estate, what had happened. Mr. Collins is indeed our cousin--our father's cousin's son. His father recently died this past Christmas. It--"

Here, Jane paused, not quite sure how to say what she wished, without giving the sisters more information than was needed about their home life.

"It was decided by the present Mr. Collins' father that Lydia and Catherine, our two youngest sisters, should stay at home until their elder sisters were married, or until they reached their majority. They--they took our father's accident very badly, and of course they are still very young."

Miss Bingley gave Jane a reassuring look, before soothingly murmuring, "Of course, Miss Bennet. From what I have heard, it is doing them a great deal to their constitutions and temperaments. Quite often, I believe, blessings come disguised as adversity. It is so wonderful that you and your family share my views."

Elizabeth gave a muted sound, as she quickly took a drink from her tea cup.

"Are you quite all right, Miss Eliza?" Miss Bingley asked sweetly.

"I am well, Miss Bingley, I merely swallowed some tea the wrong way."

 "Of course, Miss Eliza." Miss Bingley motioned for Elizabeth to bring her tea cup forward, and she replenished the cup. "As you said before, Miss Bennet, your aunt and uncle came to stay at Longbourn, after your father's accident?"

"Yes, my aunt and uncle came as soon as we wrote, and did indeed spend a few weeks at Longbourn, until

 Mr. Collins and his late father arrived, Miss Bingley." was Jane's reply. Elizabeth was able to catch the note of terseness, that underlaid her sister's tone. Replenishing her sister's tea was the only thing she could do at the moment.

Jane smiled at her in thanks, as well as relief, and returned her attention to Miss Bingley.

"And where are they from?" This came from Mrs. Hurst, who seemed to not be able to hold in her eagerness at this moment.

And so it comes, Elizabeth thought ruefully, as she opened her mouth to reply.

*****

They made it through the evening meal, Elizabeth was surprised to say, after being cross examined by the Bingley sisters all afternoon, with only a light repast of tea, small lemon, raspberry, and white cakes to sustain them. And it was not as though they could refuse such *polite* attentions from their most prominent neighbors, not with Mr. Collins as the head of their household.

 Enduring such attentions, as always, was made easier by the presence of Jane, but afterwards, Elizabeth felt the need to clasp her hands tightly together, to stop their shaking. It was not as though she were afraid of

Miss Bingley and Mrs. Hurst, but rather could not stop the influx of feelings and memories she felt every time she spoke about what happened. The face and voice of Mr. Collins danced around the edges of her mind, and she wanted desperately for the noise to stop.

Now their meal was over and it was time for Elizabeth and Jane to head back to Longbourn. despite Elizabeth's earlier teasing of Miss Bingley, the weather was quite fair.

It had drizzled a bit as they had rode in, but beyond their hats and outer garments becoming a bit damp, Miss Bingley had no need to fear for any more of their company. At least until Mr. Collins had officially sent his invitation for the Bingleys, Hursts, and Mr. Darcy to dine with them.

Miss Bingley had just ordered a passing footman to gather Elizabeth and Jane's things and pull up their carriage when Mr. Bingley and Mr. Darcy arrived from dining with Colonel Forster and the officers in Meryton. Mr. Bingley handed his hat off to a servant, and nearly dragged his taciturn friend along with him, in his eagerness to greet the Bennet ladies.

He gave them a brief, eager bow, and then started, "Oh are you both to leave already, Miss Bennet, Miss Elizabeth?"

He turned to his sister. "Caroline, allow us some conversation with our closest neighbors. Their carriage can wait another half an hour."

Miss Bingley and Mrs. Hurst glanced at each other, their expressions mirroring their surprise, and then to Mr. Darcy,

in an almost pleading way, Elizabeth thought. She followed
their gazes.

Mr. Darcy, his expression as it ever was within the company
of others was grave and foreboding. He gave them no help,
however, as he bent at the waist, to Elizabeth and Jane, and
turned to his host with an expectant look on his face.

Mr. Bingley's face lit up as he recognized the intent on his
friend's face, and offered his arm to Jane, who took it with
no change of expression. Elizabeth was startled when Mr.
Darcy strode his way towards her, in short, clipped
movements, as though he were attempting to hold himself
back, and extended the crook of his arm to her, after giving
her another bow from the waist. And thus, they were
escorted to an adjacent parlour, and were awaiting coffee
and plum cake.

Mr. Darcy, upon entering the room, escorted Elizabeth to
where she would sit with her sister, with Mr. Bingley
opposite them on a small chaise, and cloistered himself at a
small table where a quill and some papers awaited him,
Elizabeth noted. He was a man of such extremes, and why
should he pay her such favor?

First at Sir William's, when he had arrogantly declared
"every savage can dance" in response to Sir William's
repeated overtures, he then had asked her to dance out of all
the ladies attending, and now with the extraordinary

deference he paid her, now only to ignore the entire room, and write a letter!

Elizabeth wished to know exactly how he would pay suit to a lady whose company he enjoyed, for every time he received hers, his expressions and actions led her to believe that it was a thoroughly unpleasant experience.

He greeted her with deadly courtesy to her face, and given Miss Bingley's musings, she did not wish to know what was said of her behind closed doors.

Jane and Mr. Bingley had started a conversation based upon the weather; he was hoping she had not suffered any adverse affects due to the damp, and Elizabeth's concentration was taken by a bored Miss Bingley, who had declined coffee in favor of promenading about the room, passing by Elizabeth so often.

"You write uncommonly fast, Mr. Darcy." Elizabeth watched as Miss Bingley stopped at the back of Mr. Darcy's chair, peering over his shoulder to note what he was writing. Mr. Darcy gave her no answer, continuing with his writing.

A few moments passed, as Miss Bingley passed by Elizabeth, and stopped behind Mr. Darcy, again.

"To whom do you write so secretly to, sir?" she asked tartly.

Mr. Darcy addressed her then, "It is to Georgiana," he turned his way towards Elizabeth, explaining further, "my younger sister. She is but fifteen years old, and is at our home, Pemberley."

Elizabeth felt honor bound to say something, as he had gone out of his way to keep her informed of his and Miss Bingley's rather one sided conversation, yet did not quite know what to say. However, before she could speak, Miss Bingley had pounced on the subject of Miss Georgiana, with a tinkling laugh, "How is dear Georgiana faring at Pemberley alone, Mr. Darcy? You must miss her and your home."

 Mr. Darcy's eyes waited on Elizabeth's form for a brief moment, then went to meet Miss Bingley's eyes. "Of course, Caroline, whenever I am away from Pemberley and my sister, I should always miss it, but Georgiana bears the solitude well."

 He addressed Elizabeth again, "She is very fond of music and playing the pianoforte, a love she shares with your younger sister, Miss Mary, I believe." Elizabeth gave Mr. Darcy, perhaps her first true smile to anyone outside of Jane, since the Collinses had come into their lives, "She is indeed very fond of playing the pianoforte, Mr. Darcy. The only true musician among us, I am afraid."

"You played quite well at Sir William's, Miss Elizabeth." was

Mr. Darcy's reply, his timbre forthright and steady.

"I thank you sir," Elizabeth started, yet did not know how to continue on, at such a compliment given to her by the taciturn and proud man who was now attending upon her every word, "However I cannot accept such a compliment. I am well aware of my deficiencies. That is my fault, as I do not take the time to practice."

"Well, you should practice Miss Georgiana's habits and diligence, Miss Eliza" Miss Bingley interjected in a smug tone, "Dear Georgiana delights in practicing her pianoforte all day long, as she informed me at our last visit. She is growing into quite the accomplished lady, as I am sure Mr. Darcy will inform you. The last time we visited Pemberley, she showed me the most beautiful design for a table, and we had quite a time playing and singing for the assembled guests at Pemberley."

Miss Bingley shot Elizabeth a smug, satisfied look, as though Elizabeth was supposed to be jealous of her felicity with Mr. Darcy's sister, a young girl with whom she was not acquainted, and could expect to never become acquainted with.

"Indeed, Miss Bingley" Elizabeth finally said in agreement, causing Miss Bingley to send her another one of her smirks masquerading as a smile. Elizabeth gave Mr. Darcy and Miss Bingley a small smile. "I shall be happy to pass on your compliment to my sister, Mr. Darcy."

Mr. Darcy gave her a long look, surprising her with a full smile of his own, and hastily returned to his letter. Elizabeth frowned at the abruptness of his manner, and turned to her sister and Mr. Bingley, who had been in quiet conversation this entire time. She was about to suggest that she and Jane should go to their carriage, but Miss Bingley was triumphant over her.

"Charles, you really should escort Miss Eliza and Miss Bennet to their carriage, it is getting quite late. We would not wish for Mr. Collins to worry about their whereabouts."

"Of course not, dear sister." Mr. Bingley offered Jane his arm, and again, Elizabeth was shocked to see Mr. Darcy appear next to her. She had not even heard him get up from his chair. "Miss Elizabeth?" he questioned, as she did not move from her seat. Finally, she had gathered her wits enough together, to accept his arm with a soft, "Thank you, Mr. Darcy."

*****

Later that night, Elizabeth crept out of the darkened hallway, and into Jane and Kitty's room. The moonlight washed both of her sister's in silvery light, and she could see that while Kitty was asleep, Jane was still awake; staring at the ceiling above.

Carefully, Elizabeth slid in between Kitty and Jane; beyond a few cursory mumbles from Kitty, who scooted closer towards the edge of the bed once she had registered her sister's presence, she laid on her side and laid her head in Jane's breast.

A few minutes passed, and the silence was broken only with a question that Elizabeth posed to her sister. "Are you in love with Mr. Bingley, Jane?"

Her answer was only a deep inhale.

Chapter Eleven

Some days later.....

Elizabeth paused in her ministrations, as she trailed a finger down the barely warm cheek of her father. His warmth was leaving him, every day he grew weaker and weaker. Jane and Kitty had informed her of this in hushed tones earlier this morning before breakfast. They were worried, and were correct in their estimations.

Mr. Bennet would be dead soon, and once he was the Bennet women would be left at the mercy of Mr. Collins, or the expense of their uncle. Elizabeth knew that she would soon be forced to make a choice, one which would either secure or collapse her family's future. A choice that she was not even certain was hers to make anymore, not if Mr. Collins had anything to do with the matter.

She worried for her mama. Worried that Mrs. Bennet would choose today of all days to revert to her former self and show the tenants of Netherfield what they were truly missing--a peek behind the curtain, if you will.

Elizabeth doubted that Mrs. Long and Mrs. Goulding, or any of their other, loquacious neighbors had kept their tongues to themselves about the former behavior of the Bennet ladies, particularly Mrs. Bennet and Lydia, but she did not wish for that horrid Miss Bingley, nor her insipid, empty headed sister, Mrs. Hurst to even catch a glimpse of an infamous Bennet display that her mama seemed only to exhibit while she was under extreme duress.

The upcoming evening would exhibit much of that, as the Bennet ladies and servants had spent the entire week readying Longbourn to entertain Mr. Bingley and his guests. Lyddie and Mary had polished every scrap of silver they owned, Jane had painstakingly embroidered a new tablecloth for their dining table, and Kitty had spent time in the kitchens assisting Mrs. Hill.

Elizabeth--Elizabeth had done her duty, a duty for which she had been instructed on ever since the Collinses had supplanted the Bennets within their own home. She was to be mistress of Longbourn one day soon, and it would not do to have the mistress of such an estate sully herself with servants work. Not like his mother had, Mr. Collins had said, going on to remind her of why his father had hated hers to begin with.

He was not the heir of Longbourn, at least not in the manner that he had wished it. Not while his cousin was alive and could still produce an heir. Even so, he was not the master, merely cousin to the master who could not produce an heir upon an entitled estate.

Anything he inherited would be the result of another man's incompetence, and while the elder Mr. Collins would accept that, accept it as his just due, he would not be grateful for such a circumstance.

And thus, Elizabeth directed the servants and her siblings in their endeavor to ready Longbourn for such prestigious guests.

Blinking away the tears that had rapidly formed, Elizabeth gave her papa a gentle kiss on his forehead before leaving the room to ready for their guests. While crossing the hallway, she met Mr. Collins as he made his way into his own room to prepare.

"My dear," he gave her a considering, expectant glance, before she realized, with a growing twist of fear, that he was waiting for her curtsey. She did so quickly, hoping he would not take any offense at her lapse, and Mr. Collins took her lightly shaking hand within his own overly warm, moist hands.

"I had come to commend you for your prodigious attention to your duties as the future mistress of such an estate, but I fear I spoke too soon, unfortunately. My dear," he reiterated in a simpering tone, as though he were speaking to a simpleton, and his grip tightened, and she dared not even attempt to draw her hand back.

"I understand the love and affection one feels for one's own father, in that you and I are united. We both have gone through an insurmountable amount of grief in a short period, what with the passing of my own dearly missed father, and the accident that has claimed the faculties of your own father. But one should not neglect one's duty, especially on such an occasion. Mr. Darcy, Mr. Bingley, and the rest of the party shall be arriving soon. Send your sister, Miss Jane in to tend to your father, if he requires attention. Otherwise, my dear, you had better go in to ready yourself for our guests arrival."

Mr. Collins paused and puffed out his chest, as though he were a proud peacock, seeking to coax its future mate by the sway of his vibrant plumage.

"Of course, it should do me great honor if you should stand by my side, to present a united front for our guests."

Elizabeth held her face taut, soothing the muscle within her cheek, as she considered his words. His intent. She was grateful that he had not forced himself within her personal boundaries, as he had done the night of the assembly, and now she had to extricate herself from him as delicately as possible. Mr. Collins leaned into her, his eyes lingering on her form. She inhaled sharply, remaining stock still as he continued his perusal of her. She did not want to move, not wanting another moment between them.

"Of course, Mr. Collins. I do apologize. I shall go and ready myself right now." she finally managed to say softly, her voice gentle and unhurried, as his grip slowly slackened, and she was free.

*****

Elizabeth walked to her own room, and drew the door shut, her heart beating wildly. She glanced down, her hands still shaking. She drew them to her, trying to coax herself back into her natural self before getting ready for their guests. Elizabeth was determined that she should give the Bingley sisters nothing to gossip about, particularly concerning the behavior of Mr. Collins, and for that she should need to be at her best. Their neighbors had enough gossip to sustain them until she married Mr. Collins, especially with the attention Mr. Bingley paid to Jane.

His *kindness* was noted particularly among the sewing circle headed by Mrs. Goulding and Mrs. Long, and while Jane may have feelings for Mr. Bingley, Elizabeth was certain that Mr. Bingley did not return those feelings. He was simply being polite, a courtesy afforded to Jane because of her beauty, and would soon fade away.

A knock on the door startled her away, and she opened it hesitantly, to reveal her mother, and sisters--Jane and Lydia. Elizabeth was taken aback to see that her mama was *smiling*. Elizabeth allowed them into her room, staring dumbly at Mrs. Bennet as Lydia gaily skipped into the room, her arms full of gowns. Jane followed Lydia at a sedate pace, while Mama glided into the room as though she were walking on air.

"Mama, are you quite all right?" she finally asked, not able to keep the bewilderment out of her voice. "Do you need to lie down? I am sure Mr. Collins--."

Mrs. Bennet waved off Elizabeth's concerns with a gay laugh. "No, don't be silly Miss Lizzie. Am I not allowed to be happy that we are receiving guests at Longbourn? Even though I am not the mistress of mine own home, I take delight in setting a table for our neighbors and guests. I taught you exceedingly well--how to direct the servants, and of course, Kitty has taken to aiding Mrs. Hill in the kitchen with my dear Lydia, why should I not be happy, when our guests shall bear the fruits of my labour? Especially *Mr. Bingley*!"

That last name was thrown out with a note of triumph in her voice. Elizabeth's heart sank, and her gaze rapidly went to Jane, who was studiously studying the folds of her gown. She moved forward to her mama.

"Mama, I really do not think--."

Mrs. Bennet directed Elizabeth to sit at the vanity. Elizabeth did as her mother bid, her mind anxiously examining the facts, applying them to the current situation at the ready. The last thing the Bennet ladies needed was their mama throwing her crippled, eldest daughter to the most eligible man in the country, especially in front of his gossiping, elitist sisters.

Tongues were already wagging due to his attentions toward Jane, which were no more than a gentleman being courteous to lady--except Jane was not a simple lady, and Mr. Bingley was more than a mere gentleman.

"Mama--" Elizabeth tried again, to have Mrs. Bennet brush off her attempted warning once again.

"Now, now Miss Lizzie. Allow me to arrange your hair, and leave the rest to me. Oh praise the Lord!" she sighed graciously, casting her eyes up towards heaven for a brief moment. In the mirror, Elizabeth met the eyes of her sister Lydia, who rolled them in good humor to Elizabeth's expression.

"I am doing this for you, miss!" Mrs. Bennet admonished her daughter, as she continued to arrange her hair.

"Mr. Bingley is a kind and gentleman, nothing like the odious Mr. Collins or his father! I thank God everyday that that man is dead, and pray that Mr. Collins will soon follow him!" she exclaimed dramatically, clasping her hands in a beseeching prayer for a moment.

"Mama!" Elizabeth was alarmed at the thoughts in which her Mama chose to voice aloud. "Mr. Collins could hear you--!"

"Oh pish posh, Miss Lizzie! That odious man is situated quite comfortably in the master's rooms, no doubt enjoying the luxury that Mr. Bennet left behind!" her voice took on a tremor at its edge.

Lydia abandoned her fondling of the ribbons she held in her hand, and drew her Mama to her.

Elizabeth gave her sister a grateful look, thankful that her youngest sister had become so grown up and mature in the past few months. Although Mama depended heavily on Lydia and Jane, in the beginning, it had only been Mary who had the forbearance to withstand Mama's changing moods with grace. Of course, Jane had always been her favorite.

Her golden, first born child. But after Jane's accident, when she could not bear to think of what had happened, what it had cost Jane, but then some time later, Lydia had brought herself forward to be an object of contentment, no doubt at Mary's urging.

Mrs. Bennet returned to Elizabeth's side, wiping her eyes.

"Now, as I was saying, Mr. Bingley is an opportunity for us. I know what those *people* are saying of us! Of our dependence of that *odious* man! My dear Jane," she cast her eyes back at Jane, who was determinedly arranging the ribbons that Lydia had disheveled, "has always done her best to benefit her family, and this time is no different! Mr. Bingley shall be our savior, so you shall not have to marry that vile man!"

Mrs. Bennet patted Elizabeth's finished hairstyle.

"There now, Miss Lizzie. Now, let Jane take your chair so I can arrange her hair as well! She has to look beautiful for Mr. Bingley!"

*****

In the end, Miss Bingley and Mrs. Hurst did not even allow the Bennet ladies the luxury of enjoying a meal before they started in with their *inquiries,* although they were simply reiterating the same questions that had been asked of them while dining at Netherfield.

Perhaps they wished to show Mr. Bingley, first hand, where all the hopes of her mama would end. The meal had been shared with polite, if somewhat distant conversation, as Mr. Bingley struggled to come up with topics of mutual interest between the two men. Eventually they fell into a cordial conversation about the running of estates.

Mr. Darcy, Elizabeth noted furiously, was of no help in this area. He resolutely focused on eating his food, only giving short, precise answers when Mr. Bingley or even Miss

Bingley included him in the conversation. She did not understand why she had persisted in the hope that he should not do as he always did, which was silently glower at anyone who tried to speak to him, who was not of his own party.

His particular treatment of her, a tidbit Elizabeth had been surprised had not made its way into the conversation yet, was simply a false honor to bestow upon himself, she realized. That he should be one of the few to be respectable and kind to one of those poor Bennet girls, well his pride should certainly bear it tolerably well.

Mrs. Bennet was still inordinately cheerful, although Mr. Bingley had yet to address Jane with anything more than a "Good evening, Miss Bennet". On the other end of the table, Lydia, Mary, and Kitty had been clustered together, and, Elizabeth was pleased to see, amusing themselves with quiet conversation, after exchanging short pleasantries with the Bingley sisters.

"As I understand it, Mr. Collins," Miss Bingley started, "you are also new to the country of Hertfordshire. How are you finding it so far?" she asked in a somewhat indifferent tone, her eager look betraying her interest.

Mr. Collins gave an excited start, at being addressed directly. Although it should not surprise her, not with the amount of time she had spent in the company of Mr. Collins, it always shocked her at how eager he was to receive attention from those he perceived as his betters.

In regards to his and Elizabeth's relationship, she was the submissive. Every moment of time he spent with her was a gift that she should always show her utmost gratitude for. Yet it was his betters that he sought his validation from.

"I most graciously thank you for your inquiry, Miss Bingley. I am finding the country air quite tolerable, and of course, I have with me the company of my dear cousins."

Miss Bingley turned to Elizabeth, awarding her with an interested glance.

"And what of you, Miss Eliza?"

Elizabeth nearly choked on the small bite of food that she had been in the process of swallowing when Miss Bingley turned her attention onto her. Taking a small sip of water, she cleared her throat and glanced back at Mr. Collins, mindful of what had happened directly after her first interaction with Miss Bingley, as she had no wish to repeat such an encounter.

He gave her an encouraging smile, happy that such a lady was addressing his betrothed, and she returned Miss Bingley's unwavering stare, head on, her confidence somehow bolstered by the fear coursing through her body.

"I do not understand to what you are referring to, Miss Bingley. As I explained on our earlier visit, I have lived in this county all my life, and have rarely left. Generally our family would spend a few weeks with our uncle near spring, at his home in London, as my papa hated going to London during the Season. "

Miss Bingley gave her a condescending smile.

"Of course, Miss Eliza. I was referring to how you and your family were enjoying the company of your cousin, despite the dreadful circumstances." Beside her, Mrs. Hurst echoed her sister's sentiments with a murmured, "dreadful".

"I simply wished to express my condolences to your family, Miss Eliza, Mr. Collins." she said, giving Mr. Collins a significant look.

"There have been so many tragedies in your family, in such

a short period of time." she said, referring to not only Mr. Bennet's condition, but the death of Mr. Collins' father.

The table went silent, as Mr. Bingley attempted to repair the damage his sister had wittingly caused.

"Yes, as my dear sister has said, I have expressed my condolences to your cousin, but have not had the opportunity to do so to you, Mrs. Bennet," he said, addressing Mrs. Bennet, who preened under his attention, "and his daughters." he said, meeting the eyes of every Bennet lady in the room, lingering on Jane's figure.

"That is indeed very gracious of you, Miss Bingley." Mr. Collins offered, his voice booming. "It has indeed been a very trying time for our family. Especially with the death of my own most excellent father most recently. He was indeed the backbone of our father, and his loss is greatly felt to this day. However, I do my best to try and emulate his conduct, to the betterment of my fair cousins.

Miss Bingley turned to her sister with an expression of anticipation, although she concealed it with a generally pleasant, interested look on her face. Elizabeth saw it, however. If there was one thing she had learned, since her papa's accident, it was to see the motivations of the gossiping hoard of women that surrounded herself and her Mama in their drawing room in the weeks after the accident, all of them intent on squeezing as much detail out of them as possible, to go and spread to the neighbors.

"Is that the reason that you recalled Miss Lydia and Miss Catherine from society, sir?" Miss Bingley inquired, a baffled and bewildered edge overtaking the tone of her voice.

A clatter of cutlery was heard, as Mrs. Bennet aggressively used her knife and fork to cut herself a bite sized piece of meat. Her mouth was now within a narrow line, as for once she fully comprehended the intent of Miss Bingley's question.

Elizabeth felt Mr. Darcy stiffen beside her, yet he said nothing. She should soon have to train herself to not be surprised at that, for the duration of his company.

She glanced to and fro from Mr. Collins, Miss Bingley, and Lydia and Kitty. Lydia and Kitty, who had been talking quietly amongst themselves, as they had been warned by Mr. Collins that he would send them to bed early, in front of their guests if he shamed them by acting as vulgar and free with their manners as they had before he entered their lives, and had now stopped talking entirely, and focused their attention on their plate of food.

Mr. Bingley, of course, attempted to come to their rescue.

"Now, now Caroline, I do believe that is not appropriate conversation for our evening. We are having a wonderful meal." He turned to Mr. Collins. "I apologize for my sister, Mr. Collins."

Mr. Collins shook his head grandly, "No, no, my dear Mr. Bingley. It is quite all right, I am quite happy to answer your dear sister's question."

He turned to address everyone at the table, his eyes especially fixed on Elizabeth's pale face. She did not know which to feel first--anger, shame, or embarrassment over what was about to happen, and only wished, not for the first time, that she and her family could disappear all together.

"When my beloved father and I arrived at Longbourn, after our dear Cousin Bennet's accident, which robbed him of his faculties, we found our dear cousins were abiding under a rather *lax* household. Of course, before his own senseless death, my dear father implemented some new rules for my fair cousins to abide by."

Mr. Collins rambled on, unaware or uncaring the look undisguised looks of interest and consternation Miss Bingley and Mrs. Hurst were giving each other, shocked at how much he was revealing, yet that only piqued their appetite. Mr. Bingley clearly did not know what to do, as he looked from his sisters, to Mr. Collins, to Jane, his mouth falling open in surprise.

"That is not to say that my own dear cousins, Miss Bennet and Miss Elizabeth were not the most amiable ladies you should ever have had the pleasure of keeping company with, although my fair cousin Miss Elizabeth's tongue is rather sharp at times."

At Miss Bingley's knowing look, he rushed to assure her, "Something, we are of course, rectifying, aren't we my fair cousin? Fordyce's Sermons, a favorite of mine while I was in seminary. It has been very useful in the instruction of my youngest cousins, Miss Lydia and Catherine, who, I am afraid were led to be very wild and unsociable girls. Too young for society and the amusements offered."

His voice took on a cheerful lilt, "And, as you can see Miss Bingley, my fair cousins have certainly learned to temper their behavior!"

Miss Bingley and Mrs. Hurst followed his gaze to a red faced Lydia and Kitty, and exchanged knowing glances.

*****

It was only afterwards, when the Bennets, Mr. Collins, and their guests were gathered in the small sitting room for coffee and tea, that Mr. Darcy drew near to Elizabeth, who was seated by the fire, alone. He held Elizabeth's eye, and her breath caught in her throat as he simply fixed her with an unreadable look. His eyes softened minutely, and then spoke.

"I do not believe Miss Bingley meant to be quite so brusque, Miss Elizabeth." he said, his voice almost gentle. She watched his face, as the shadows from the lanterns and fire played with his features. Elizabeth looked away, unable to meet his gaze. There was something akin to pity, except she would have felt insulted had he pitied her, given his understanding of the situation she and her family found themselves in.

She also felt another flare of anger, for he had said or did nothing while his *dear friend's* sister humiliated her family, and thoroughly enjoyed herself while it happened. Any apologies from him, or from Miss Bingley would also register as false and insincere.

"But I would like to take the opportunity to offer my condolences, since the subject has been brought up. After a long illness, one that lasted several months, my own dear father died when I was barely at the age of my majority. I have a sister, Georgiana, who is the same age as your sister, Miss Catherine, who also suffered an unjust amount of pain due to our father's long illness. It--it robbed us both, but especially my sister of having a father for a very long time, before he died."

Mr. Darcy paused awkwardly, before stating "I experienced feelings of extreme grief, it was only the love of my sister and cousin, Richard Fitzwilliam, that pushed me through to the end. I only experienced relief when my father died--I-I-" here he stammered, looking away, "I was happy that he was no longer in pain." A grave expression fixed his face. "It does get better, Miss Elizabeth. But the pain will never go away."

Elizabeth cleared her throat, finding her voice at long last. She gazed at Mr. Darcy in bewilderment. What a man of many contradictions! Yet again, she still did not know why her mind dwelt on the character of Mr. Darcy.

A proud, arrogant man, who thought nothing of teasing his friend for being disappointed that the most beautiful woman in the room was lame, yet here he was, exposing himself to her in the most private of ways! It was only she, of the whole of Meryton, Elizabeth surmised, that had seen something of the true Fitzwilliam Darcy. She doubted Miss Bingley had seen such a side to Mr. Darcy, or if she had, she had dismissed it just as well as she had dismissed Elizabeth's pain at her father's condition.

Elizabeth felt a twinge of pity for Mr. Darcy at those thoughts, and for that she did not know why. He was nothing to her, and would most likely be gone in a few months, with Mr. Bingley right along side him if his sister did not have anything to say about it.

"Thank you, Mr. Darcy. I thank you for your kind words. It is the most understanding anyone has been since the accident."

Mr. Darcy gave her another low bow, at the waist, and stalked back to his friend's side. Watching him go,

Elizabeth's eye was caught by Mr. Collins, who gave her a significant look. She withheld a fine tremble, as she knew there would be a *conversation* to be had about her private conversation with Mr. Darcy.

Chapter Twelve

Elizabeth lay abed, aware that it was long past the time she would usually get out of bed. But it was no use, as she had not been able to take her usual morning walks, generally two or three miles before breakfast, and while she was still abed, she did not have to interact with Mr. Collins.

Jane and Kitty generally took a walk of half an hour or so along the lawns of the estate, but even that had diminished after the elder Mr. Collins had declared Jane to be fit enough, and his son would hardly question his father's claims--as it was, it hardly mattered that his father was dead. His word was law. A fact Elizabeth was slowly realizing would always hold true.

A short rap on her door was the only notice she received before it was thrust open. Before Elizabeth could comprehend her actions, she had flung herself onto the floor. And waited--hoping and praying for what she knew not. All she knew was that she was afraid.

"Lizzie?" a feminine voice was heard.

Elizabeth sighed in relief. It was her sister Lydia. Who, in her usual brashness, a trait that the Collinses had not managed to completely train out of her, had barged into her room. Elizabeth hauled herself up from the floor awkwardly, and then faced her sister, a sheepish look dominating her face. Lydia furrowed her brow.

"Lizzie what were you doing on the floor?"

Elizabeth said nothing, for she could not tell Lydia, nor Jane for that matter of the previous night and early morning, when she had laid awake, listening to Mr. Collins heavy steps stop, and pause on the other side of her door.

She did not wish for her sisters to realize that she could only wait, and see what happened.
Without waiting for an answer, Lydia leapt into other matters.

"Lizzie, today is Aunt Phillips card party! Mary and I want some new ribbons to trim our bonnets." Continuing on, she faltered, suddenly looking elsewhere.

"W-would you speak to Mr. Collins?" she asked timidly. "About allowing us to walk to Meryton to go the milliner's shop? Even if we could only go to one shop that would be wonderful!" she exclaimed enthusiastically, as though that would be the basis of Mr. Collins allowing them to go anywhere.

Due to their partial mourning of his father, and the assumption that they would soon be mourning her own father, the Bennet ladies had spent a ratherlimited time in the actual town of Meryton, only leaving for assemblies, and even then, rarely. Mr. Collins wished to allow them time to prepare themselves for more mourning, and it benefited him as he could keep Elizabeth under his thumb for the time being.

Elizabeth studied the anxiously hopeful face of her younger sister for a few moments, before conceding with a small nod.

"Of course Lydia, I will speak to Mr. Collins after our morning meal. Will you go see if the horses are needed on the farm? If not, that may persuade his opinion more in our favor, if we should go by carriage." she said nonsensically.

Lydia gave Elizabeth a tight, enthusiastic hug, before rushing back to the door, now trembling in excitement and boundless amounts of energy as every fifteen year old girl had. Stopping in the doorway, she curiously composed herself and turned to look back at Elizabeth.

"Lizzie?" she asked, her voice low.

"Yes?"
"Are you quite all right?" The question was asked in so sincere a tone that Elizabeth wanted to cry, but did not wish to frighten her sister.

Swallowing raggedly, she replied, "I am well, Lydia. Go on, I shall follow you in a few moments time. I need to get dressed."

Lydia shot her a look that stated she clearly was not fooled, but left anyway.

Wiping the coming tears from her eyes, Elizabeth moved to her closet to get dressed, and to compose herself for the coming conversation that she must have.

*****

Mr. Collins had confined himself within his study when he heard a short knock breach his study's sanctum.

"Yes, you may come in." he said, presuming that it was Hill arriving with the tea tray. He always liked to take tea and a few pieces of toast while he worked the ledgers in the morning. The door was opened, and to his immense pleasure and satisfaction it was his betrothed, his dear cousin Eliza--holding his tea tray! Even more perfect!

He leapt to his feet.

"Yes, my dear, come in, come in! Set the tray down here." he said, gesturing to the empty place he had set aside for such occasions, every morning.

His betrothed did as she was bid, and it warmed his heart to think that his father had gone to the lengths he had to choose such a fine bride for him, his only son and heir.

Although his betrothed still had a rather sharp tongue, she had not used it in quite some time, and for that he was grateful.

She was learning,and he was very eager to instruct her. Soon she would be the perfect Collins bride, the perfect Collins heir. Just like his dearly beloved mother, whom God had taken too soon from his family.

His betrothed sank down onto the chair opposite his own with as much grace as he would expect from a woman who was to be mistress of such an estate, and regarded him respectfully--a trait that he and his father had worked hard to instill upon her from the early days of their residency.

Once again, he thanked God that he had had his father with him when he had arrived at Longbourn. Heaven help him if he had to take upon all of this *himself*! He was entirely sure that he would have been driven mad and sent to Bedlam, and *then* where would his fair cousins be without his guidance?

"How may I help you my dear?" he asked condescendingly, entirely sure that there was some matter that his fair cousin needed his help with, otherwise why should she be here, disturbing the master of the estate while he worked to improve their livelihoods? As a point in her favor, how he knew that she would make him an excellent bride, even before his father had chosen her for him, was that she was extremely respectful of his privacy, and had never sought him out early in the morning. Not for her trivial, feminine needs.

He watched as his dear cousin swallowed nervously, and then responded to his question.

"Sir, I was simply wondering if my sisters and I could walk into Meryton, if you should not be able to spare the horses from the farm, to go the milliner's shop after breakfast. You see," and her his lovely cousin rushed to explain, for she knew that he would be entirely displeased if she had interrupted his work for some foppish request, although he had immensely enjoyed her visit, and was considering having her join him every morning--to encourage their natural felicity, of course.

"You see," she repeated, and his heart warmed at her soft, feminine voice. He considered it a mark of extreme pride and attraction that when she addressed him, and only him, her voice had changed into something that was more feminine and docile. Another mark, surely that they were completely made for each other, two halves of a whole, as God had said.

"As you know, Mr. Collins, my dear Aunt Phillips has invited us to her card party, later this afternoon. And we were hoping that we should be able to go into town and buy some ribbons for our hats. We should like to show Longbourn at its best. Would that be all right, Mr. Collins?" she asked uncertainly.

Mr. Collins leaned back in his chair, not showing his fair cousin what he was thinking. He was, of course, going to allow her and her sisters into town for this brief visit.

It would be a reward with how well they had behaved themselves when Mr. Bingley and his party had dined in his home. Such behavior deserved a reward, especially for the younger two girls, who had been shameless hoydens--loose women, they were sure to become if there was no one who would take the trouble to check them. And so he did.

He was sure that Mr. Bingley had heard the rumors of their former behavior, and now he had seen first hand that Mr. Collins was an intelligent, knowledgeable master of his own household and estate--a very valuable neighbor.

But he should also like to give his fair cousin the knowledge that what she has will not come for free, that her days as being able to sit, read Fordyce's Sermons, and embroider cushions would soon come to an end. In the beginning, his father had instructed that his fair cousin should sit with him in this very study, and learn how to work the estate properly, as its mistress, and so those lessons had taken very few days. Now, her mornings were spent directing the servants with her mother, but he thought that she should also learn how to work with himself. Learn just how often he had to make the most difficult decisions, and how that affected her pin money, for instance.

He gave his fair cousin an alluring smile. Licking his lips, he leaned forward and said "Of course my dear cousin. Your youngest sisters, of course, deserve a reward for their sensible and modest behavior for the meal with Mr. Bingley and his guests. However," he said sharply, when she opened her mouth to thank him. She closed it rather fast, and looked rather wounded, so he rushed to assure her.

"I do apologize my fair cousin. But I was simply wishing to be able to speak without any interruptions, you understand, do you not my dear?" He waited for her to nod hesitantly, pleased that she had grassed his intentions so thoroughly, and so quickly.

"However," he repeated, "I should wish that you would start taking your mornings her in this study, with me. I believe that God intends to take your father not too long before nigh, and it should be a wonderful idea for us to begin on our intimate felicity, do you not agree, my dear?" He knew that she would, that she was grateful to be marrying an intelligent man who wished to secure her comfort before they were even formally engaged!

"Yes, Mr. Collins." she finally said. His fair cousin sounded a bit unenthusiastic, but Mr. Collins reminded himself that she was a proper lady, and that proper ladies her age did not encourage men of his station. It was natural for them to wish to be seen as chaste individuals, and he thoroughly agreed with his fair cousin on that score. How wonderful that their fundamental values had thoroughly matched together!

"You may go my dear, you and your sisters, after our morning meal."

He gestured that she should leave, so that he could get back to his ledgers. His fair cousin, ever the proper lady, gave him a deep curtsey, as she had been taught, and smoothly glided away. A small smile came over his face, and remained there the entire morning, as he thought of their future together.

*****

A walk. A glorious walk. Elizabeth sighed in pleasure as at the cool breeze drew gently across her face. She was keeping a sedate pace, as to not outmatch Jane. All the sisters were. Lydia, Mary, and Kitty were all arm in arm, chattering about something, anything. Although Mary was new to the world of giggling, she had quickly matched Lydia and Kitty, excited and happy to bond with her younger sisters.

She had often felt the odd sister out, and Elizabeth had felt even more guilty, after everything had happened, that she had allowed her younger sister to be as ignored as she had been. They were together now, truly together, and that was all that mattered.

The sisters entered the shop, it was curiously empty for the time of day, and Elizabeth watched in amusement as her younger sisters swooped into the remaining ribbons, examining them critically for their differences in color, texture, material, size, and cost. She had tucked her extra allowance into her reticule for such an event, as she was entirely sure that her sisters, most likely Lydia--whose boldness would never leave her, but, perhaps be dampened somewhat--would ask to borrow money.

"Lizzie, are you quite all right?" The question came from Jane, who had not gone off with their sisters to peruse the ribbon, nor gone off on her own. It should not have surprised her, but it did. She turned to her sister.

"I suppose Lydia spoke to you." It was not a question.

"Yes, she told me that when she came into your room this morning, you were on the floor, next to the bed. And that she had heard you fall."

"I am fine, Jane."

Jane slipped her hand into Elizabeth's. She gave a meaningful squeeze, and Elizabeth was reminded of the conversation they had some weeks ago, while in their carriage to attend upon the Bingley sisters. She was certain Jane had remembered it too.

At that moment Lydia and Kitty came to her side, each with pleading expressions, and allowing their gazes to follow Mary, who was still critically examining the ribbons, as she used to do for her books. With an exaggerated, long suffering sigh, Elizabeth dramatically flourished her reticule containing her money, and handed it over to her sister Kitty's eager hands.

With a quick kiss to her sister's cheek, Kitty glided back to Mary with as much feminine grace as she could muster. Lydia stayed with Elizabeth and Jane, a curious expression dominating her face.

"Are you sure you are well, Lizzie?" she finally asked, seeing the confusion on Elizabeth and Jane's face.
Elizabeth rushed to assure her.

"I am quite well, Lydia."

Lydia's face transformed into understanding, as she

whispered, "I am not a child any longer, Lizzie." She gave a mournful pout, reminding Elizabeth of her youth, as she flounced off.

*****

"I say, is that the Bennet ladies!" a masculine voice was heard behind them, and Elizabeth turned to see the owner of such a voice, only to see that it was an officer--Denny if she remembered correctly.

One of the very officers that Lydia and Kitty had shamelessly flirted with previously. Beside him was a rather handsome man, who especially stood out due to the sharpness of his dress. He and Denny, if Elizabeth could still voice such thoughts, even to herself, looked very dashing and smart in their uniform and dress, and she could see why Lydia and Kitty had fallen for the men in regiments.

Looking beside her, at Lydia and Kitty, she was pleased to see that although they had returned Denny's greeting, they had done so respectively and in a normal tone. None of the shrieking and giggling of yesteryear.

"I say, I have not seen you ladies in quite some time." Denny said, when it was clear that Lydia and Kitty were not going to fall over themselves giggling over him.

"Our family has decided to stay somewhat close to home, because of the death of Mr. Collins' Papa and our Papa." Lydia finally said, her gaze betraying to Elizabeth's face, wishing for confirmation that she had said the right thing. A smile from Elizabeth told her she had.

Denny bowed dramatically, Elizabeth sardonically noted, but the man beside him did not. He simply gave a short bow, tipped his hat before murmuring that he was very sorry for their loss. Sarcastic feelings swept Elizabeth's mind as she realized that he had probably heard exactly what had happened to their family from Denny himself, or from some other gossip in town.

"You ladies still are going to Mrs. Phillips card party, are you not?" Denny gave them, especially Lydia and Kitty a roguish smile, that Elizabeth did not like at all.

Lydia opened her mouth to respond to his inquiry, and Elizabeth stepped forward to answer, intent on getting Denny's attention off of her younger sisters, when out of the corner of her eye, a shadow drew. She turned to see what it was.

It was Mr. Bingley and Mr. Darcy, both on their magnificent horses. Mr. Bingley swung off his horse, haphazardly, and gave the Bennet ladies a low bow. Beside him, Mr. Darcy had not gotten off his horse, and was regarding the man next to Denny with something akin to loathing.
Their eyes met, his dark and furious, and he gave Elizabeth a short nod, before directing his horse to gallop off.

Mr. Bingley gave the Bennet ladies an apologetic smile, before excusing himself to gallop after his friend.

The man next to Denny spoke.

"I have been entirely rude, I have not introduced myself. I am George Wickham," he said with a bow to each of the sisters. He then said, with a nod in the direction of Mr. Darcy, "That was Mr. Darcy, of Pemberley, correct?"

"You are indeed, sir, correct. He is staying with Mr. Bingley, the tenant of Netherfield--the closest neighbor to our estate." Jane said quietly.

Mr. Wickham gave her a charming smile, his eyes lingering on her cane, and then spoke of other matters.

"What is this I hear of a card party, eh Denny?" he asked jovially.

Denny turned to answer his friend, but not before giving Lydia and Kitty an alluring wink.

"Their Aunt Phillips throws card parties once or twice a month, and these lovely ladies are sure to attend it for the first time in a year or so, to my recollection."

Mr. Wickham gave them another bow, "Then I should be entirely remiss if I did not attend such an event." He added considerately to his friend, "Perhaps we should go out of their way, Denny. I am sure these ladies have other important tasks to accomplish before the day is over, and we are blocking their way."

With bows and curtsies exchanged, the gentlemen and ladies were on their way.

*****

Elizabeth massaged the spot upon which her arm ached, as she sipped some punch slowly. Mr. Collins had forcefully grabbed her arm when they had gotten out of the carriage, because she had not gone to his side quick enough, and it still stung. She hoped it would not bruise, that he had not left his mark upon her. He had been grabbing her more and more, and it was getting quite difficult to conceal even the lightest of marks.

Mr. Collins was attempting to play Vingt-Un, drawn into the game by her shrewd Aunt Phillips, who gave her a gentle smile; Lydia and Kitty were in a game with Maria and her dear Charlotte, Mary was playing a light, merry tune upon the pianoforte, and Jane sat next to Mama, who was holding court with some other ladies.

The officers had indeed been surprised when Lydia and Kitty had not chased after them, as they always had before, nor even to really speak with them, but generally pleasantries. It had taken them but a few moments to get over their shock, and sport with some other young ladies.

A man drew near her, and Elizabeth was shocked to see that it was the man from before, Mr Wickham!

"How do you do, sir?" she asked, as he carefully poured himself a cup of punch.

"I am very well, Miss Elizabeth. How are you enjoying the party?" he asked. Elizabeth responded, and they exchanged general pleasantries for a few minutes or so.

Elizabeth smiled in genuine pleasure. If she had been the same person, she should have already been half in love with such a man. He was everything that was polite, charming, and witty. He had informed her that he was soon to join the regiment, and she was sure that his charms, while in uniform, would go very far.

"I wonder, Miss Elizabeth, if it is not too much trouble to ask--but how long has Mr. Darcy been in Netherfield?" Elizabeth answered with some curiosity, wondering if he had some connection to Mr. Darcy or his family. She recalled that she had heard from Mrs. Goulding that his uncle was an earl. "About six weeks or so, I believe. Why do you ask, Mr. Wickham?"

He regarded her with a curious intent, before searching around to see if anyone was watching or listening to them. When none were found, he answered her.

"It may shock you to know, Miss Elizabeth, but we were boyhood friends. My father was the steward of Pemberley, and his father, the old Mr. Darcy was my godfather."

Elizabeth frowned in confusion. "Then why had--" Even before he answered her, Elizabeth was not sure why she was confused. Mr. Darcy *was* proud and arrogant, disregarding his sometimes complementary behavior towards her. Speech, without actions to fortify the words were rather useless, a hard learned lesson she had comprehended very quickly

"Mr. Darcy's father died some years ago, close to his majority. And old Mr. Darcy had been very fond of me, indeed he was my godfather and treated me like a second son. And Darcy had always been jealous, and that jealousy manifested in an unforgivable manner."

Mr. Wickham's voice lowered here, and became very raw.

 "We had been estranged for several years, when I had heard that Uncle George-I beg your pardon--Darcy's father had been dying for several months, and I had begged and pleaded for Darcy to allow me to attend upon him at his deathbed, but Darcy refused. As if that were not enough, in further injury, his father had left for me the living that is currently vacant on his estate, Pemberley. I had always meant to join the Church, and had gone to university in preparation. Darcy refused, giving the living to another."

He took a sip of his punch, and laughed at Elizabeth's shocked expression.

"So I have had to make my own way in the world."

"How cruel!" Elizabeth could only say. Mr. Wickham gave her another bow, and said "It is not so terribly bad, Miss Elizabeth. I have prospects for a new career, I have food and water in my belly, a place to lay my head at night. I have been in worse situations before."

Elizabeth wondered at his abrupt change in manner,

"Were you not able to find any legal recourse, my Uncle Phillips is a solicitor, perhaps he could--"

Mr. Wickham shook his head thoughtfully. "It is indeed a terrible situation, but it is best to forget about it. My love for his father's memory is the only thing that keeps me from any retaliation."

And with that, he excused himself to go and dance with a red headed girl she had noticed earlier, flitting among the officers--a Mary King--and Elizabeth was left to consider her conflicting thoughts alone, aware that she was again, thinking upon Mr. Darcy's fractured character.

Chapter Thirteen

Netherfield Ball

Elizabeth settled behind the vanity, and watched as Jane carefully made up her hair. Jane was already dressed for the ball, a simple white gown with blue accents at the waist and hem, her hair arranged in a simple bun. Elizabeth smiled into the mirror, where her sister was watching her.

"You look beautiful Jane."

Jane returned her smile with a sad look.

"Not beautiful enough, it would seem."

Elizabeth turned to Jane, rather abruptly, causing half of her hair to fall out.

"Lizzie!" Jane admonished. "Lydia and Kitty still wish to use your vanity, and they have spent their time taking care of Papa and Mama while we are in here to use it before we have to leave!"

Elizabeth saw the wisdom of her sister's words and submitted to her sister's gentle instruction.

Mary had taken more of an interest in her appearance, as a consequence of sharing a room with her formerly scatter brained, brash sister, Lydia, and that inclination had followed to her hairstyles Previously, she had arranged her hair, simple and unadorned, as something she was able to do herself, and without a mirror.

Being that Lydia and Kitty had been recalled from society, they had transferred all of their attentions to Mary. Not surprisingly, due to the upcoming ball, Lydia and Kitty had spent half the morning, when they were able to dodge Mr.

Collins, arranging Mary's hair, and had come up with a number of interesting and creative styles that suited Mary, as they said.

Lydia and Kitty, however wished to use the large vanity that now resided in Elizabeth's room, and had unfortunately made their desire clear in Mr. Collins' presence. He had ordered that should they wish to use something that was not theirs, and in fact belonged to the future mistress of the household, never mind that she was their sister, then they would have to *earn* the time spent in Elizabeth's room.

And so, Lydia and Kitty had spent part of the morning and early afternoon in papa's room. As more and more time passed, more and more of the duties in his care were heaped on the Bennet ladies, as Mr. Collins required Mr. Hill more and more frequently on the farm.

They had shaved the growing hair on his face, had fed him, given him a short sponge bath on his face, arms, and chest, and then had changed his bedding with the help of Mrs. Hill. She assured them that Mr. Hill would come in later to attend to Mr. Bennet's private needs, and that was that.

Mary and Lydia had then spent the rest of the time comforting their mama. Elizabeth's mouth compressed into a thin line, each time she thought of the situation. Mr. Collins had been informed by several gossips, that at her Aunt Phillips card party, that her mama had been holding court with the neighbors, spreading the notion that Jane would soon be courted by Mr. Bingley, due to the attention and care he had bestowed upon her each time they met in company.

Mr. Collins admonished her mama for spreading such falsehoods, and unfortunately the invitation for the Netherfield ball had come to their home that very morning that Mr. Collins had been informed of her mama's deeds. He had determined that for her punishment in maligning such an honorable man, she should say that she were not feeling well, and stay home for the ball.

Mrs. Bennet had called for her smelling salts soon thereafter, and was now enclosed in her rooms and had refused to leave. It had been a week since then, and neither Lydia, nor Jane, nor Mary could persuade Mrs. Bennet to leave her room.

They had been bringing her trays every morning and night, but Elizabeth feared that soon Mr. Collins would grow weary of submitting to her mama's nerves, and order that she should have no food, if she would not come downstairs and eat with the *family.*

Her mama had already suffered enough blows to her pride and sense, and Elizabeth did not wish for it to worsen any further.

Perhaps, after papa was gone, and they were wedded and bedded, Mr. Collins would have everything he wanted, and their situation would not seem so dreadful.

She could only hope.

*****

Elizabeth sat on the end of the bed, with Jane and Mary, watching as Kitty finished Mary's hair. It was an elaborate style that Elizabeth would have thought was too much for Mary's simple gown, but she found that it enhanced her entire being. She noted with more than a touch of pride that Kitty was very much becoming an accomplished hairdresser. They did not even need a maid anymore, not that they could spare Maria with mama's nerves, nor from Mrs. Hill.

"Lydia, Kitty, Mary--" Elizabeth started, her eyes darting to the door, checking to make sure that it was closed. "I should like to speak to you about something, a matter which I have done some thinking of, for the past few days."

"What is it?" Mary asked softly, noting the serious look on her sister's face.

"It is about Mr. Wickham, Mary. I do not know if any of you noticed, but while we were at Aunt Phillips', Mr. Wickham approached me at the punch bowl."

"Oh yes!" Lydia said with a devious grin. As she spoke, everything came out with a rush, "I saw you--Maria and I both did. He seemed very interested in *you* Lizzie."

She sighed dreamily, "Isn't Mr. Wickham frightfully handsome? It would be awfully romantic if you should marry him instead of that stodgy Mr. Collins, Lizzie! I know! You should run off and elope to Gretna Green--I would cover for you by sleeping in your bed--or perhaps Mary should, you are both around the same size, and I am so much smaller than both--"

"Lydia!" Elizabeth said sharply, much more sharper than she intended. Lydia's mouth closed, and her mouth turned downward, as she looked at her hands. On both sides of her, Kitty and Mary put an arm around her in comfort.

Elizabeth gave a soft sigh. "I am sorry, Lydia. But what I have to say is important."

"What is it, Lizzie?" Jane was curious, as Elizabeth had not said anything to her about Mr. Collins. She too had noticed that Mr. Wickham had approached her, as she was trying to ignore the boasting her mama was doing on her behalf, for an event she was certain would never occur.

"I think," Elizabeth started hesitantly, "that we should stay away from Mr. Wickham. I do not trust him."

"Has he said anything untoward, Lizzie?" Jane wanted to know.

"No, Jane. He has been very proper, a gentleman. But I feel that there is something sinister about him. We spoke for a few minutes of general topics--the weather, how he liked it her Meryton, and so on. And then he turned the conversation towards Mr. Darcy. You all saw how rude Mr. Darcy had acted towards him, when we met in Meryton. Well, he informed me that he had known Mr. Darcy since he was a child, and that his godfather had even been Mr. Darcy's father!"

Jane knit her brows together. "Then why should Mr. Darcy have treated him thus?"

"He claims it is because he was the favorite of Mr. Darcy's father, and in consequence, refused to allow him at his deathbed, nor claim the inheritance that Mr. Darcy's father left in his will."

"And you do not believe him?" Kitty asked, speaking up for the first time.

Elizabeth shook her head. "I do not know. But what I do know is that it is very odd that he should have relayed all of this information to me! I had barely been introduced to the man, and he has told me all of his woes in short order!"

Lydia's eyes grew wide at her implication, caught between her glee and happiness at being able to at least *view* the officers at her aunt's card party, and the knowledge that one of her new favorites was
dishonest.

Ever since she was a little girl, her mama had waxed rhapsodies over the honorable nature of the officers that she had met in her youth, before marrying her papa, Mr. Bennet. So kind! So honorable! So brave to sacrifice one's life for one's country! One of them would have made an excellent husband, had she not succumbed to Mr. Bennet's charms.

Elizabeth shifted her tone into that of a soothing presence. "I do not know if he is lying, Lydia. But I do think it odd that he should tell all of this to me, after one brief introduction. And, I went to the market today with Mrs. Hill and asked the vendors of Mr. Wickham, and they have all reported that he has told them all the same story! I know that Mr. Darcy is proud and arrogant, but--" and here her voice softened, and she hated herself for her weakness, for her reliance on the scraps of kindness and propriety that Mr. Darcy had deigned to convey to her, and only her, "he has been very kind to me, while we have been in the same company."

The Bennet sisters exchanged knowing looks, as Elizabeth had already informed them of the conversation they had after the disastrous dinner with Mr. Bingley.

"He and Mr. Bingley were abominably rude about Jane when they first met, although I believe due to the pressing circumstances, they have more than made up for their slight." Elizabeth said lightly, aware of Jane's discomfort, yet also wishing to be fair to Mr. Darcy, for it pained her to be aware that he truly behaved in a more gentleman like manner, when it came to her sister, than the majority of men that Elizabeth had grown up with! The day that one of those gentlemen would do more than stare at Jane, when they believed they were being discreet, and come up to her and speak, then that should be the day that Mr. Darcy should be overruled.

"Mr. Darcy, especially is hated and everyone in town is disgusted by his pride and arrogance. But I believe him to be an honorable man. His actions have revealed that to me. I do not trust this Mr. Wickham, as we do not know enough about him, and I simply wish for you all to be on your guard against him. As we have already seen, he is a determined flirt, and at the very least we should get into some trouble with Mr. Collins--especially you, Lydia and Kitty. If it comes back to him that you are encouraging his attentions while at Aunt Phillips' card party, then he may ban you from going to them as well, no matter if she is our aunt."

At the threat of no longer being allowed to attend their sole societal amusement, Lydia and Kitty both nodded in agreement, and made rapid promises of never flirting with him or the officers.

*****

"Miss Elizabeth!" Mr. Bingley greeted her enthusiastically, as Elizabeth made her way down the receiving line at Netherfield.

"Mr. Bingley." she returned his greeting. She was slowly warming up to him, his eager and gentle manners made it quite hard to dislike him. Of course, her mama had done an admirable job of helping her along, with spreading the rumors that Mr. Bingley should like to court Jane.

After spending half the night awake in anger, Elizabeth simply realized to herself that she was angry because Jane was in love with him, and no matter what, no matter what attentions he bestowed upon Jane, he would never make her an offer. However, that expectation came not from him, nor the town, but from mama, and Elizabeth knew that it was not fair to him, nor to Jane. She was amazed that he even paid them the particular attentions that he had, knowing that it would fuel the rumor mill. And his sisters.

He was a good man, and it was not his fault they were in this situation. That was what she had to tell herself. That was what Jane had to tell herself, as he bowed over her hand with a flourish.

"Miss Eliza, how droll to see you!" Elizabeth kept her smile plastered on her face, as she curtseyed for Miss Bingley.

"Of course Miss Bingley, it is an honor for my family and I to be here. I thank you for the invitation." with another curtsey, she was about to leave and look for Charlotte, as behind her, Miss Bingley was already questioning Jane as to why their mama was not present,when a warm and moist hand grabbed her arm. She froze.

Mr. Collins.

"Do remember, my fair cousin," he said, his tight grip not loosening, "that I have claimed your hand for the first two dances."

She gave him a curtsey, after he had let go of her arm, "Of course, sir. I was about to find my friend, Charlotte. I shall look for you when the dances are started."

He inclined his head, "Of course my dear cousin. You may go." he said, giving his permission. Giving him another curtsey, she left to find her friend.

Charlotte was across the room, nibbling on a small tart, when Elizabeth found her.

"I do not have long, Charlotte," she said, as her friend embraced her, "as I have promised my first two dances with Mr. Collins."

"Is he so very bad, Lizzie?" Charlotte asked, her head tilted to the side.

"Not as bad as his father. He is a rather poor imitation, but an imitation none the less."

Charlotte patted her hand.

"You simply need to decide what you are willing to settle for. There are many who would give an eyeteeth to be in your position, Lizzie. However, you have other prospects." she said slyly, her eyes moving across the room--to where the glowering Mr. Darcy stood, stiffly with his hands at his side.

Elizabeth looked at her friend, aghast. "I swear Charlotte, every time we meet you come up with new fantasies in order to amuse yourself. Mr. Darcy is not interested in me!"

"He is watching you at this very moment, and has been watching you since you arrived. Do you fault his taste?" she asked tartly.

Elizabeth was spared from answering, as Mr. Collins had arrived to claim his dances.

"My dear cousin." He bowed, and they went to their positions in the line, and the dance began, with Mr. Bingley leading it with his sister, Mrs. Hurst.

Elizabeth, although as a rule always made it a point to speak during a dance, she had learned that she may as well keep her answers limited to "Yes, Mr. Collins" or "Of course, Mr. Collins", as he was excessively fond of imagining their future together, while they were dancing. Something about the act, she supposed how intimate it was, always spurred his thoughts and feelings--thoughts and feelings that were best left unspoken.

"How wonderful, my dear cousin! That we should be able to tell our children that we have danced together at Netherfield, for the first time in three generations! I imagine that it should be a point of great pride and pleasure, even many years in the future, should Mr. Bingley choose to stay, that he had such a prominent, betrothed couple attend his ball."

"We are not betrothed, Mr. Collins." Elizabeth cursed herself as the reprimand slipped out of her mouth before she could stop it.

Mr. Collins eyes and mouth tightened, and she knew she had gone too far.

"Of course not, my fair cousin. Not yet." he said, ominously, and then continued on, as though she had not said anything.

He had then shocked her by allowing her to return back to her friend Charlotte, while he attended upon Sir William and Mr. Bingley, who had been joined by Jane and Mary, and she knew that the ball had granted her a reprieve.

For now.

She had been speaking to Jane and Mary, as Charlotte had gone to attend to her father for something or other, and was shocked to see Mr. Darcy stalk up to her, his face tight, as though he were in agony.
He addressed her with his usual low, grave bow, and then gave her a long look before asking brusquely, "May I have this next dance, Miss Elizabeth?"

She was so stunned that she could only murmur an affirmative, and he was gone before she could even curtsey.

Her expression was still stunned when Charlotte arrived, who questioned her appearance.

"Mr. Darcy has just asked Lizzie for the next two dances." Mary helpfully informed Charlotte.

Charlotte gave Lizzie a knowing look, saying "And now who is fantasizing, Lizzie? You shall see that I am right."

*****

Mr. Darcy had collected her for their dances, offering his arm in his usual grave manner. As they walked past the assembled throng to line up for the dance, with some small satisfaction, she was glad to see the briefly horrified face of Miss Bingley, who then quickly found a partner for the coming dance.

She did not understand why Miss Bingley had thought to be so jealous of her, especially when she knew that Elizabeth was as good as betrothed and united in marriage to Mr. Collins.

Their dance began, and it was utterly silent. Elizabeth felt almost unnerved as she felt Mr. Darcy's eyes follow her, yet he never said a word.

"Come Mr. Darcy, we must speak of something while dancing."

That shook him out of his almost dazed state. "Do you speak as a rule, while dancing then?"

"I do indeed, Mr. Darcy. I find silence, generally makes for an uncomfortable dance."

"Uncomfortable for yourself?"

"Indeed, sir."

"You do not seem to be the type, to wish for conversation while dancing. I understand that you were an avid walker."

"I was, Mr. Darcy."

"An undertaking that you did alone."

Elizabeth gave him a knowing look. "Yes, Mr. Darcy. We all of us have our inconsistencies and faults."

Mr. Darcy startled at her reference.
"I did not mean to imply--"

"It is of no importance, Mr. Darcy. I am only teasing."

Their moves were silent for a few more minutes, as Mr. Darcy ventured with, "Do you and your sisters often walk to Meryton?"

Ah, so here it was, she thought. He wished to know what Mr. Wickham had said to her. "We do not, Mr. Darcy. I accompany our cook on some occasions, but lately we have not had the time. The day we met with you and Mr. Bingley, it had been our first outing in quite a while--for our aunt's card party, you see."

"And the gentlemen you met?"

"Mr. Wickham." Elizabeth helpfully supplied. "Yes, we had just met him as well. A very charming and witty man, I also spoke to him at my aunt's card party. He had been invited along with the other officers."

That Mr. Darcy did not, Elizabeth noted, as his face grew more grave and grave with each word that spilled from her lips.

"Mr. Wickham is blessed with happy manners, he is very sure of making friends wherever he should go. Whether or not he is capable of retaining them, is of another matter entirely." Mr. Darcy spoke angrily, so much so that Elizabeth faltered in her steps and nearly lost her footing, and it was only his actions that kept her in part with the other dancers.

"Miss Elizabeth?" he said worriedly, his anger transformed into caring. "Are you quite all right?"

Elizabeth was tired of that question.

"I am perfectly well, Mr. Darcy." she said coldly.

He seemed surprised at her answer and manner, but made no more attempt at any conversation throughout the dance. After it was over, he escorted her back to Mr. Collins and her sisters, who were speaking to Mr. Bingley, Miss Bingley, and Mrst. Hurst.

As they drew near, Mr. Darcy appeared to recover some of his earlier pride, and stated confidently, "I would advise you, Miss Elizabeth, to tread carefully when it comes to Mr. Wickham. He is no gentleman."

Coolly, Elizabeth replied, "I am not a child, Mr. Darcy. And as for Mr. Wickham's birth, he has informed me himself that he is the son of a steward, no great deception on his part."

Mr. Darcy spoke no further, but simply delivered her to Mr. Collins, and stalked away. Elizabeth watched him go, paying half a mind to the conversation at hand. How dare he speak to her as though she were a child! As though she had not one lick of sense in her head!

She had tried--had tried to give Mr. Darcy and Mr. Bingley the benefit of the doubt, regarding her sister. As it was, despite their disgusting joke, they were the only two gentlemen who actually looked at Jane as a person, and not as someone who was on the shelf, but it was becoming increasingly difficult. She did not even know why she cared.

If Miss Bingley had her way, Mr. Bingley would soon be gone--back to town, or to purchase an estate that was closer to Mr. Darcy's home. They would soon be out of her life, and she would have to focus all of her attentions elsewhere.

Mr. Darcy, she decided was a walking contradiction. He had shown understanding and sensitivity regarding her father, yet decided the majority, if not the entire town of people, people she had grown up with her entire life were unworthy of any attentions. Except her, apparently. Try as she might, she could no longer ignore Charlotte's teasings.

Elizabeth had excused herself to look for some punch, when Miss Bingley intercepted her.

"My dear Miss Eliza, I had simply thought to warn you."

"Warn me of what, Miss Bingley?" Elizabeth asked in what she hoped sounded like a pleasing tone, as she was already starting a headache with all the people who had apparently attempted to warn her tonight.

"I have heard that you have taken a fancy to Mr. Wickham. I understand you met him in Meryton, and then at one of your aunt's quaint card parties," Miss Bingley smiled, showing all of her teeth, "He is a scoundrel of the first order, and has abused Mr. Darcy most abominably."

"And how is it that he abused Mr. Darcy, Miss Bingley?" Elizabeth asked, actually interested in the feud between the two men, and whether or not there was more than an appearance of truth to Mr. Wickham's story.

Miss Bingley hemmed and hawed for a moment. "I don't know the particulars, but I do know that it was not Mr. Darcy's fault!" she exclaimed.

Elizabeth smiled. "Of course not, Miss Bingley. Mr. Darcy is without fault."
Miss Bingley's mouth twisted as though she had sucked on a lemon. "Excuse me, Miss Eliza. It was kindly meant."

The two ladies curtseyed, and Elizabeth was left to continue her journey, her thoughts wandering more and more to Mr. Darcy and Mr. Wickham.

Chapter Fourteen

A few days after the Netherfield Ball

"My dear I think we need to speak of your conduct at the Netherfield ball."

Elizabeth's head jerked up from the embroidery she was clumsily stitching. Embroidery had never been a strong point in her *accomplishments*, however she had brought it into her daily "meetings" with Mr. Collins in an attempt to dissuade Mr. Collins from any further contact. So far, it had worked. Of course, he had interrupted her stitching with mundane comments and prattle that she was forced to treat as the height of intelligent and interesting conversation, but it was not the worst that she had endured so far at the hands of a Collins.

"Did Mr. Bingley find anything inappropriate in my manner or conduct, Mr. Collins?" Elizabeth asked, unable to keep the sarcasm from her voice.

She had kept her anger towards Mr. Darcy very well hidden, and the only person who had anything to do with her attitude was Miss Bingley. Elizabeth recalled that Miss Bingley had danced with Mr. Collins after the supper set, so she supposed that was when Miss Bingley had told him of their conversation.

Mr. Collins frowned at the inflection at her voice. His dear cousin was certainly becoming a nuisance. Such an attitude would not be tolerated after they were married, nor before even! He remembered that his benevolent, wise father had told him before he died, that he had to take the trouble to check the Bennets, especially his lovely betrothed, for if he did not, they would become an ill sort of manner of woman, and that would not do for a Collins.

"Mind your tone, Cousin Eliza. No, Mr. Bingley did not find any fault with your comportment during the ball, through God's mercy. If he had been near, when you had acted thus towards his sister!" Mr. Collins sighed dramatically.

"Thank the merciful God above, Miss Bingley did not deem it fit to trouble her brother with such troubling news, but instead went to me. What is this business that she speaks of? She speaks of you favoring an officer at your Aunt Phillip's party. If this is true," his tone turned cold, in a manner that she had not thought him capable, although she supposed it was because she had not tried his manner, as she had his father's, "then we shall take steps to correct such a lapse in manners. As it is, I am very much disobliged to allow you or your sisters to attend those shameful parties if that is behavior that your aunt encourages in young people. I suppose she has no knowledge of how families behave in higher circles, being that her husband *is* a solicitor, but you, my dear cousin, know better."

"I have done nothing, Mr. Collins, that would shame my father's home." Elizabeth withheld the biting remark that she wished to say, but could not for fear of retaliation. "Miss Bingley was simply making inferences from information, I know not what."

Mr. Collins leaned back in his chair, and her mind immediately went to her dear Papa, of how he would indolently lean into the back of the high, padded master's chair, while reading one of his beloved novels, instead of attending to the figures on the ledger.

Her eyes drifted upwards, to the ceiling, as she pictured, in her mind's eye, of her poor father lying unconscious in that awful bed, in the smallest room of the entire estate, and she fought the tears that pricked her eyes.

Elizabeth delicately coughed, reaching across the desk for the tea that lay proffered before her. "I met Mr. Wickham while my sisters and I walked to Meryton, before Aunt Phillip's card party. We had left the milliner's shop, and were on our way back home when we ran into Lieutenant Denny and Mr. Wickham. We spoke a few minutes, after we were introduced to him, by Lieutenant Denny."

Here she paused, wondering if she should mention Mr. Darcy, and his reaction to seeing Mr. Wickham. If she did mention it, as his name was going to come up again in a few moments, then it may send Mr. Collins into a shock and God knew what horribly embarrassing speech Mr. Collins should tell Mr. Darcy afterwards, when the opportunity presented itself, but if she did not, would he still find fault with her? In the end, she decided not to mention Mr. Darcy. It was enough.

"And then, as you know, we arrived at my aunt's gathering. I had gone to retrieve a cup of punch for myself, when Mr. Wickham addressed me."

"And what exactly did he say, dear cousin of mine?" Mr. Collins asked, leaning forward intently, his mouth hanging slightly open as he hung upon her every word. Elizabeth though, in a moment of churlish glee, that despite his anger, despite how he frightened her, he rather looked like a dog, drooling with its mouth open.

"He asked me how long had Mr. Darcy been a guest at Netherfield. He then told me that he had known Mr. Darcy his entire life, as his father had been a steward at Mr. Darcy's estate, when Mr. Darcy's father had been alive. In fact, he told me that Mr. Darcy's father had been his godfather, and that he had willed him a living on the Pemberley estate, but that Mr. Darcy had been jealous that his father loved him, and so he had denied him the living, or any other portion of his inheritance."

Mr. Collins leapt back in his chair, looking visibly frightened. Elizabeth furrowed her brows together--was Mr.

Collins well? That he should care that much for a man he deemed beneath him would be surprising and entirely strange.

Mr. Collins put a hand over his heart. "Oh, excuse me my dear cousin, but I cannot imagine a man of his status joining the church! The horror! It was indeed correct of Mr. Darcy to deny him such a thing. His dear father must have had his wits addled when he wrote such a will, for I have heard it said from Sir William that his father died after an especially long illness."

"Of course, Mr. Collins." Was Elizabeth's only reply. She repressed the sigh of annoyance, she wished to make. Speaking to Mr. Collins about such matters was entirely useless.

"And that is the extent of your contact with such a man?" Mr. Collins sternly questioned Elizabeth once more.

"Yes, Mr. Collins. That is the only conversation I have ever had with that man. And I have taken the precaution of warning Kitty, Lydia, Mary, and Jane away from any prolonged conversation with him, as I did not feel he behaved entirely proper in telling me such a history on our first meeting!"

Mr. Collins stroked his chin, appearing to be thoughtful, "Indeed my fair cousin, indeed!

"Now, before you shall leave, my dear Miss Eliza, there is a matter of your manner not simply towards me, but also towards Miss Bingley, that needs to be corrected." he said, advancing upon her slowly, knowing that she would not attempt to leave her nor, even the room.

Mr. Collins tutted nonsensically, "I should have hoped that we should never have reached this point, my dear cousin, but I cannot allow such behavior to go unpun--", Mr. Collins speech, as well as his advance was interrupted as her mama's shrieks reached the din of the room.

"Oh my dear Lord, I shall go and see what confounds that woman right now!" Mr. Collins shrieked, his face abruptly turning puce in his frustration, as he left the room at an ungainly run.

Elizabeth stayed shrunk in the chair, aware of the fact that her mama's fortunately timed tantrum had saved her from the threat of escalating, physical violence.

For now.

*****

Later that night, Elizabeth reached into the back of her closet, and gathered every single blanket she had spirited away from the open cabinets, and piled them underneath her coverlet, saving two for herself. When she had arranged them to her satisfaction, she undressed for bed, and spread her blanket upon the floor, and settled herself for the night.

And it was only then, that she allowed herself to cry, as she had so many other nights previously.

Papa was dead, and it was only a matter of time before she should be forced to marry Mr. Collins. It was Mama who had discovered him. Most days, Mama had not been able to look upon Papa, and Elizabeth did not blame her. In the beginning, she had, but she understood now the burden that Mama had been under. But now, now that she had missed the Netherfield ball, had not been able to push Mr. Bingley and Jane together, or, at the very least watch their interactions together, she had taken to sitting with Papa in the morning. Elizabeth was glad, simply because Mama had stopped shrieking about her nerves, "her poor Jane".....,"her brave Lizzie".

Now Papa was dead, and Elizabeth would have to be brave

for her family.

Withholding a hiccup, even from herself, she buried her face within her arms as she tried to go to sleep. To forget, even if it were just for the night.

Before Elizabeth fell asleep, her last thoughts were of gratitude that she should at least see her Aunt and Uncle Gardner and cousins again, as Jane had taken it upon herself to immediately write to their Uncle, and inform him of her father's death while Mr. Collins was preoccupied with the doctor and directing the servants.

***

Elizabeth fidgeted nervously, as she awaited her aunt and uncle. They had written, sent an immediate express back that their Uncle was going to finish the day's business, and then they would be leaving directly from their home in Gracechurch street to Longbourn, without any stops. Elizabeth was grateful for her aunt and uncle's attendance to such matters, for she was sure that when they arrived they should be in desperate need of a meal, a hot bath, and a bed, after traveling through the night. She hoped her cousins were not entirely exhausted.

Standing beside her, Mr. Collins walked the length of the room, always pausing to adjust the fit of his garments, taking out a handkerchief and refolding it, and running a nervous, sweaty hand through his hair. It was driving Elizabeth mad, as each time he walked the length of the room, he did so silently, and always past her by the nearest breadth. Her chest caught each time he did so, and she wished to have peace for a bit longer.

"Will you not sit down, Mr. Collins?"

Elizabeth looked over in shock to see that her youngest sister had addressed Mr. Collins. He had been in such an agitated state, ever since he had been told that her father was dead, that she did not know what to make of him. Whether or not it was a good indication of their future, or a negative one.

Kitty went to the window, as they heard horses come.

"Aunt and Uncle Gardner are here!" she said excitedly.

Mr. Collins all but ran from the room, and Elizabeth gently coaxed Kitty from the window, and into her seat next to Mary and Jane. Mrs. Bennet was in her room,

having been given a sleep aid with a small glass of wine, and was now sleeping. Mr. Collins had wanted them to be displayed as proper ladies, and here she was, doing as she was bid.

Her Aunt Gardner came first, enveloping Elizabeth first into a tight hug, and doing the same to her siblings.

"Girls, how are you? Where is your mother?" Elizabeth's uncle asked as he tightly gripped Lydia.

"Mama is sleeping, uncle." Lydia replied, looking uneasy. "She was screaming and crying, so we gave her a glass of wine and helped her get ready for bed. Not even her smelling salts helped this time." she said.

"This time?" her uncle questioned.

Elizabeth shot her sister a look, causing Lydia to clasp her mouth shut, and Elizabeth answered for her. "Mama has had a hard time adjusting, uncle. Generally when she would get like that, we would give her a glass of port and her smelling salts, but this time we had to give her a sleep aid from the apothecary, as she refused to calm down."

Her uncle nodded sagely. "Yes, of course. I only wish we could have been here."

"Where are our cousins, uncle?"

He looked sheepishly to their aunt, and replied "We had left them at home. More space in the carriage for the journey back, and it was a rather tiring journey to begin with. It was better for them to stay at home with their nurse than to come to Longbourn at this time."

"Yes, uncle." Elizabeth replied, not knowing how to react. He had left behind her cousins because he intended to take her and her sisters and mama back home with him to Gracechurch street.

With all her heart, she wished that she could go with, but she was caught between two wants: a want to unburden herself from Mr. Collins, and a want to not place any undue stress upon her uncle. He was not at fault for her papa's poor planning for his daughter's futures

Mr. Collins swept into the room, gesturing for Mr. Gardner to follow him into the study, "As I do not believe that the subject of a funeral is an appropriate conversation in front of the ladies, and their delicate constitutions." he explained pompously, full to the brim of the knowledge that he was the superior of the room.

Her uncle left, but not before giving a significant look to his wife

Elizabeth's Aunt Gardner settled into the settee closed to the tea, one that Elizabeth had left intentionally open."

How is it that you are all doing, my dears?" she asked, pouring herself a cup of tea and sipping at it delicately.

"I understand that it must be very hard for you, but also, in some ways a relief. I am here to comfort you girls in any way that I can, while we are here."

"Are you we going to come and stay with you, Aunt Gardner?" Lydia wished to know, leaning forward from her seat almost anxiously.

Her Aunt smiled gently at Lydia, her eyes cataloging the difference in her speech, comportment, and style of dress, as well as Kitty and Mary's, as they all bore the same, marked changes.

"That is our purpose in coming here." Her eyes strayed to Jane, and then lingered on Elizabeth. "If the situation had been different--" she paused, not knowing how to explain the matter for her youngest niece's ears, although she was quite sure that they understood the situation better than anyone else could ever describe it.

"Aunt Gardner--" Elizabeth started.

"No, no my dear. We shall not hear a single word against it. Our minds are quite fixed. We have not received a letter from anyone in this household, excepting Mr. Collins for nigh on nine months. We should have come months ago, but we did not. And that shame shall stay with us."

Elizabeth occupied herself with her tea, unable to express the emotion she felt, without sobbing.

*****

One week later...

The day they buried Mr. Bennet was a cold and dreary day. Elizabeth thought rather sardonically that it was just as well, for it was her father's favorite type of day. All the better for him to be indoors, away from the farm, and inside his library, occupied with his favorite book. Elizabeth stretched her dyed black gown over the length of her lap, studying the material as the parson droned on and on about her father's unfortunate passing.

The parson did not understand the turmoil that her family had gone through, after her father's accident, and what they would go through now that he was dead. Her father had been dead from the moment he had not woke up; he had left them all behind nearly a year ago. He had left them to pick up the pieces he left, and the reality of that was hitting Elizabeth harder and harder with each passing moment, now that he was truly gone.

Afterwards, when they had stood in the receiving line at the church, to thank the mourners, before proceeding to watch their father be buried, Elizabeth saw down the line that Mr. Bingley and his sister, Mrs.

 Hurst and her husband, and Mr. Darcy, even, had attended the service.

Mr. Bingley came forward first, his countenance heavy as he approached them. He went first to Elizabeth's mama, who had wept loudly throughout the service.

"My dear Mrs. Bennet, if there is anything I can do to comfort you, you shall name it." he stated in a quiet, uncharacteristically somber intonation to his speech. He moved down the line of Bennet sisters, stating the same in the same tone of speech, his expression betraying how serious he was.

When he reached Jane, he gently reached out and briefly laid a warm palm on top of the cool hand that was gripping her cane.

 Jane turned her head away, as she squeezed her eyes shut, and dried her tears with her other hand. "Thank you, Mr. Bingley." she said breathlessly, at last.

Mr. Bingley repeated the same to Elizabeth's shocked aunt and uncle, who had little idea that Mr. Bingley had been such a good friend to the Bennets, indeed even Elizabeth had only realized the significance of Mr. Bingley's actions until this day.

Miss Bingley, Mrs. Hurst, and Mr. Hurst--the latter she had never seen less than a spans' away from the wine cask, nor without a glass in hand--offered their sympathies in short, formal tones, and moved away as quickly as possible. It was only Mr. Darcy now.

Elizabeth heard his low tones before she saw him, he being away from his party, and beside a rather tall gentleman.

"Miss Elizabeth." There he was, he had said her name once again, as always had, in the same, precise timbre.

She gave a curtesy.
"Mr. Darcy." she said. It was all she could say without her voice catching.

She felt as if she should look away, as his usual scrutiny of her was fixed as always, but returned his scrutiny for her own. She was still offended by his behavior at the Netherfield Ball.

"I most humbly apologize for your loss, Miss Elizabeth." he finally stated, after they had held each other's gaze for more than a few moments. "The loss of a father is a cruel deprivation, from which we shall never forget.

With that, he moved on, leaving Elizabeth to receive the others.

*****

It appeared as though Mr. Collins had simply wished to wait until after the funeral to speak of the future. In that, Elizabeth supposed he was entirely proper. Propriety held no favor with her, as she had spent the next week sleeping next to her bed, although she was sure that Mr. Collins would not try anything while her aunt and uncle were here, and not after he had won--her papa was dead.

Elizabeth and her uncle had been summoned into the study of Longbourn's new master, and Elizabeth's uncle escorted her in, on the crook of his arm, Elizabeth had an unparalleled view of Mr. Collins' smug countenance.

"Now, Mr. Gardner, now that my dear cousin, Mr. Bennet has been called from this earth, and it has been an appropriate amount of time, I had thought we should discuss the matter of the wedding, before you leave for London."

Her uncle shifted beside her, and Elizabeth stared resolutely at the wall behind Mr. Collins' head.

"Am I to understand, Mr. Collins, that my niece was in a courtship with you, before her father's death, and that she accepted your proposal of marriage?" her uncle asked, his speech rigid and clipped. Elizabeth betrayed a glance to her uncle's face. What was he on about?

He knew, simply from his meeting with Mr. Collins' father that there had been a courtship nor a proposal, but a presumption, based on the innate superiority that Mr. Collins felt within his own mind, as the eventual master of Longbourn.

Mr. Collins sputtered. "Well, no, of course not Mr. Gardner. That would have been highly improper, due to the fact the fact that I was, in effect, acting as my fair cousin's guardian." "Indeed." her uncle echoed.

"I shall be blunt, Mr. Collins. Your father put us in a bind the last time we met, and we had been so shocked and overcome with my brother in law's condition, that we had not the strength, nor the will to refuse him. But today that weakness ends. My niece shall not be marrying you."

With her uncle's words, Elizabeth expected Mr. Collins to leap to his feet, the disgrace and indignancy he felt from her uncle's words to be shown clearly on his visage, which would be dark red, and that they should have to hear his blustered, but no less correct threats about their future.

Mr. Collins did not lose his temper for once, when faced with such information. Perhaps he felt, as he always did, that he held the upper hand, and Elizabeth would, eventually, come crawling back to him, as any other woman would in such a situation.

Perhaps he was right.

No, Mr. Collins leaned back in his chair, comfortably, casting his hands down the smooth, worn leather of the chair. "If we do not come to an accord this very moment, Mr. Gardner, on whether or not my fair cousin and I are to be married some three months thence, then I shall be forced to inform my fair cousins and Mrs. Bennet that they shall need to find lodging elsewhere tonight, and for the rest of their natural, God given lives."

There, he had played his trump card, and now he had only to wait and see if it had shaken Mr. Gardner enough, for if that happened, he should then have to immediately bear the added expenses of six more ladies to his household.

Therefore, Elizabeth was not surprised when her uncle stood up, and gave Mr. Collins the bare minimum of a bow, stating "We shall leave, immediately after the girls have packed their clothing, Mr. Collins."

Elizabeth faced Mr. Collins uneasily--surely he was not quite so angry and changeable, that he should set them out of the house with only the clothing on their back.

However, Mr. Collins simply waved them away, in the same manner as his father had dismissed him from earlier times, and before Elizabeth closed the door behind her, to the study, she was left with one last remark from Mr. Collins-- "I would not keep me waiting long, my fair cousin."

Chapter Fifteen

In the immediate aftermath of Mr. Collins' ultimatum, the Bennet-Gardner family found themselves with only a few articles of clothing, and childhood mementos tucked away between layers of muslin and ribbon, on their Aunt and Uncle Phillips doorstep. Mrs. Bennet was still weeping, although she had managed to quiet herself a considerable amount, when she had been informed that she was to stay with her brother at his home, instead of living at Longbourn, with her second eldest married to its heir.

"London!" she sighed between sobs. Elizabeth, despite the circumstances and the tension she felt, could not help but laugh. It seemed that nothing would ever keep her mama's spirits low.

Her uncle rapped on the door of his sister's home, and waited. A few moments later, the woman, arrayed in black with accented grey took one look at the assembled party, and ushered them in quickly.

"I am indeed not surprised that you have come to us, brother. I do not give one fig what the neighbors should say, that Mr. Collins is an odiously hateful man, and any woman who shall be bound in matrimony to such a man, shall be very vexed indeed." Throughout her speech, she brought them all to the morning room where she received callers. Gesturing for them to be seated, she rang a bell, and a servant arrived a few moments later.

"Lucy, go and fetch Stevenson, and tell him to gather our guests bags, and situate them in the guest rooms. Then inform the cook that we shall need tea and biscuits."

Here she turned to her nieces and sister. "Brother, you and my sister shall share a room of course, Mary and my poor sister shall share, Lyddie and Kitty will have a room to themselves, and Jane and Miss Elizabeth shall have the last. There, shall that do?" she asked, obviously wanting their satisfaction.

"I am afraid that we do not have much room, I am forever asking of Mr. Phillips to expand upon our home, but as you know he does not see the need, being that we have no children." Mrs. Phillips continued to get them situated, still prattling on--a trait she shared with Mrs. Bennet--" Mr. Phillips is at his practice, I shall send a servant to send word to him that you are staying with us for the time being."

Mrs. Phillips, who truly was a mirror image of her only sister, Mrs. Bennet, excepting the fact that she had no children, let alone daughters to marry off, smiled in satisfaction as she had her family all along side her.

Elizabeth was shocked at the reception she and her sisters had received from her mother's family, but her aunt's next words calmed some of her shock, as her aunt revealed that Mr. Collins had paid her a call after the infamous card party visit.

"The nerve of that man!" she exclaimed. "He and his odious father kept my nieces and dear sister away for the majority of a year, and the first time they have any amusements at all, in an especially proper environment--their aunt's home, no less--he comes here, calling my home a den of iniquity, and questioning whether or not my niece spoke to another gentleman--no an officer!"

Mrs. Phillips shuddered delicately, offering a handkerchief to her sister, who had begun a fresh round of tears at her sister's words. She patted Elizabeth's hand consolingly.

"I should have refused such a man, as well Miss Lizzie! Chin up! Besides, you shall be going to London, and I am sure there are quite a few gentlemen with three or four thousand a year that shall be swanning around you and your sisters as soon as your mourning period is over!"

Elizabeth smiled at her aunt's words, but it was a false smile. Her aunt knew as well as she did, that the only one of them who should make an advantageous match would be Jane, and that was simply not possible anymore.

***

A few days later....

They were to only stay a week, to catch their breath, before traveling by carriage to their aunt and uncle's home in Gracechurch street.

Mrs. Bennet, although initially inconsolable, had stopped her wailing, and was now counting her blessings, that she should be able to live in London! She had wanted to do so all her life, for although she was shrewd enough to land an estate owner, when she herself was the daughter of a humble solicitor, she had never been able to convince him to spend any more than a few weeks, once or twice a year at most, in London--to see her brother and his family, and to take advantage of the shops.

Elizabeth could not help that they were making a mistake of a colossal size. She had always thought, that when faced with the choice--of marrying someone she did not love or respect, and saving her family, that her pride, her convictions should save her from making such a misstep, of repeating her mother and father's mistakes in terms of their marriage together.

Yet she found that she did not think she could do it, now that her choice was looming before her face.

At best, she should always have to shuttle between her Aunt and Uncle Gardner, to her Aunt and Uncle Phillips. She did not know if she should be able to watch Mr. Collins and some other, nameless, faceless woman inhabit her dearly beloved home, Longbourn, and why should her uncle bear the majority of her and her siblings expenses when they brought in so little?

Elizabeth and Jane lay in their borrowed bed, wrapped in each other's arms in a way that they had not been able to for many months.

"Lizzie?"

Elizabeth closed her eyes, and deepened her breathing, hoping that she could fool Jane into believing that she had fallen asleep. A few more moments passed and Jane repeated her name, this time a bit louder. Again, Elizabeth ignored her sister, and resolutely snuggled deeper into her pillow.

"Lizzie," Jane's hand reached to smooth Elizabeth's hair from her face, and returned back around her waist. "I know why you refused Mr. Collins, Lizzie. The real reason. Lydia told me." At that, Elizabeth stiffened minutely, and Jane's hand returned to her hair, gently stroking, petting. "I understand. Mama and uncle--everyone understands Lizzie."

"That does not discard the facts, Jane." Elizabeth finally rolled over to face her sister.

"Do you think our Uncle Gardner and Uncle Phillips have not considered the facts?" was Jane's rebuttal.

"Of course they have Jane, but I do not think that I could forgive myself if I---." Elizabeth paused, carefully considering her next words. "I had always considered myself a strong, disciplined woman, Jane, but it appears I am not."

Jane weighed her sister's words, comprehending the intent behind them.

"Lizzie, whatever you decide, I shall always be with you.

Even if I have to stay with Aunt and Uncle Phillips."

Elizabeth grasped her sister's hand tenderly, before brushing a kiss to her forehead.

"I know, Jane."

After that, it seemed that Jane was finally content to sleep, having communicated her apprehension and loyalty to Elizabeth. Elizabeth lay awake for many hours afterwards, unable to fully fall into a sleep, and so, when the sun had began its peak, she deftly slipped out of bed, and had quickly dressed.

Grabbing a thin shawl that belonged to her sister Lydia, she informed a passing maid that she was leaving the house for a walk, along the tract to Sir William's home, and that she should inform her family that she should be back before their morning meal.

Elizabeth flitted down the countryside, taking in the crisp, cool, clean morning air. despite the immense pressure she was still under, she had never been more, nor felt more free. Mrs. Bennet had often complained of her stubborn, independent nature, citing her daily walks along the countryside as visible, visceral proof that her only ambition in life was to flout the rules of society.

Mr. Bennet, of course had taken her side, as she *had* been his favorite, and he enjoyed the fact, Elizabeth thought, that she was so entirely different from her mother. That while Jane was the image of everything she had desired of a daughter, so Elizabeth was his. She was better than a boy, he had always declared, something that had always made her laugh.

Elizabeth had come down the winding road that led to her dearest friend, Charlotte's home. Elizabeth grimaced as she thought of the previous visit that Charlotte had paid shortly after the Bennets and Gardners had vacated Longbourn.

Charlotte was indeed surprised that Mr. Collins had thrown them out so quickly after the funeral, and had informed her that the entire town was speaking of it. She had laughed when Elizabeth archly informed her that people did little else, and that she was used to strangers sticking their noses into her family's affairs.

"I am not surprised you refused Mr. Collins, Lizzie. Something within you altered, with his presence. However, I caution you to be fully aware of what you are yielding."

Elizabeth exhaled deeply. Charlotte was too resolute, despite her double handed advice.

***

Elizabeth, not wishing to end her walk so soon, had elected to carry on, realizing that she was now quite close to Longbourn. Only a mile or so, an easy distance. She faltered, and could take no more steps forward, nor bring herself to turn around and return to her Aunt Phillips. She was at a standstill, and she cursed her weakness in being unable to break it.

Some long minutes passed, and Elizabeth noted a figure on a white horse approaching.

"Mr. Darcy!" Elizabeth called out, immediately embarrassed that she had shouted his name as though she had stumbled upon him committing some wrong doing.

For his part, he seemed surprised to see her, and Elizabeth was reminded that had her family's circumstances been different, he and she may have run into each other several times before, in the time he had spent in Netherfield. Perhaps they may have become better acquainted, and even become friends. Perhaps they should have loathed each other.

"Mr. Darcy, I do apologize," she expressed, still disconcerted, "I was surprised to see you here."

Mr. Darcy was on his horse, and he during her speech, he slipped off, and walked towards her, leading the horse by the bridle.

"Miss Elizabeth," he greeted her solemnly, sweeping his tall, black hat off of his head, transitioning into a smooth bow. She curtseyed, not for the first time feeling as though they were key players in a dance that did not seem to end. After a few moments of awkward silence, Mr. Darcy cleared his throat, and asserted, "I have heard here in Meryton that you and your family are to live with your uncle in London."

Elizabeth swallowed a grimace, as she noticed that he was, rather politely, avoiding the fact that she had refused an offer from her cousin, the new master of Longbourn.

"Yes, we shall be leaving at the end of the week to travel to my aunt and uncle's. They are very eager to return home to their children."

"Indeed."

A lengthy silence reigned, and Elizabeth was about to bid Mr. Darcy good day and return back to her aunt's, when she heard her name.

"Miss Elizabeth?"

Her eyes met Mr. Darcy's

"Yes, sir?" she asked, wincing minutely, as even the title reminded her of Mr. Collins, and of the decision she did not wish to determine, and yet she had no other choice, if she wished for her family to be comfortable after the trials they had endured on her behalf. While her family, especially her aunts and uncles were understanding, only she, Mrs. Bennet, Lydia, Kitty, Mary, and Jane knew the truth. And while they may not resent her now for making the choice her uncle had wished of her, they would, in the future. Of that, Elizabeth was sure.

Mr. Darcy clasped the brim of his hat in his hand, twisting it cruelly. He spoke softly, but full of authority, that Elizabeth hardly reconciled what he was expressing.
"Miss Elizabeth, I understand that you and your family have gone through a tremendous loss recently, and if there were any other option, I should have taken it, but the present circumstances are what they are, and there is no changing them. It will not do. I must confess to you how ardently and violently, I admire and love you."

At that last confession, one that he nearly whispered, Mr. Darcy's hat fell uselessly from his hands, and onto the ground. He did not notice it lying upon the ground, and Elizabeth was far too shocked to mention it. Immediately, her mind returned to Charlotte's previous teasings, and then to the current predicament she found herself in.

Could Mr. Darcy be the answer to her prayers? She had not time to contemplate that notion for Mr. Darcy had said--

"I have fought against my family's expectation and reputation, the inferiority of your rank and circumstance, and I am of the utmost willing to put your circumstances aside and ask for you to end my agony. Please do me the honor of accepting my hand in marriage, Miss Elizabeth."

Elizabeth rapidly flitted from astonishment to acrimony to astonishment again. *Mr. Darcy had actually proposed to her*, albeit in the most insensitive, arrogant method. She was reminded of Charlotte, who had said shortly after their first meeting with Mr. Darcy, that a man so illustriously wealthy in connections and money, had a *right* to be proud, as though there were no other way.

Mr. Darcy was now staring at her, intent on upon her answer, and Elizabeth rushed to say something, anything that did not make her sound like a fool, let alone an outright refusal. The barest trickling of an idea crept into her mind, and she contended that it was not the worst idea, and certainly not a trial.

"I--I appreciate your sentiments sir, and I am very sorry to have caused you any unjust pain. It was unconsciously done."

Mr. Darcy scowled at her answer.

"Is this your final reply, Miss Elizabeth?"

"No, sir."

He seemed surprised at her response.

"Then please, Miss Elizabeth, I should like to know the intent behind your reply, if you are not refusing me. Is this a convoluted attempt at determining the depths of my *affection* for you?" Mr. Darcy spat out the word affection, as though it were an infection that he was determined to be rid of as quickly as possible.

"No, sir. I am simply trying to sketch out your character before I agree to marry you. I hear such different accounts of you that puzzles me exceedingly. Your insult of my family circumstance seems to confirm at least one account."

Mr. Darcy seemed dumbfounded for a moment, before he remembered himself.

"Forgive me, Miss Elizabeth. I-I meant no offense."

Elizabeth had meant for it to come as a gentle admonition, something that could be construed as teasing, for no matter what she had said to Mr. Darcy about sketching his character, she had its essentials firmly in mind, and in that he was her choice. However, her response came more bitterly than she had anticipated.

"I do find it odd, Mr. Darcy, that you should insult me in one breath, and insult me in the next. Although I should be used to such a thing, for you behaved in the same manner at the very first assembly in which we met."

Mr. Darcy frowned.

"To what do you refer?"

"I refer to the remark that you made to Mr. Bingley after you had both been introduced to my family--to my sister, Jane." Elizabeth could not even shame him further, by spitting out the remark afterwards, for it pained her every time she thought of the incident.

Mr. Darcy's face colored a deep red, and he stared at the road.

"I apologize, Miss Elizabeth. There is no excuse for what I said, and I should have apologized sooner had I know that I had been overheard. I shall apologize to Miss Jane, posthaste, no matter what your answer may be."

Elizabeth nodded in satisfaction, glad that she should invoke such an action from Mr. Darcy. It would not take away the pain, nor the feelings Jane held for Mr. Bingley. But it would satisfy. For now.

"What else is it that you wished to know, Miss Elizabeth?" Mr. Darcy finally ventured after a few moments silence. "Mr. Wickham." There was no triumph in her voice, though the gentleman in question was her trump card. His name had provoked such a strong reaction from not only Mr. Darcy, but Mr. Bingley, in barring him from the Netherfield ball, and Miss Bingley, in her impassioned defense of Mr. Darcy's non-existent faults.

At the mere mention of the man's name, Mr. Darcy had tensed visibly and Elizabeth noted that his fists had clenched within his hands. When he noticed her looking, he tucked his hands behind his back.

"What has he told you, Miss Elizabeth?" Mr. Darcy asked, his tone soothing and encouraging.

"I do not appreciate being spoken to like a child, Mr. Darcy, as I told you at the Netherfield ball." Elizabeth stated coolly, her anger roused at his patronizing tone. "Mr. Wickham informed me at my Aunt Phillip's card party that he was your father's godson, and that you had been jealous of his relationship with his father, to the point to where you had not allowed him to see your father on his deathbed, and had cheated him out of his inheritance--a position in the Church."

Elizabeth continued on, before Mr. Darcy could speak, glad that she, for once, had the upper hand. "I did not trust Mr. Wickham. I did not trust that he should tell me such things, personal, intimate details of another's family upon our first meeting. I told my sisters to stay away from him, whether or not his story was true." she said, lifting her chin to face Mr. Darcy square on.

Silence reigned, as Mr. Darcy, Elizabeth supposed, was struggling to keep his agitation under wraps. Finally, he said,

"That was indeed very wise of you, Miss Elizabeth. If you would permit me, I should like to tell you the true story of our estrangement."

When Elizabeth nodded her assent, Mr. Darcy rushed to explain, unable to bear the agony her her opinion of him being tainted by Wickham's falsehoods.

"Mr. Wickham and I were indeed close, boyhood friends, and my father was his godfather. My father loved him, sent him off to university with me. It was there that our paths began to diverge. Wickham began to spend more time with immodest women, indolent heirs to fortunes, and the gaming tables. He lost and borrowed quite a bit of money. Always, my father paid his debts. Less than two years into university, Wickham left, and I heard nothing from him until years later when my father was nearing death."

It was here, Elizabeth noted that his breath had turned ragged. Even speaking of his father's death still wounded him to this day.

"My father wished to see Wickham before he died. I had spent a large amount of money trying to locate him, and when I did, Wickham refused to see to my father. My father died without ever seeing him, and it was weeks afterwards that Wickham came, asking about my father's will. He declined the living, and wanted the value of it--some three thousand pounds--and which he was given. He disappeared again, and I had hoped to never see him again."

Elizabeth had listened to his story in rapt attention, and so when silence lapsed around them again, she somehow had a feeling that the story did not pick up to the period where they had met here in Meryton. Mr. Darcy swallowed roughly, looking anywhere but at her.

"It was a year ago, when I came across him again. I have a younger sister, Georgiana, who is your sister Kitty's age. After our father's death," here he stopped, and then contradicted himself, "no, Miss Elizabeth, if I should be completely honest, it was after the death of our mother that Georgiana's woes began."

He gave her an apologetic look.

"My father loved my mother, and fell into a deep depression after my sister's birth coincided with her death. He was an excellent father, to me, but not to Georgiana. She has very few memories of his full attention. When I returned home from university to take my place as the master of Pemberley, I found a timid, mouse of a girl, instead of my inquisitive little sister. As a remedy, I had slowly exposed her to more society, and in part of that was sending for a holiday in Ramsgate, with a companion."

His visage darkened, and Elizabeth nearly withdrew. She understood the pain that Mr. Darcy's sister felt, how she had transformed. It only took one person to make the transition, and belatedly, Elizabeth realized, Mr. Darcy was hers.

"It was there that I had discovered, but for the fact that I had decided to arrive a few days early, that her companion was in league with Wickham and had conspired to elope with my sister. She is to inherit thirty thousand pounds upon her marriage. Once I informed him that he should never receive a penny of her inheritance, he left immediately. My sister was thrown into a deep depression, one from which she suffers to this day."

His gaze met hers, his eyes somber and heavy. Elizabeth's heart ached for Miss Darcy, for she understood the shame and worry she felt. It was a heavy burden, to have come so close to disappointing, and shaming your family in the pursuit of happiness.

"Do you understand now, Miss Elizabeth?"

"I—yes, Mr. Darcy. I understand."

"And if your inquiries are thus satisfied, shall I have your final reply as to my original question?"

"I should like for my sisters to be able to stay with us, Mr.

Darcy." she finally said. "Not all the time, but I want--."

Elizabeth felt breathless and though she were about to faint. Mr. Darcy walked towards her, offering her the crook of his arm, as he led his horse alongside.

"We shall be able to discuss such things later, Miss Elizabeth. Allow me to escort you to your aunt's. I should like to speak to your uncle straight away, before your party leaves."

Elizabeth and Darcy walked, arm in arm, and once they had reached her Aunt Phillip's house, she was swept inside, and the last she saw of Mr. Darcy, was requesting an audience with both of her uncles.

Chapter Sixteen

Mr. Gardner ushered in the strange gentleman--for he could note that he was a gentleman by his dress and the uprightness of his figure--who had escorted his niece home. The gentleman bowed at the waist, and introduced himself.

"Sir? My name is Fitzwilliam Darcy, of Pemberley, and if it is not too much of an inconvenience I would have an audience with you and Miss Elizabeth's other guardian, Mr. Phillips."

Mr. Gardner shot a confused look at his niece, who returned his without a hint of what she was thinking, nor feeling. What on earth could a man of such stature have to do with his niece?

Both of his sisters--Fanny and Alice--had spent the last few morning retelling their woes to his wife, who gleaned out the necessary information to relay to him. It gave him a clearer picture, gleaned from information that his niece had not, or did not wish to tell him.

To that end, he was very familiar with the name "Fitzwilliam Darcy", for Alice had called him the most horrid, disobliging man who had ever come to Meryton, so unlike his closest friend, the amiable Charles Bingley--who had taken a fancy to Jane, and had she not been thus injured, they should be posting wedding banns by now, indeed!

Mr. Darcy danced but rarely, and generally only members of his own party, although, now that he was thinking upon the subject, he recalled that he had been informed that Mr. Darcy had danced with Elizabeth twice.

He was now also recalling that Mr. Darcy was known throughout Meryton not only for his arrogance and pride, but for his betrayal to his father's memory. Mrs. Phillips had told his wife of a Mr. Wickham, a man who had grown up with Mr. Darcy, and was loved by Mr. Darcy's father--only to be cast away, and cheated of his inheritance when Mr. Darcy's father died after a long illness.

The poor, young gentleman, now an officer in the militia was determined to make his own way without causing any more pain to the memory of Mr. Darcy's father, so he had graciously forgiven Mr. Darcy, but the rest of the town had no!--Mrs. Phillips declared.

Mr. Gardner returned the gentleman's bow, and answer him, "Of course, Mr. Darcy. Right this way." Leading him into his brother in law's study, he gave another bow and excused himself to collect his brother in law. A few minutes later, they returned and situated themselves.

"Port?" Mr. Gardner asked, as he poured himself a small glass. Mr. Darcy's eyes shifted for a moment, before he acquiesced with a nod of his head.

"What service may we perform for you, Mr. Darcy? I am at a loss as to how we should have any mutual business, having never been introduced before this very moment." Mr. Gardner asked, curious as to whether or not he would be witness to a display of the now infamous Darcy pride and arrogance.

Mr. Darcy's reply was not a reply that he could immediately forget, nor did he comprehend what he was hearing. He *must* have misunderstood his reply.

"Excuse me, Mr. Darcy. Would you repeat what you just said?"

"Of course, sir. I am here to request your permission to marry Miss Elizabeth. I have proposed, and she has accepted."

Mr. Darcy finished his port with a careless swallow, and sat back in his seat to await their reply. Mr. Gardner and Mr. Phillips looked askance at each other. Although Elizabeth had not technically been proposed to, she had refused an offer from Mr. Collins less than a week ago! And now she apparently had accepted a man who was known as proud, rude, and arrogant. A man who was used to getting what he wanted.

Mr. Gardner and Mr. Phillips held a silent conversation for a few moments, before both nodding in agreement, and Mr. Gardner turned to Mr. Darcy,

"If you would excuse us for a moment, Mr. Darcy. We should like to speak with our niece, and then we shall return with your answer."

Mr. Darcy inclined his head in agreement.

"Of course, sir. I am at your convenience."

"Of course, thank you sir. We shall return in a few minutes." Both men left the study, carefully closing the door behind them, before they went to look for their niece--who was now eating in the parlour with her sisters and mother.

Mr. Gardner cleared his throat, not wishing to announce the business he concerning Elizabeth, in front of his grieving Fanny, for he would give Elizabeth a way out if she should wish to take it. God knew what state of mind she was in, and it was his fault. He should have taken his nieces, at the very least when he had realized the character of both the Mr. Collins, but he had not, and he would regret it to his dying day.

"Lizzie, would you join myself and your uncle for a few minutes? We have a matter to speak of."

He watched as his niece, the youngest one, look from

himself to Elizabeth, confusion and interest evident in her dark eyes. Elizabeth smiled at her, and excused herself from the assembled party. She followed him and Mr. Phillips into another, empty parlour.

"Elizabeth, I have a Mr. Darcy of Pemberley in my study, asking for your hand in marriage." Mr. Phillips started. "Am I to understand that you have accepted him, of your own free will."

Elizabeth's eyes flashed, "Of course, Uncle. He is nothing like Mr. Collins!" she said, rather defensively, her tone brusque and unyielding. Immediately she chastened herself.

"I do apologize, Uncle Phillips. It was a surprise. Mr. Darcy proposed this morning. I do believe that it was due to the fact that we should be leaving for London soon."

"And you wish to marry him?" Mr. Gardner wanted to know. "Truly? I have not heard good things about this man, niece."

Elizabeth regarded her uncle with a cool gaze.

"Uncle, I am not permitted to speak to you openly of Mr. Darcy's affairs, however I suggest that you should question him directly. I have settled all of my concerns with Mr. Darcy directly, and am satisfied. But uncle--" here her voice lowered, "he truly is a good man, and he is one of the few, along with Mr. Bingley, who have treated us, especially Jane with respect."

Mr. Gardner's eyes widened in surprise, as he recalled his first meeting with the elder, now deceased Mr. Collins, and his reaction to his niece's injury.

"I do not deny, uncle, that his proposal comes at a fortuitous time," here, she wavered slightly, not wishing to alarm her uncles, "but his proposal came as a surprise. A happy surprise."

"And you are sure, Elizabeth?" Mr. Gardner scrutinized her carefully, watching her expression for any minute changes.

"I am sure, uncle." she responded confidently.

"Then we shall grant him permission, niece."

"Thank you uncle." Mr. Gardner and Mr. Phillips embraced Elizabeth one last time, before returning to the study, where Mr. Darcy sat, still as ramrod straight as before they had left. "Well, Mr. Darcy, we have satisfactorily ascertained our niece's acceptance of your proposal, however, before we grant you permission to marry her, we have a few questions concerning a Mr. Wickham, and other matters."

At that, Mr. Darcy's entire body tightened further, although he relaxed moments later, slightly.

"Of course, sir." he said in a strained voice. "What would you like to know?"

"Everything."

***

"Are you surprised, aunt?" Elizabeth asked, a few hours later as they took tea. It was just her and her aunt, who had requested a private audience with her. Beyond informing Jane of her engagement, Elizabeth and her uncles had elected to not inform the rest of the family about their engagement before they left for Gracechurch street in two days.

This meant, of course, that Mr. Darcy could not pay a call to her before they left, but Elizabeth found that she did not mind. Or, rather she did not wish for the attention it would cause if he should call again.

There were most likely quite a few whispers going around as to why she had been escorted back to her home on the arm of Mr. Darcy, but she was hoping that they would disregard it, when they saw that he had paid her no special attention afterwards, and that they would be departing soon thereafter.

Her Aunt Phillips had already done her duty in informing the assorted callers that the Bennets should be leaving very shortly, at the end of the week, to live with their uncle in London.

Her Aunt Gardner smiled gently at her, behind her tea.

"I was surprised, Lizzie, but I realized that I have hardly known you until now." she said.

"I hardly know myself, aunt." Elizabeth responded, more airily than she felt, her mind drifting to where Mr. Darcy had found her, on the road to Longbourn. If he had been but a few minutes earlier or later, they would have missed each other entirely, and she should be sitting across her aunt for a very different sort of reason.

"Lizzie, I was simply shocked, as you were, I imagine." Mrs. Gardner took Elizabeth's hand within hers. "Although, your sister has informed me that Mr. Darcy, despite the insulting remark he made after your first meeting, has always acted very kindly towards the both of you, even apologizing for the faults of others." she said, referring to the disastrous dinner, where Miss Bingley and Mr. Collins had both insulted and denigrated her younger sisters.

Elizabeth smiled distantly. "Yes, aunt. We have had a rather tumultuous beginning, but Mr. Darcy has always been very kind to me and Jane."

Silenced reigned, as both ladies sipped their tea absentmindedly, both wishing to speak, yet neither knowing which subject to broach next.

"I imagine the wedding shall be soon?" Mrs. Gardner said

delicately.

"Yes, aunt. Uncle and Mr. Darcy agreed that under the present circumstances, it should be soon. So he shall come and call on us at Gracechurch street, where he will have the banns published, and we shall be married by special license in six weeks."

"My, that is sudden." her aunt remarked blandly.

Elizabeth ducked her head down into her tea, unsure of why she suddenly felt shy and unsure.

"Yes. Mr. Darcy wishes to inform his family and bring his sister, for us to become acquainted before the wedding."

"That is indeed very wise."

"Aunt."

"Lizzie." Elizabeth's aunt responded to her, matching the same exasperating tones Elizabeth had produced.

"I simply want you to be sure that you are making the right decision, my dear. That is all. Marriage is a lifetime commitment, and not an undertaking to be taking lightly."

Elizabeth glanced out the window, her yes following the men and women that walked through the streets of Meryton, each and every one of them passing by her aunt and uncle's home, every single day on their way to the shops.

"I know, aunt."

"Lizzie, I did not mean--"

Elizabeth grasped her aunt's hand into her own. "I understand. I do not love Mr. Darcy, Aunt Gardner, but he is, in his essentials a good man, and after everything that I have now learned, that is all I require."

"Well then," her aunt said brightly, changing the subject, "you shall have to write to me and describe the grounds of Pemberley. I believe you shall be very pleased with them. From what I remember of my girlhood in Lambton, Pemberley, indeed Derbyshire has some of the finest woodland areas in the country."

***

Fitzwilliam Darcy strode into the study of his best friend, Charles Bingley, who, uncharacteristically had his head buried in a large pile of correspondence. Fitzwilliam resisted the urge to laugh at his friend, for this morning had brought him two impossibles: the woman he had hardly admitted, even to himself, that he loved had accepted his pig headed proposal, and his best friend, a man who, despite his desire and drive to fulfill his father's dying wish and become the master of an estate, absolutely loathed the letter writing responsibilities that were entwined with the workings of an estate, was seeking to improve his personal defects by applying himself to the task.

Charles head poked up, his dark hair crazed and wild, as though he had spent the entire morning running his hands through it.

"How was your ride, Darcy?" he asked good naturedly, using the arrival of his friend as an excuse to take a break from the piles of correspondence that lay before him.

"It was....productive." Fitzwilliam finally settled onsuch a word.

"Really, how so?" his friend asked eagerly.

Fitzwilliam decided to simply say it.

"I met Miss Elizabeth on the road to her home," he said, matching Charles' wince as he mentioned Longbourn, as he and Charles had endured a dinner of Miss Bingley and Mrs. Hurst tittering and play slapping each other's hands due to the fact that Miss Elizabeth had apparently refused to marry Mr. Collins, so soon after the death of her father, and as a result of her decision, she and her sisters had been ordered to vacate their home by Mr. Collins. A perfectly legal decision, but still, one that had made him not only uneasy, but had kept him up for quite a few nights, until he had admitted to himself the cause of such feelings. "and I proposed to her, Charles. She has accepted."

Charles gaped at him, and then fell back into his chair, doubled over, and began to laugh.

"Charles? Are you well?"

Charles sat up, wiping the tears of mirth from his eyes, as he composed himself. When his breath had finally steadied, he replied, "Oh I am quite well, Darcy. I am simply imaging my dear sister's reaction when you tell her of your engagement."

Fitzwilliam shifted uncomfortably within his seat. He had been lucky enough to avoid Caroline on his journey into Charles' study, but he would not be able to avoid the woman forever. His eyes slid over to Charles form in a silent plea.

"Oh no, my dear friend. It is your engagement, and you should be the one to tell Caroline. I shall of course, be by your side, to console Caroline afterwards."

Fitzwilliam frowned. "That is unkind Charles. I have never encouraged your sister."

Charles ignored his concerns with a wave of his hand. "As

you know, that has never stopped Caroline. Now that you are engaged, she shall be forced to cast her hook into another fish. Perhaps a more willing one."

Charles walked to his old friend, and clasped him on the shoulder. "Congratulations, Darcy. I should have guessed that you had feelings for Miss Elizabeth, but I should not have predicted that you should be so forthright about them!"

Fitzwilliam returned his friends clasp with a warm smile, glad that he had the friendship of such a man. "Of course, Charles, there were circumstances that hastened my proposal, but I should hope that you would stand up with me in six weeks."

Charles agreed readily, though his joy and happiness for his friend was tinged with sorrow.

Later that evening, after Miss Bingley and Mrs. Hurst had elected, not surprisingly to retire early, both feigning headaches, and Mr. Hurst too had left Charles and Fitzwilliam to their own devices to retire to his rooms with a bottle of port, the remaining friends elected to retire to the study.

Fitzwilliam watched as Charles stared moodily into his port glass, and then finished it with a long swig, grimacing as he did so. It had never failed to amuse Fitzwilliam how little tolerance Charles had for strong drink, and that he only imbibed simply to fit in with his fellows. Another manner in which he and Charles were different, Fitzwilliam supposed. A voice reproached him, its pleasing tone familiar, in the back of his mind, sardonically noting the differences between a gentleman related to an earl and descended from one of the first land owning, ancient families in England, and from the grandson of a tradesman who had recently purchased his first estate.

The difference between a gentleman of good standing and wealth, beholden to no one but his own mind, marrying where he wished, and a newfound gentleman wishing to gain more than a foothold into a new world.

Fitzwilliam winced. Caroline was convinced that Jane Bennet nurtured a burning passion for Charles, while he had been convinced that Caroline thought so because of Charles' infatuation with the blonde beauty, despite her impediment.

He had never seen anything other than general pleasantry on the lady's face, although he noted that she had not been often addressed by other gentlemen, at least not in his presence. Therefore, her behavior he could only compare to when she interacted with himself, Bingley, and Mr. Collins. The voice, still so pleasing and sweet, encouraged him in his thoughts, and he, at once made up his mind, to speak bluntly to his fiancee--oh how he loved to even think the words--and ask her opinion, for, now that he was completely being honest with himself, he realized that Charles was the master of himself, and his decisions were his own.

First, he had to be honest.

"I have something to confess to you Charles." he said, rousing Charles out of his dejected stupor.

"What say you, Darcy?"

"I proposed to Miss Elizabeth this morning."
"Yes, Darcy, I know." Charles replied, confused.

"I bungled it." Fitzwilliam said, his chin hanging low in dejection.

"What do you mean, Darce?" Charles asked, still confused.

"I insulted her family. Her father has not been cold in the

ground a week, she has been thrown out of her childhood home by a dejected suitor, and I found her walking towards her home, and I stopped and I proposed. I had been thinking of doing so, to my chagrin, almost immediately after meeting with her again, when your sisters had invited her and Miss Bennet for supper."

He hung his head lower, unable, or unwilling to face his shame.

"Charles, I must apologize. I had arrogantly thought that she should immediately accept my proposal not simply because of my stature, but because of hers. She accepted my proposal, but not before setting me to rights. I had--if it had been any other lady, I think that I should have walked off immediately."

Charles studied his friend carefully.

"But what should you have to apologize to me for, Darcy?"

"It is about Miss Bennet."

Charles protested, not wishing to hear another laundry list of why he should not propose to her, love her, and Darcy lifted a hand to stay his complaints.

"Charles, you are of your own mind. I know that your sister has only teased you so far, because she does not believe that you are willing to court or propose to Miss Bennet due to her disability, and for a time I had tacitly agreed with Caroline, as in terms of fortune and connections, it should not have help your social status. Had your sister felt your feelings were serious, and not simply a fleeting crush, she would have enlisted myself to assist her to dissuade her, and I most likely would have agreed and helped her. For that, I apologize."

Charles clapped his friend on the shoulder in gratitude,

which his friend gratefully accepted.

"You are my closest and only friend Darcy, and I am glad you are marrying Miss Elizabeth. You proposed to her some dozen hours ago, and already you are losing some of your fastidiousness! It is a Bennet influence, I am sure of it." he joked.

Fitzwilliam regarded his friend with a serious mien.

"I do not know, Charles, if Miss Bennet is in love with you, for I do not know enough of her character to make such a judgement. If you are willing, I shall ask Miss Elizabeth when we meet in London in a week, and gain her opinion then. I shall help you, if that is what you wish."

Charles acquiesced to his friend easily, a ready smile touching his lips.

"A chance Darcy, that is all I require."

*****

Gracechurch Street, London

"Are you really going to marry Mr. Darcy, Lizzie?" Lydia asked eagerly, as she lazily sprawled over Elizabeth and Jane's bedroom.

As with staying at their Aunt and Uncle Phillips for a short period of time, Elizabeth and Jane had to share a room, as well as Lydia and Mary--who had both elected to continue sharing a room--and Kitty had a room to herself, for all of her cousins were still in the nursery.

The sisters were gathered in Elizabeth and Jane's room, all of them eagerly asking questions about Elizabeth's engagement. Elizabeth had already granted them, a much edited version of his proposal, leaving out the information that Mr. Wickham had attempted to seduce and run away with Mr. Darcy's sister, only confirming for them that Mr. Wickham was not a man to be tolerated or trifled with, though it was unlikely that they should ever meet him again.

"Yes, I am Lyddie." Elizabeth said absentmindedly as she searched for a nightgown and wrap to change into from her shared trunk.

"Are you in love with him, or are you marrying him because of Mr. Collins? I think you are marrying him because of Mr. Collins," Lydia said in a rush, continuing her speech, not noticing the effect it had on her now trembling sister. "I saw him. He thought I was loud and stupid and silly, but *I am not*, and I saw him!" Lydia exclaimed.

"Lyddie!" Mary admonished, "You are upsetting

Lizzie."

Lydia pouted for a moment, before realizing that her sister was right. She slid off the bed in a most unlady like fashion, and curled up to Elizabeth, who still stood trembling in front of the open trunk.

"I'm sorry Lizzie." she repeated sorrowfully, over and over again, into Elizabeth's shoulder. Elizabeth could only nod, unable to stop her trembling.

Chapter Seventeen

Netherfield Hall

Darcy had been packed, ready to leave for nigh on a week now, and had forced himself to stay the extra days here in Netherfield, as he had already promised Mr. Gardner that he would stay with Charles until early December. The morning before Miss Elizabeth and her party had left, Mr. Gardner had arrived to Netherfield, and they had used Charles' study to have a frank discussion about the expectations Mr. Gardner had for the betrothed of his niece.

Fitzwilliam smiled to himself, as he poured a steaming cup of coffee that had been left on his desk by his valet. The man had made it perfectly clear, he may have been Fitzwilliam Darcy of Pemberley, but should his niece wish to end the engagement, up to the morning of their wedding, he would assist her in anyway that he could. His smile ended, though, as his thoughts drifted to the rest of the conversation that Mr. Gardner had been forced to have with him, wanting to give him that extra time to process the information.

Fitzwilliam slammed his cup down, harder than he intended, as he thought back on the words of his betrothed's uncle, as he had informed him of what his niece had gone through in the months leading up to her father's death. He should have known, should have not been wound so eagerly within his own pride and embarrassment over loving such a woman, that he should have almost entirely dismissed Mr. Collins' behavior at the evening they had spent in Longbourn.

He was loath to admit that he had been more interested in ignoring the pointed barbs of Caroline, and the general foolishness of Mr. Collins that he had only paid attention when Miss Elizabeth either spoke, or her name was drawn into the conversation. Even so, he had seen that she had been embarrassed, and had only come to her defense when it was *safe* for him to do so, when he was safe from the sharp, wagging tongues of Caroline and Louisa Hurst. Fitzwilliam vowed to himself that very moment that he should always put his family--which now included Miss Elizabeth, Mrs. Bennet, her sisters, and her loving aunts and uncles--first before any societal or prideful concern. He knew Miss Elizabeth did not love him, and marveled and thanked God that she had indeed accepted his proposal, after all that she had been through, and he promised himself that he should endeavor to be worthy of her, and perhaps, one day soon, she would welcome his love, and return the favor.

***

Finishing his coffee, Fitzwilliam stared at the empty sheets of paper that lay in a neat pile upon his small desk, a faint look of distaste graced his features. He had already written the much more pleasanter letters required--the first to Miss Elizabeth, of course, and to her uncle. Two separate letters that he had sent by express.

The letter to Mr. Gardner had simply informed him of his travel plans, and gave a brief overview of his intentions in the coming weeks, such as informing his family of his engagement, and when he should elect to have the banns published. He also wrote a letter of credit, instructing Mr. Gardner to place any purchases of new gowns and other fripperies, including Miss Elizabeth's wedding gown under his name, and he would take care of the bill.

The other letter, sent to Miss Elizabeth, contained a brief version of the same, and contained his rather paltry attempts at conversation, which had never been his strong suit. He hoped the news of Mr. Bingley coming to London the week after his own arrival would please her and her sister, Miss Bennet, but that was all he could note within the letter, except to wish her good health and enticement to enjoy her time with her sisters.

Otherwise, Fitzwilliam had already written to instruct his sister's new companion, Mrs. Annesley, that she and Georgiana should ready themselves to travel to London, and that he should meet them as soon as possible, from Pemberley.

He was now in the process of informing his aunt, Lady Catherine de Bourgh that he was to marry another, shortly after the New Year. He knew, his entire family knew that she had more than nurtured hopes that he should marry his cousin, Anne de Bourgh, even claiming that his mother had wished for such a union while he was still in nappies.

Fitzwilliam could not help but doubt such an idea, mainly because his father had never allowed Lady Catherine to utter such foolishness within his presence. One public set down in front of the entire family one dreary winter morning, less than a year after his mother's death, and Lady Catherine had retired the subject, at least in front of his father and himself, until his father's death.

He supposed that she thought he was weak willed and easily manipulated, due to the fact that he had not been like his cousin, the Viscount, who was still sowing more than a few wild oats with women of ill repute, spent the majority of his time at his club, or gambling, and subsided on port and imported wine.

He had always been of a rather studious bent and had focused almost entirely on his studies, and applied the same application to his care of Pemberley--all things that his father had drilled into him from childhood. Pemberley was to be his for only a generation, and it was his duty to keep its care and its inhabitants well. It was a duty that he should pass along to his son, a son that Miss Elizabeth, God willing, should give to him.

Fitzwilliam sighed, not being able to put off such a matter much longer. He was due to leave after breakfast, and wished to post his letter when he immediately arrived in London, so it would reach Lady Catherine before she read about the banns in the morning paper. She deserved that, at least. He thought about sending a letter to Anne, for she was his cousin, but ultimately he decided against it, due to his feeling that Lady Catherine most likely would read her mail before she should even receive to it.

Dipping his pen in the inkwell, he applied himself to the unpleasant task, not sure which would be easier--writing this letter, or informing his uncle, the Earl of Matlock that he should be taking a penniless bride, in person?

*****

Fitzwilliam patted his horse's head in relief as he saw the familiar road that led into the city of London. A few more hours' time, and he would be in his London townhouse. A hot bath, a good night's rest, and he would leave early the next morning to pay a call on his uncle the Earl before breakfast.

One of the many differences from his father's family from that of his mother's family was the relatively minor insistence that his father would keep country hours no matter where he was, and the Earl had always insisted on keeping London hours--which meant a later start to the day-- a rather interesting experience as a child.

While Fitzwilliam doubted that the Earl and Countess of Matlock should immediately disown him--they were of a rather cautious nature, neither of them as hot headed, temperamental, nor quite so easy to offend as Lady Catherine, it was more likely that they should wait to see how the wind blew--if his betrothed should be seen as nothing more than a country miss who had been blessed by the Almighty, or a shameless fortune hunter who had seduced the upright, rigid Fitzwilliam Darcy--and whether or not he truly was the master of his own household, and could managed Lady Catherine.

He was prepared for such a challenge, for he knew that Lady Catherine would not go away quietly. At least, he had Richard to count upon.

***

Edward Fitzwilliam, the Earl of Matlock, his wife, the Countess, his son, the Viscount of ___, and his second son, Colonel Fitzwilliam returned the stately bow of their nephew and cousin, Mr. Fitzwilliam Darcy, and all they could see then, was his rapidly retreating back, as he stalked his way out of their London home.

Almost immediately, his wife had settled down, and resumed her embroidery, her pretty pale blue eyes focusing intently upon her work. A bit of her tongue peeked from between her lips, and Edward wished to capture the stray wisp of hair that escaped her chignon, and lay artfully across her brow.

His wife, the Countess, was still just as beautiful as she had been all those years ago, when they had been introduced by their parents, at the start of her first season--when she had been Miss Eloise Spencer.

She had been just as serene and pleasing as she was now, and Edward did not understand it. His nephew, of an old, respected name had just arrived, virtually unannounced, and had upset all of their appetites by declaring that he was to marry some country miss without any name or fortune, less than two months after her father had died. Edward looked to his sons, who looked just as shocked and dismayed as he felt.

Although his eldest son had been somewhat of a disappointment, as he had elected to spend more time in the gaming hells and his club and frequenting whores than applying himself to estate management, or any other useful activity, he knew that his son would never go out and marry without attention to connection or fortune--of that, he was entirely sure. Not unless he wished to be disinherited sooner than he could swallow down a glass of wine.

He studied his wife. She gave a put on sigh, as she set aside her embroidery for the moment.

"Edward, dear, are you quite all right?" she queried in her gentle, pleasing voice.

Her voice shocked him out of his apathy, and he waited an appropriate amount of time to reply, unable to confess to her that she had shocked him, "Of course my dear. I was simply pondering the news our nephew brought."

His sweet Eloise scoffed at the notion. "Oh, that." she said lightly, as though it had been so very long ago that he had brought the news to them, and not merely five minutes past. "I should not worry too much, Edward."

"And why not, Mama?" came the question out of the mouth of his indolent, eldest son.

Richard, his younger son, ever the soldier, had not betrayed an expression, except shock at when his cousin had given them his news. It was from that, that he guessed that Fitzwilliam had not informed his favorite cousin, and boyhood friend of his intentions.

"Your cousin Darcy is enchanted with a country miss. Darcy keeps his affairs close to his heart, and is a private man. He is also very conscious of his duty. In time we shall see whether or not he has chosen well, and in the meantime, he shall have your Aunt Catherine to deal with."

Both of their sons shuddered in reminder.

"She shall not be pleased," the Countess mused calmly, as though she were speaking of a bonnet or lace, "And the first thing she shall do is attempt to pay off or run off the woman to whom your cousin is engaged to--the sooner the possible. If she is a fortune hunter, then she shall take the money, if not, then she shall be your cousin's problem, not ours. I am confident that he is master enough to settle his own affairs, husband." she said, her voice gaining a bit of tartness, as she addressed her husband directly

"Darcy has ten thousand a year, Mama," came the almost petulant whine of the Countess' eldest son. The Countess sighed, as she felt a headache coming on, almost certainly induced by the pettiness of her eldest child.

"Perhaps if you spent less time whoring and drinking, son of mine, then perhaps your father would allow you more levity in matters of the estate." she replied coolly, regretting the manner in which she had coddled him as a baby, to his growth as a young man--his birth had been terribly difficult, and she had been convinced by the doctors that she should never have another child, and so she had lavished so much, too much attention on her only child, doting upon him in a manner that was extravagant, even for the wife of an Earl.

Her summer child, Richard had come as a surprise six years later, and named for her dearest grandfather, who had died shortly before her marriage to the Earl.

"Mama, I only wish to point out that if she is a fortune hunter, than there is little that Aunt Catherine may do to persuade her otherwise, of marrying Darcy. Not when she shall have ten thousand pounds, and very likely more--God knows that Darcy does not speak of such things to me!--at her disposal!" her son cried out dramatically, flinging himself around his chair.

"Sit up straight, dear." she said softly, however her son detected an undercurrent of steel, and thankfully obeyed.

The Countess of Matlock gave her son a full smile, one in which showed all of her teeth, and replied, "If you do not believe that your Aunt Catherine could not bribe, nor persuade a fortune hunter to give up your cousin Darcy, then, my dear son, you understand even less of the wiles of woman. A lesson I should have expected you to learn quite well, due to the debts that your father pays, in your name, every month."

Her son had enough sense to hang his head, although she supposed it was due to the blistering headache he had, no doubt due to the amount of wine he had drank the night before, and she supposed she should be grateful that he was here, as it *was* the holiday season.

Her summer child, Richard, moved to bow over her hand, to grant her a kiss, and excused himself.

"Do speak to your cousin, Richard." she encouraged gently.

Richard gave his mother another kiss, this time to her cheek, and murmured that he would.

The Countess picked up her embroidery, content that it would end, one way or another, by the New Year.

*****

Gracechurch Street, one week previous

As Elizabeth had predicted, Mrs. Bennet had gone into hysterics when she had been informed of her daughter's engagement. At least her uncle had given them time to unpack their clothing and spend a good night's rest from the road, before unleashing their mama upon them. Elizabeth supposed that her Uncle Gardner had thought that her mama would not quite be up to withstanding an attack of her nerves, and would spare her this time, however it appeared that he was wrong.

Elizabeth had been in her cousin, Eliza Jane's nursery, watching her pick and discard the ribbons that she wanted to wear *especially* with her gown that matched her pretty cousin, Jane's, when Mrs. Bennet swept through the room, clutching in one hand a handkerchief, and in another a vial of smelling salts.

"My dear, sweet girl! God has been very good to us!" Mrs. Bennet wailed, as she clasped Elizabeth to her tightly.

"Mama, I cannot breathe!" Elizabeth protested, although it was muffled by the material of her mother's gown.

"Oh, oh, oh my poor dear, I do apologize!" Elizabeth stood there and waited, as her mother determinedly brushed every speck of non existent dirt and dust from her person.

"Mama, I am perfectly well." Elizabeth said, although she truly could not *reprimand* her mother, not now, when this was the first bit of good news that her mother had received in a long while.

"Of course my dear, I apologize!" her mama repeated excitedly. "Now I have come to fetch you, your young man has sent you a letter--oh! indeed he has sent you more than that, my child!" Mrs. Bennet exclaimed enthusiastically. "You must go downstairs to eat your breakfast Lizzie, for afterwards we are going to the shops!"

Elizabeth was alarmed almost immediately. "Mama, we do not need any clothes, not yet. We should wait for Mr. Darcy to arrive, I should hate that he would think---"
In her eagerness, her mama interrupted her-- "It is Mr. Darcy who has given his permission, Lizzie! Go and see for yourself! He wrote to your uncle, giving us permission to spend the money!" Mrs. Bennet sighed dreamily, "I always knew you should do your duty to your family, Lizzie!"

At that, Elizabeth all but repressed a snort, but followed her mama out of the room, and downstairs.

Shopping, it seemed, was to be the order of the day. Of course, they should need mourning clothes, for they were all living on three recycled gowns each, all they had been able to pack when Mr. Collins had thrown them out, and Elizabeth would need to see to her wedding gown.

Once downstairs, after settling down to her breakfast, Elizabeth blushed to see a letter addressed to herself, in a fine, elegant hand that was unknown to her.

Mr. Darcy, her mind supplied, and she hurriedly placed the letter in her pocket, before Mrs. Bennet could see, her blush returning in full force as her sister Jane watched her place the letter in her pocket.

***

It was hours later, in the relative privacy of her bedroom, shared with her dear Jane, that she allowed herself to open the letter and read it. She had waited until Jane had fallen asleep, unwilling, for some reason, to share her letter with her closest sister.

Miss Elizabeth, it read, *I have sent this letter by express, and so I hope that it should arrive shortly after you yourself have arrived at your uncle's, if not previous. I hope your journey was pleasant, and it was not too cold in the carriage, although I suppose you had your sisters to keep you warm.*

Elizabeth smiled at the reference, for she had indeed not moved from her spot, unwilling to give up the body heat generated by her sister Lydia in the middle, and her sister Jane on the other side, no matter how uncomfortable the carriage was. *I have also sent a letter to your uncle, and within it explaining some of the finer details of our upcoming wedding, and have enclosed a letter of credit, for which you and your sisters and mother may go to the shops and obtain a general wardrobe, as well as special gowns for our wedding.* There it was, the line that had excited her mama so much that she had to have a glass of wine to calm herself down before leaving the house.

The letter continued, speaking of general pleasantries, and Elizabeth was astounded to note that Mr. Bingley was to stand up for Mr. Darcy in their wedding, and that he should be arriving a week after Mr. Darcy would! She had some thoughts of waking Jane to tell her the news, but decided against it, and then decided to go and tell Mary, for Mary had confided in her the last night that they had spent at the Phillips' that she thought Mr. Bingley should be very sad to see Jane go.

Elizabeth took great pains to make her tread light, as she did not wish to disturb, nor excite her young, exuberant cousins, whose nursery room was located next to hers and Jane's, and so when she had reached what she thought was Mary's room, she opened the door, to find not Mary's, but her mama's room, the candle still going, but her mama was nowhere to be found.

"Mama?" Elizabeth whispered tersely. There was a muffled sob, that came from the bed, but Elizabeth knew that it did not, for the curtains had been drawn, and her mama was not in bed.

"Mama?" she repeated, going around the bed, dreading what she might find. And find her mama she did. Dressed in her night clothes, red faced and clutching an empty bottle and glass, her sobs becoming hiccups due to their frequency.

"Oh dear Lord!" she whispered, as she pried the bottle from her mama's hand, and helped her up from the floor. Her mama started crying again, sobbing that she did not wish for her girls to see her like this, that she was a failure as a mother, and Elizabeth shushed her, assuring her that she was the strongest mother that had ever lived, and that she would help her.

As Elizabeth tucked her into bed, Mrs. Bennet grabbed her hand, raising her palm to her cheeks, rubbing her tears into her daughter's hand.

"I miss Mr. Bennet!" she attempted to cry loudly, but the wine had now dulled her voice so that the entire household was not awakened.

"As do I mama, we all do." Elizabeth said soothingly.

"I should never have allowed him to go into that carriage, I have always said that we should hire a driver, but Mr. Bennet refused! My poor Bennet! My Jane!" she cried quietly, already halfway to falling asleep, Elizabeth's hand still clutched within her own.

Elizabeth waited until she was asleep, and quietly returned to her room, her letter all but forgotten.

***

It took a small amount of coaxing, but Elizabeth had persuaded Kitty to start sleeping with their mama. She would have asked Lydia, but according to Kitty's protestations, Lydia kicked, and to which Lydia replied hotly that she *did not*, and it took a calm and practical

 Mary to settle the sisters. Kitty would sleep with their mama for she was uneasy with sleeping alone, as she had always slept with either Lydia or Jane, and it was a perfect situation for all of them.

It was now drawing close to Mr. Darcy's first visit to her uncle's home, as her betrothed, and as every day passed, so did her apprehension increase. She did not wish for him to encounter any difficulty or hardship concerning her family, during their engagement period, and worked very hard to counter that notion. She was sure her aunt had noticed while they were shopping, but she did not say anything.

She hoped she would not.

Chapter Eighteen

Elizabeth smoothed the stiff black material of her gown nervously, as she awaited near the window overlooking the road below to note if and when any carriage should stop in front of her aunt and uncle's home. Beside her, Jane patted her hand soothingly, having elected to stay and wait for her sister.

Elizabeth had never been more grateful for her sister's attention as she waited, her nerves on fire, trembling because of the wait.

Today, Mr. Darcy was to arrive with his sister, Miss Georgiana, and his cousin, Richard, the younger son of his uncle, the Earl of Matlock--as he had written to her previously. Mr. Darcy had arrived in town a week after they had, and he had spent the three days he had been in town to settle, inform his family of their engagement, receive his cousin and sister, collect any and all legal documents needed, and now, to visit her in her aunt and uncle's home.

Elizabeth had been immensely gratified that Mr. Darcy was not to come visit immediately, but was to wait a few days, for it gave her time to comport herself, to think. She had already taken care of the issue of her mama, and her Aunt Gardner had spent almost every moment she was not with her children, with her sister in law, after Kitty and Elizabeth had informed her the next morning of what Elizabeth had witnessed in her mama's room that night.

Right now, she was attempting to persuade her mama to keep herself busy. Elizabeth hid her smile, as she considered the image of her mama studiously bent over needlework. For all that her mama used to wail and groan over Elizabeth's propensity for taking long walks, Elizabeth was now entirely sure that she had inherited her temperament not from her papa, as she had always thought before, but from her mama.

Currently, her mama spent her mornings keeping an eye upon the younger children as they played in the back garden, and in the afternoons poured over the fashion magazines that their Aunt Gardner had thought to buy from the shops. Mrs. Bennet poured over the French fashions, watching fondly as Lydia, Kitty, and Mary tore apart their bonnets to mimic the new styles that were introduced to them. Elizabeth was glad, for between that and her upcoming wedding.

The sound of a knocker startled Elizabeth, as she realized, with a start that she had missed Mr. Darcy's carriage in the drive. Standing up, she smoothed her skirts again, and made to walk downstairs. Jane grabbed her hand before she could go.

"Calmly, Lizzie." she said soothingly.

Elizabeth nodded gratefully to her sister, and calmly glided down the stairs.

Mr. Darcy was waiting for her at the bottom of the stairs, imposing and grave as always, and beside him stood a lighter haired man, who was not even attempting to hide the grin on his face, and a fair haired young girl, whom Elizabeth realized with dismay was Miss Georgiana Darcy.

That was whom Mr. Wickham had attempted to elope with? In her mind's eye, Elizabeth had sketched a rendering of Miss Georgiana Darcy, and *that* was not whom she had been able to form into her mind. To be sure, she had a womanly figure, but Georgiana Darcy looked painfully young, in the same way that her sister Lydia looked younger than her years. However, unlike her sister Lydia, she looked painfully shy and timid, unable to meet Elizabeth's eyes.

Mr. Darcy bowed in greeting, "Miss Elizabeth," he said

warmly, and Elizabeth saw for the first time his smile, and that he had dimples in the grooves of his cheeks, "allow me to introduce my sister, Miss Georgiana," and at that introduction, Georgiana dipped into a low curtsey, which Elizabeth returned, "and my cousin, Colonel Richard Fitzwilliam." the friendly looking man also bowed, looking fairly amused as he did it.

He explained it a moment later. "I have not seen my cousin Darcy this nervous in quite a long while, Miss Elizabeth," he said with a roguish wink. "I shall need to know your secret."

Elizabeth led them to the parlour, where the servants had already laid the area out with tea, scones, biscuits, fresh preserves, and butter. They settled down and Elizabeth poured tea for her guests, noting the way that Mr. Darcy preferred his, and when they were contented with their tea, she poured her own.

"I should say this, before Darcy keeps you all to himself, Miss Elizabeth, but I am truly sorry for your loss. I cannot imagine what you must be going through." Colonel Fitzwilliam was the first to offer his condolences, Elizabeth's soon to be sister in law, falteringly echoing her cousin, although Elizabeth could tell that it did not make her sentiment any less real, nor false.

"I thank you both, Colonel, Miss Georgiana," she smiled pleasantly at them both, and then turned to Mr. Darcy, "although truthfully I am glad that he is no longer in any pain. It was a long...." here she stumbled over how to describe her father's death, what it was, what it was not, "illness" she finally settled on a word, "and I am glad that he is at peace now." There, Elizabeth was satisfied that she had not embarrassed Mr. Darcy at all in her description of her father's passing to his family.

Elizabeth turned to address Mr. Darcy, and then his sister, "Are you well, Mr. Darcy?" When he replied that he was, she then asked Miss Georgiana if her journey was tolerable, to which her soon to be sister in law replied very quietly that it had been a smooth journey, although she had no wish to undertake it again quite so soon.

They maintained pleasantries for a few more minutes, until her Aunt and Uncle Gardner arrived with her sister Jane, Lydia, Kitty, and Mary. Her mama was still preoccupied with her cousins, an occupation Elizabeth was grateful for.

Mr. Darcy stood up, almost at some prearranged signal with her uncle, and offered her his arm. "I was wondering, Miss Elizabeth, if you would take a walk in the gardens with me for few minutes?"

Elizabeth glanced back at her aunt, who gave her an encouraging nod, and took Mr. Darcy's arm.

Mr. Darcy led her to the gardens, and they walked a bit, Elizabeth still holding on to Mr. Darcy's arm. For his part, he seemed content to let her clutch at him, and continue taking a turn about the garden.

"Shall we say something, Miss Elizabeth?" his words startled her, for she recognized them as her own, cloaking the anger and bitterness she had felt at the time, in levity and tartness.

"I suppose we must, Mr. Darcy," Elizabeth agreed quietly, unsure how to process the feelings that were now welling inside of her--reminders of things she wished to forget, of a previous life.

"Miss Elizabeth, are you content?" Mr. Darcy was looking at her now, concern dominating his features.

"I am well, Mr. Darcy. Simply tired." she rushed to assure him. To keep him distracted, she spoke of his sister, "Your sister seems like a lovely girl, Mr. Darcy. I am sure she is a credit to you, as Miss Bingley often stated."

"Yes," Mr. Darcy replied distractedly, "Georgiana is very accomplished."

"Perhaps she could play for us later, Mr. Darcy? I am sure my cousins would enjoy such a lady playing for them. Unfortunately," she said with a laugh that sounded even tight to her own ears, "only one of their cousins play, and I am sure listening to Mary or myself play are vastly different than hearing someone who has been trained play."

Mr. Darcy frowned at her belittling jabs, and regarded her with serious eyes,

"I am sure that we shall be just as entertained if you or Miss Mary should play, but for you, I will ask my sister if she would be willing to play. She is rather shy, you see." Mr. Darcy trailed off uncomfortably, and Elizabeth held back a flinch as she had distressed Mr. Darcy..

She searched for a subject that might distract him, anything.

"And would you tell me of Pemberley, sir?

She knew she had made the right choice, when his eyes lit up in a manner that she had rarely seen of him, and he led her to a nearby bench, and began to speak in a most animated manner. Later, when she had gone to bed, Elizabeth would realize that the ghost of a smile still touched her lips, as she thought about the beautiful grounds, as described by Mr. Darcy, who had been kind enough to take great care in describing the grounds to her.

*****

Two weeks later......

In the coming weeks, Elizabeth's days were divided into the time period where Mr. Darcy was not visiting Gracechurch street, and the time he was.

Generally most mornings Elizabeth and Mr. Darcy would take tea and some small pastries, as Elizabeth found it difficult to adjust to Town hours--a trait she shared with Mr. Darcy--then taking a turn in the garden or the park for a few hours before joining the rest of the family for breakfast.

She found that each day she spent with Mr. Darcy, simply walking, was a day that she found it easier to breathe. His sister and the Colonel often joined him in domestic felicity with her sisters, as more and more days passed.

Elizabeth worried about bonding with her soon to be sister, as she had no concept of her true character, once the shyness had been stripped away, other than what Miss Bingley had spoken of her--a demure, well bred lady who delighted in the arts--the complete opposite of her younger sisters, who, although were a great deal better behaved than before, had little in the way of a lady's education.

While Miss Georgiana was too well bred and mannered to note such a thing, Elizabeth could see the differences--the way in which Miss Georgiana devoted herself to her music and her studies, and the way in which her younger sisters focused on their bonnets and lace.

Hopefully, Elizabeth sighed as she turned a critical eye over herself in the mirror, that Mr. Darcy was as willing to overlook their deficiencies--her deficiencies--as he claimed to during his proposal. She would admit, as she reflected criticisms at her sisters, that those same criticisms, excepting any obsession with her dress and hairstyle, could also be accurately targeted at her.

Miss Bingley's voice drawled through her mind, as she recalled that night that Miss Bingley praised Miss Georgiana for her talent at the pianoforte, her beautiful drawings, her sweet disposition--all of which pointed to the makings of a substantive, accomplished lady.

The cobbled steps of horses and a carriage jostling to a rest in front of her home shook Elizabeth out of her thoughts.

She peered out of the window in curiosity, as her Uncle Gardner was away, visiting one of his warehouses, Mr. Darcy had informed her only the day before that he should be gone for a week or ten days to attend to some business concerns within Derbyshire, and her mama,

Aunt Gardner, and younger sisters were out shopping--for they would have special gowns made for Elizabeth's wedding, which was less than a month away.

Jane had settled down for a much needed nap after wrangling with her niece and nephews all morning, and Elizabeth was alone in her sister Mary and Kitty's room to give Jane some privacy and quiet.

Elizabeth watched as an older lady, formidably dressed in black and gold swept out of the carriage, and descended upon the steps of her uncle's home, followed by a footman dressed similarly.

A few moments later, a maid knocked urgently on the door, telling her that the lady was none other than Lady Catherine de Bourgh, and she was requesting an audience with Elizabeth.

"Yes, thank you Lucy. Please tell her ladyship that I shall be down presently.", wincing for the maid, as she could now hear the querulous tones of the lady below.

 She was not stupid, she knew why the lady was here--through their conversation the very first day they had interacted after their engagement, he had spoken very little about either of his extended family members--Lady Catherine de Bourgh, the Earl and Countess of Matlock, the Viscount of ____--and had instead focused on his sister and his cousin--and it was common sense to propose that they should not have been pleased to hear of his engagement to a country bumpkin.

Elizabeth steadied herself, mentally preparing herself for the lady's attack, as she turned the corner into the parlour where Lucy had situated the woman and her footman--who stood silently in the corner, his face expressionless.

She curtseyed. Lady Catherine regarded her with cool, disapproving eyes. Before she could introduce herself, Lady Catherine barked,

"Are you Elizabeth Bennet?"
"I am your ladyship." Elizabeth replied, despising how weak her voice was.

"I do not wish to stay in this part of London for any longer than necessary, Miss Bennet," the lady started, her voice tinged with scorn, as she had to travel to *Cheapside*, in order to speak to the woman who was so presumptuously engaged to her nephew, "so I shall be brief and to the point. I presume you know who I am, but I shall state my identity to begin with,"

Here, she drew herself up as though she were preparing herself for battle, "I am Lady Catherine de Bourgh, the daughter of the late Earl of Matlock, and the widow of Sir Lewis de Bourgh. My nephew, Mr. Darcy, is your supposed fiancee, and I wish for you to break off the engagement. I am willing to pay you a substantive amount of money, Miss Bennet, for you to do so."

She then spread her hands, bejeweled in several rings,as if to show off the supposed wealth she could delugeElizabeth in.

Elizabeth lifted her chin, and said firmly, not wishing to speak to Mr. Darcy's aunt in a manner that would displease or embarrass him, yet not wishing to bear her company any longer, after paying her such an insult, "I will not accept your offer, Lady Catherine," and then, seeking to move towards the door, "I shall walk you to the door" she said politely.

Lady Catherine gave her a look of rigid disapproval, a look that did not scare Elizabeth, not anymore for she had endured worse, and said harshly, "You are making a mistake of improbably magnitude, Miss Bennet."

"How so, Lady Catherine?"

Lady Catherine screeched in outrage at her bored tone, her eyes glancing to the open window, as though there were several of peers watching her breach of propriety. Elizabeth waited for her to compose herself, which, unfortunately was a relatively short amount of time.

"Do you honestly believe that my nephew should marry you! You! A young woman of inferior birth and no fortune, who had not the good sense to thank the Good Lord that her own honorable cousin, heir to her father's estate was willing to marry her, when he shall be able to marry *my* daughter, the heiress of all that her father left behind! Mark my words, Miss Bennet, this union shall not stand! My nephew may have forgotten himself to your wiles for a brief time, but he shall soon set himself to rights, and that includes you and your family!"

The tirade, and oh Elizabeth could not categorize it as anything but, continued on as Lady Catherine began to list her family's deficiencies--prior or otherwise--as though she were reading aloud from a list.

"And do you honestly think that my nephew should seek to align himself with a woman whose younger sisters are shameless, vulgar hoydens, flitting after any male in a red coat, a cripple elder sister who also seeks to use mean, shameless arts in the capture of another wealthy man, as well as a shameless mother who advocates such behavior and arts from her daughters! It shall not be born! You do not know my nephew very well Miss Bennet, and you shall understand this soon enough!"

These words were delivered in such a biting tone, that Elizabeth almost did not catch the note of desperation that clung to each and every word that poured out of Lady Catherine's furious form.

"And then, I wonder, Lady Catherine, that you should wish to have your illustrious name sullied with such a man!" Elizabeth noted drolly, mentally cataloging each micro expression that dominated Lady Catherine's face."I will not stand for this! I shall make this offer one last time, you headstrong, impertinent girl! I have with me thirty thousand pounds, and all of that shall be yours the moment I have confirmation that you have refused my nephew."

"I will not." was Elizabeth's reply, and without waiting for anything further, the grand lady swept out the house, her ever silent footman trailing her form without notice.

***

Safely situated in her carriage, Lady Catherine looked out the window to see the horrid area, Gracechurch street, leave her view as her carriage swiftly carried her out of *Cheapside.*

Glancing down at the letter gripped tightly in her hand, she mentally catalogued all that she should need to accomplish when she reached Rosings Park. A letter to Mr. Collins would be sent out posthaste, requiring his arrival to Rosings as soon as possible.

One way or another, the country chit would be taken care of.

*****

Elizabeth had debated whether or not to inform Mr. Darcy of his aunt's visit, when he returned from his trip, but she found that she did not have to, as he had immediately apologized for his aunt the moment they were alone in the garden, Jane and Mr. Bingley trailing a discreet distance behind them.

"I must apologize, Miss Elizabeth, for Lady Catherine's behavior." he said before she could even open her mouth.

"There is nothing to apologize for, Mr. Darcy" she rushed to assure him before he could self flagellate himself at all. "I was expecting there to be disapproval from your family, although I was not expecting it to be quite so," here she paused, seeking a word that would not sound as condemning as she wished it to, "*direct*, although I am used to such directness," she awkwardly joked, her mind retrieving Lady Catherine's references her younger sisters' and mama's former behavior, "so it was not quite so bad." she ended, peering into her betrothed's face.

He gave her a strange look, and opened his mouth to say more, but was interrupted with the girlish cry of her mama, calling out enthusiastically to Mr. Bingley and Jane.

Elizabeth turned away, the corners of her mouth downturned, as she studied the flowers. It was moments like this that she realized that her mama truly favored Jane above everyone.

When Mr. Darcy had written to inform Elizabeth that Mr. Bingley had to delay his visit due to some unexpected business coming up, her mama had wept and had to be consoled by Kitty and Elizabeth for the rest of the day and the majority of the night, so convinced she was that Mr. Bingley was never coming to visit Jane.

And when Mr. Darcy had informed her that he should be bringing Mr. Bingley with him after his business concluded in Derbyshire, it were as though God himself had proposed a visit, for mama spent the next two days directing the servants and the cook to her increased demands.

Not even at her engagement to Mr. Darcy had her mama displayed as much enthusiasm or happiness for *her*--she had indeed thanked Elizabeth for her actions to save the family, her cunningness in refusing Mr. Collins, and had been ecstatic on the news that Mr. Darcy was willing to pay for their new gowns, but never had she greeted Mr. Darcy and Elizabeth on a stroll throughout the garden with as much happiness and pride as she had with Mr. Bingley and Jane.

She missed her papa, so much that it ached.

Beside her, Mr. Darcy must have sensed her thoughts, as he smoothly slid his bare hand to hers, gripping tightly. Neither of them said a word, and Elizabeth found, that for once, they did not have to.

***

Elizabeth and Darcy's wedding day.....

"Shall I leave you alone for a moment, Lizzie?" her sweet sister asked, as she watched Elizabeth pace up and down the length of the room.

Elizabeth was dressed, had been dressed for nearly an hour now, and was now awaiting the carriage to take her to the church in which she would be married.

Jane had barred the door to her younger sisters and mama over an hour ago, sensing Elizabeth's distress, and had offered to leave the room to leave Elizabeth alone with her thoughts, but Elizabeth had wished her to stay.

Jane looked at the small plate of uneaten fruit and toast, and then back at her sister.

"I shall bring these to the kitchen Lizzie." she offered, and without awaiting her sister's reply, took the place and quietly left the room. Elizabeth's eyes followed her. With more regular exercise, Jane's movements were becoming less stiff, less painful, and it showed in her attitude.

Jane did not return, and a short time later, a small knock alerted her to a presence at the door, and Elizabeth turned her gaze towards the door, expecting her sister, but instead it was her future sister, Miss Georgiana with a small package in her hands, shyly standing in the doorway, unable to enter without permission.

Elizabeth gave her an encouraging smile, and said "Come in, Miss Georgiana."

Georgiana blushed prettily and closed the door behind her.

"You look lovely, dear." Elizabeth complimented her on her simple and plain gown, although she could clearly see Lydia's influence in the detailing of her small reticule that she held loosely in one hand.

"Thank you." A few moments passed, and Georgiana pressed the small package, rather clumsily, into Elizabeth's hands.

"These are from my brother," she rushed to explain, blushing furiously at the thought of being a mediator between any type of flirtation between her brother and Elizabeth.

Elizabeth was not surprised. She had received several gifts-- some large, such as the shopping trip Mr. Darcy had provided--and some small, such as a simple gold bracelet with their initials inscribed, and a small cross necklace, tastefully encrusted with seed pearls and tiny rubies--a replica of the one she had lost to Longbourn. She wore both today.

Aware that Miss Georgiana was anxiously waiting her to open the package, as well as watching her face directly, no doubt to inform her brother of what she thought of his gift, Elizabeth carefully opened the package, and enclosed of the package lay a pair of pearl and diamond earrings, that would go wonderfully with her dress.

Elizabeth glanced to Miss Georgiana who was visibly excited.

"My brother especially wanted you to wear them, Miss Elizabeth. They belonged to my mother, and my father gave them to her before their wedding as well."

Elizabeth gave Miss Georgiana a fond smile, carefully noting the tightness around Georgiana's eyes as she spoke of her parents. If Elizabeth had not known better, she would have thought it a wonderful anecdote from a young girl who had been raised by loving parents, or, rather a loving father. She knew Georgiana had neither, and before she could stop herself, she embraced Georgiana gingerly, minding her dress.

Georgiana stood ramrod straight in her arms for a few moments, and then relaxed, and returned her actions.

They stood there for a few minutes longer, wrapped in each other's arms, and then at the sound of another knock, parted from each other. Elizabeth checked herself in the mirror to see if she was still presentable, and when she saw that she was, she followed Miss Georgiana out of the room.
In a few short hours, she would no longer be Elizabeth Teresa Bennet, but would be Elizabeth Bennet Darcy.

Elizabeth Darcy.

Chapter Nineteen

Rosings Park

Although Mr. Collins was a proper gentleman, ever mindful of his station and situation in life, he found that he could not keep his eyes away from the splendors that Lady Catherine had introduced him to, by dint of writing to him, and informing him of Elizabeth Bennet's deceitful, underhanded ways, the paltry arts for which she used to trick, nay, *deceive* Mr. Darcy, Lady Catherine's beloved nephew, to *marry* her.

Indeed, he had read of the wedding of Elizabeth Teresa Bennet, of Hertfordshire to Mr. Fitzwilliam George Darcy, of Pemberley in Derbyshire in the morning's paper.

It had not been a shock to him, no more than a shock that Mr. Darcy had actually forgot himself and had married his inferior cousin, because Mrs. Bennet's infernal sister, whose company and tongue he *knew* he should have forbade Elizabeth Bennet and the other Bennet chits from, had spread the word all over Meryton, from one of her paltry card parties, that Mr. Darcy had proposed to his cousin days after she had refused him!

Not for the first time, since refusing him, had Mr. Collins wished he had come across his fair cousin before she had left town.

Beside him, the man that he had brought with him--a Mr. George Wickham--snorted as he took in the glory and splendor of Rosings Park, and Mr. Collins resisted, barely, the urge to cuff him for his sheer cheek in the face of such a splendid home.

He had resisted thus far, because Mr. Wickham had not acted in this manner in front of Lady Catherine, although he supposed it was due to the fact that he and Mr. Wickham were meeting with Lady Catherine for the first time, as she had humbly, and generously invited them into her beautiful estate.

But if he should act thus in front of a woman such as her ladyship, Mr. Collins was sure to give him the proper hiding he deserved for such disrespect.

A butler, dressed in somber black opened the door to the grandest estate, and without even taking their names, led them into a parlour where an imposing, fiercely handsome woman sat awaiting them.

Mr. Collins, unable to keep himself from being overwhelmed by the splendor that was presented to him, nearly tripped over himself in his eagerness to bow to her ladyship, yet did not wish to keep his eyes off the chimney piece nor the paintings that dominated the walls of that great estate.

"My dear Lady Catherine de Bourgh," he said reverently soft voice, a feat which he found most impressive, as he was out of breath from keeping himself upright from falling, "I am Mr. Collins of Longbourn. And my companion, " he said, unable to keep the lurid distaste from his lips, "is Mr. George Wickham. I had thought he might be useful to your ladyship, and so I persuaded him to join me on my journey to your magnificent estate, my lady."

He jostled the man beside him to bow, which the man did with an exaggerated lowness. Mr. Collins mouth twisted at the gall of Mr. Wickham!

Perhaps some time in debtor's prison would improve his disposition towards his betters, Mr. Collins thought cruelly, as he examined the reasons behind Mr. Wickham becoming his traveling companion.

Elizabeth Bennet had indeed been correct to be suspicious of his story of Mr. Darcy cheating him out of an inheritance, although Mr. Collins was of the opinion that Mr. Darcy, will or no, had clearly done what any other man of his station would have when faced with acknowledging and rewarding the son of a steward as though he were part of his own *family*!

After Elizabeth Bennet had related to him the story that Mr. Wickham had relayed her, he had summoned Mr. Hill to ask around Meryton as to the character of Mr. Wickham, although Mr. Hill had told him, quite honestly, a mark in which he valued in such a servant, that Mr. Wickham charmed the ladies, but had was already gaining a reputation for being unable to pay his debts, and such charms were wearing thin on the shop owners of the town of Meryton.

To add insult to injury, Mr. Darcy, before leaving town, a week or so after Elizabeth Bennet had left to live with the Gardner's in *Cheapside*, he and Mr. Bingley, as he understood it, had visited Colonel Forster, the head of Mr. Wickham's regiment to inform him of Mr. Wickham's misdeeds. He had also found out that Mr. Wickham was engaged to a Mary King, who had recently inherited ten thousand pounds, an engagement that had ended after word got out of Mr. Wickham's behavior.

Mr. Collins felt pity for the man, Mr. Darcy, the estimable Lady Catherine's nephew, for he had clearly been tricked and deceived by Eliza Bennet, but he had portrayed a sound mind and head in informing Colonel Forster of Mr. Wickham's misdeeds in spreading an egregious story around Meryton. If Mr. Collins had been in the same position, he should have also done the same thing.

"Mr. Collins." rang the authoritative lady's voice.

Mr. Collins focused upon her in panic, for he had been lost in his own thoughts once again, and had gotten distracted, a trait that his benevolent, dearly missed father had done his best, with God's hand, to train out of him.

Mr. Collins bowed as low as he could go, as second time, his apology pouring out of his mouth like water rushing over a high fall, "My dear Lady Catherine de Bourgh, I am indeed mortified! I most heartily--"
"That is enough, Mr. Collins!" the lady spoke over him, and Mr. Collins instantly quieted. "You and Mr. Wickham, sit, over there." she said, gesturing to the open chaise to the left of her.

Mr. Collins meekly did as he was bid, and Mr. Wickham followed lazily after him, clearly uninterested in the proceedings. An attitude, Mr. Collins was pleased to note, that Lady Catherine did not seem to tolerate.

"Mr. Wickham, I should hope that you would take an interest in these proceedings, given the vendetta you hold against my nephew." she informed him, calmly.

Mr. Wickham's face drained of color, and before he could say anything, her ladyship, Lady Catherine had him closing his mouth with a single look.

"Now, Mr. Collins, Mr. Wickham, I only require that you should listen." she said authoritatively, her dark eyes roving over their forms.

"My nephew has made a grave mistake, a mistake in which I had given him ample time to correct before it became too late, and unfortunately it has become too late for he has married the chit, and they are most likely now in Derbyshire, in my dear, late sister's home!"

Mr. Collins knew that he should do as her ladyship had requested, that he should stay quiet, but he could not help himself, and rushed to comfort Lady Catherine as best he knew how, given that their companionship and knowledge of each other consisted of only a two letters between them--

one from Lady Catherine directing Mr. Collins that he should come to Rosings Park, posthaste, so that they could speak of her nephew and Eliza Bennet, and the other, he was proud to say, he had sent by express, stressing to the clerk that the rider should not stop but continue to ride straight to to Rosings Park, so that her ladyship should receive his reply as quickly as possible.

"It is not entirely your nephew's fault, your ladyship," he said in what he hoped to be a soothing tone, "for I have spent nearly a year in close quarters with Elizabeth Bennet, and I do believe, Lady Catherine, that she is entirely capable of those mean arts that some, ill bred ladies employ to capture such a man. Indeed, my own dear father, whom God took away too soon from this world, had sensed it in the Bennet girls, and had done his best to instruct me in the best way to handle them, for their own benefit."

Seeing encouragement from Lady Catherine's stern features, Mr. Collins continued on, ignoring Mr. Wickham's garbled laugh.

"Indeed, my lady, I found that strict access to only the most polite and refined company was the key to dealing with such a family of females, yet I am saddened to note that even when they were properly chaperoned, and in the direct influence of a fine woman, such as Mr. Bingley's sister, Miss Caroline Bingley, Eliza Bennet still managed to go back to her former behaviors. It is indeed shocking, and I most heartily apologize for her behavior, your ladyship, although there was not much else that I could do." he finished with, gazing hopefully into Lady Catherine's eyes, hoping that she should hear him, that she should understand him.

There was a long moment of silence, the longest and most horrid silence that Mr. Collins had ever felt, and he had only relaxed when Lady Catherine addressed him thus,

"I see."

Calling for tea, Lady Catherine graciously directed her servant to pour it especially to their tastes, and returned to the task at hand.

"I want you to tell me of the Bennet sisters, Mr. Collins. All of them."

Her ladyship was so direct in her wants, that Mr. Collins had no choice but to comply, and eagerly, he did.
 Of the eldest Bennet--Jane, who was the most beautiful of the Bennet sisters, but was now crippled in the same accident that injured and killed her father, and was now unable to wed because of it.

Of Eliza Bennet--Mr. Collins took great pains to explain the amount of time his father had spent with her each morning, until her death, in instructing her and guiding her away from the unfortunate arts that seemed innate in the Bennets.

Of Mary Bennet--the plainest of all the Bennet sisters, who had spent a great deal of time practicing on her pianoforte, although she played very badly, and had since been tarred with the same brush as her hoydenish sister, Lydia, due to their close proximities.

Of Kitty and Lydia Bennet, both of whom had been loud, silly, obnoxious girls who had openly lusted and ogled and chased after officers--after men, and had gone out to seek them, unchaperoned! Lydia Bennet especially displayed such behavior, for she was the ringleader.

He regretfully informed her that that was most likely where Elizabeth Bennet had learned such behavior, in her capture of Mr. Darcy, despite his and his father's best efforts to dissuade such behavior.

Her ladyship seemed pleased with his information, for she asked him several more questions, before saying "Good, thank you, Mr. Collins", an accolade that he should remember for the rest of his days, before turning to Mr. Wickham, and questioning him as well, on his financial situation.

As Mr. Collins listened to his ladyship's plan and what she had intended to do, to free her poor, obviously confused and deceived nephew, he could not help but

 allow his smile to take over his entire face.

Once Eliza Bennet had been dealt with in a satisfactorily way, as her ladyship was making sure happened, he could move on with his life, and proceed to select a bride to birth the Collins heir. He was not quite sure that he should choose anyone from Meryton, for they had all whispered behind his back when Eliza had rejected him, for why should any one of their daughters be worthy, or have any right to become the mistress of such an estate as Longbourn after such disrespect, but he still had some time to make a final decision.

All would be as it should, soon enough.

*****

Darcy Townhouse, London

Directly after their wedding, the Darcys, Bennets, Gardners, and Colonel Fitzwilliam had gone to the Darcy townhouse, across town, for a lavish dinner, at least to Elizabeth's standards.

She and Mr. Darcy had been seated next to each other in the middle of the long table, and were surrounded by their friends and family--a small party for the wedding of such a man, but it was to be expected. None of Mr. Darcy's family, save for his sister and the Colonel had attended the wedding, and as for friends, it was Mr. Bingley who carried that distinction, although Miss Bingley, Mrs. Hurst, and Mr. Hurst were all in attendance.

On Elizabeth's side, her family--the Gardners, the Phillips, and the Bennets--her mama and sisters--had all attended, but her day had been made when her beloved Charlotte, escorted by her eldest brother, and younger sister Maria had arrived at the church just before the service was to start.

Elizabeth had supposed correctly that Sir William was attempting to placate Mr. Collins by only allowing Charlotte a few days to spend in London for her wedding, before returning to Meryton. As with his usual generosity, Mr. Darcy had paid to hire the coach that brought Charlotte to London.

All around them, they had been surrounded by noise. On Mr. Darcy's side, his sister sat between himself and Colonel Fitzwilliam, while Jane was on Elizabeth's left side, and she spent the afternoon conversing with Mary and herself-- although Elizabeth did not miss the longing looks that Jane and Mr. Bingley exchanged across the table, despite the consternation and dismay his sisters, especially Miss Bingley, displayed.

Across the table, sat Elizabeth's Aunt and Uncle Gardner, and Charlotte, and then farther along was Mr. Bingley and his sisters, and Mr. Hurst.

Everyone was speaking all at once, Lydia, Kitty, and Maria's excited tones shushing their youngest cousins, the Gardner children, whom had been allowed to attend such an event, providing they watched their manners. Elizabeth glanced at her sister in law, wondering if she should have been seated nearer to Mary.

"Are you enjoying yourself, Elizabeth?" came a voice beside her, and Elizabeth turned to Mr. Darcy. He had called her by her name for the first time, and she found that she quite enjoyed it, despite herself.

She laughed lightly and said "I do not think I have ever enjoyed myself so much, Mr. Darcy."

She was shocked to see that Mr. Darcy moved his hand from above the table, to below, and moved towards her lap, reaching for the hand there. Lightly splaying his hand over hers, he said, "Fitzwilliam. I would like you to call me by my name, Elizabeth."

Elizabeth tried to smile again.

"Fitzwilliam."

***

Night had fallen, and Elizabeth had dismissed her new maid, ironically named Charlotte, and now waited by the window for Mr. Darcy to come.

A week ago, her Aunt Gardner had taken her aside to speak of her wedding night, of what should happen, which had not saved her any embarrassment when her mama had cornered her the night before her wedding, nearly dragging her by the arm to her own room to speak to her away from the prying, young ears of the innocent, and had proceeded to, for lack of a better word, expound on her Aunt Gardner's advice in very passionate terms. Elizabeth should not have been surprised, for her parents had produced five children in rapid succession.

She could not be sure that either woman had helped. Mr. Collins' father had shattered any illusions or questions Elizabeth had about the act itself, and now she hoped that Mr. Darcy would come to her and get it over with, so she could sleep.

Elizabeth waited a while longer, her mind going to other places, but always listening for any hint of a rap on her door, when the door that connected her room to Mr. Darcy's was opened.

Before her brain could catch up to what had happened, she had fallen off of her seat by the window in panic.

It *was* Mr. Darcy, she realized belatedly, dressed in a rather warm looking, dark red robe, and leather slippers on his feet. He rushed to her side.

"Mr. Darcy," she said softly, looking to the ground, "I apologize."

She forced herself to keep her face serene, composed, as his large, warm hand went to lift her chin to face him.

"Fitzwilliam." he gently corrected\

"Fitzwilliam," she echoed, embarrassed that she had forgotten his wish, earlier, that she should call him by his Christian name, as she had refused to do so during their courtship. "I apologize sir," she said in a rush, "you startled me." Embarrassed and shamed, she looked to the ground again.

Mr. Darcy helped her to her feet, and she quickly looked to her own robe to see if it was still securely tied, and whether or not it had gotten disheveled in her fall. She righted herself quickly, not wishing to anger Mr. Darcy.

He secured her arm within the crook of his, and led her gently into the connected room--the master's bedroom.

He allowed her a few moments to take in the room, and she did. While her room had clearly not been updated, fashion wise, since there was last a mistress of Pemberley, she found its style very similar to her own, namely that it was not overbearing in its decoration. Mr. Darcy had promised her that she should be able to make as many changes as she wished to the room, but she found that she did not wish to make many.

Mr. Darcy's room, however, bore the traits of not simply the master of the house, but of his own personality. She was amused to see a small shelf of a personal library adorning both sides of the fireplace, and a small table equipped with paper and an inkwell for him to write his personal correspondence within the privacy of his own room.

Her gaze fell to the bed, and she could not tear her eyes away from it, no matter how much she wished.

She had stared at the bed for a long moment, minutes even, before she snapped out of it, and looked back at Mr. Darcy who was still holding her arm, ever the proper gentleman. He was looking at her with an indecipherable expression, one that made her remember their first introduction, and how impertinent and rude she had been, and before she knew it, a lone tear had rolled down her cheek.

Before she could wipe it away, Mr. Darcy's hand had already gone to do it for her. He clasped her face, gently, with both hands, and laid a kiss upon her forehead.

She opened her mouth to say something, anything--to get him to go to the bed, but he shushed her.

Giving her another kiss to the forehead, he gently tucked her arm back into his own, and escorted her from the room, and back into her own.

Once there, to Elizabeth's confusion, he pulled back the covers to her bed, watched as she climbed into the bed alone and situated herself comfortably, and then pulled the covers back over her form.

With a whispered, "Good night, Miss Elizabeth", Mr. Darcy was gone, disappeared on the other side of the door.

Elizabeth cried as she slept that night, although she

was not sure if they were tears of sorrow or happiness.

***

Pemberley, Derbyshire

Elizabeth had been married for precisely a month now, and she had been surprised to note how the time flew by. She and Mr. Darcy had stayed a week in London after their wedding, before traveling to Pemberley with Miss Georgiana.

When Mr. Darcy had first suggested it to her, that she should be able to spend a bit more time with her sisters and family before going to live in Derbyshire, where she knew no one but her own husband's family, she had been grateful for his generosity, yet again.

But after what had occurred on their wedding night, or, more precisely, what had *not* occurred on her wedding night, she had found it difficult to face her mama, her Aunt Gardner, and even her dear Jane.

When she had received Jane two days after her wedding night, in the parlour of the grand Darcy townhouse, it had simply been the two of them, sharing an afternoon tea, and her sister had asked her, in a delicate tone, if she and Mr. Darcy were well, and Elizabeth had opened her mouth to tell her, but found she could not. So she had not.

It was a secret she and Mr. Darcy kept to themselves. Life at Pemberley was a dream. She had not been able to keep the look of wonder out of her face, as she had gazed upon the beautiful grounds, and had started to memorize its details, as though she were on a tour of the area, instead of it being her new home! Mr. Darcy, and even Miss Georgiana had chuckled at her reaction.

Mr. Darcy had quickly introduced her to Pemberley's

housekeeper, Mrs. Reynolds, who was a warm, motherly type of woman, but did not brook nonsense. Elizabeth instantly liked her, as she reminded her of a more refined version of her beloved Mrs. Hill.

Mrs. Reynolds was to assist her in managing Pemberley, and while Elizabeth had received more of a thorough education on estate management than she would have on her own, Pemberley was on a grander scale than she had ever been expected to be mistress of, and her duties reflected that fact.

She would have to be very diligent in her duties, and that first duty entailed going through the correspondence from the neighbors, acquaintances, and family members who had, at least grudgingly, offered their congratulations at their marriage.

Thankfully, on her second day at Pemberley, Mr. Darcy had shown her to her own study, which was equipped with everything she should need to enact her duties as Mistress of Pemberley.

Unfortunately though, her eagerness to not neglect her duty also meant that she should not be able to walk the grounds. Her mornings were now spent dealing with correspondence, servants, and accepting calls from the neighbors, while her afternoons were spent in the music room with Miss Georgiana, often listening to her play, or they would adjoin to Elizabeth's study and share tea and pastries.

Sometimes they were joined by Mr. Darcy, but not often for he was needed at the farm and elsewhere along Derbyshire, where he owned various properties. He had told her that the first month or two of their marriage, he would be very busy for he had been gone for some time, and so she let him alone.

During the nights, though, she waited. Waited for him to one day open the door that connected their rooms; waited for him in the pitch darkness.

He never came.

***

"Elizabeth?" came her nervous sister in law's voice. Elizabeth frowned in concern, for Miss Georgiana had lost a great deal of her shyness towards her, and they were able to converse as friends.

"Yes, Georgiana?" she replied.

"I was wondering if you would wish to walk on the grounds with me." came her answer.

Elizabeth smiled at her sister in law, as she realized what she was doing, although she desperately wished to take her offer.

"That is quite alright, my dear. I am fine."

"But--." Miss Georgiana protested, Elizabeth's eyes widened in shock, as she expected Miss Georgiana to simply do as Elizabeth said she wished, no matter what her body language may have told her.

"It is fine."

"Fitzwilliam says he would like to join us on the walk, Elizabeth." Georgiana finally managed to get out.

"Fitzwilliam said that?" Elizabeth asked, hastily, tripping over her words. If Mr. Darcy wanted to.....

"He did indeed." a male voice was heard from the doorway, and Mr. Darcy strode into the room. He gave his sister a soft kiss, and held out his hand for Elizabeth, who was still seated at her correspondence.

"Elizabeth, you deserve a break. And it would be good for us to spend some time together," he said lightly.

"You wish to walk on the grounds with me, Fitzwilliam?" she said, not stumbling over his name anymore.

"I wished for Georgiana to ask you to go on the walk," he answered confidentially, keeping an eye on Georgiana as she had left the room in preparation of their walk, "for I know that you are still skittish of me. I had thought it would make you more comfortable."

"Mr. Darcy--I--Fitzwilliam." she said helplessly.

"There is nothing wrong, Elizabeth." he said gently. "Now", he said with a renewed vigor, "let me show you where Richard and I landed in the most trouble, as boys."

Chapter Twenty

Pemberley, Derbyshire

Elizabeth had been married for nearly three months now, she realized as she sipped tea with her new sister inside of their personal sitting room, located just off to the side of her personal study, where she performed various duties, such as writing her personal letters, responding to invitations and general correspondence sent by neighbors, balancing the weekly budget for Pemberley itself, and so on.

Her husband, Mr. Darcy had not claimed his marital rights in that period of time, and she did not know what to make of it, of him.

Thankfully, now that she had a better understanding of Mr. Darcy--and their marriage had certainly opened her eyes to a hidden side of Mr. Darcy that she had not seen before--she could say in truth that she no longer hated him, that she no longer saw him as simply a proud and arrogant man.

Starting with their wedding night, she realized ruefully. She was not a naive young miss--she understood why Mr. Darcy had looked at her as often as he had--from the very beginning of their acquaintance, when they had been introduced to one another at Meryton's local assembly.

Yet he did nothing. Every morning, Mr. Darcy rose from his bed around the same time as she did, and they both dressed for the day, and would meet for a period of half an hour in the small sitting room that lay between their connected rooms, and they would eat a brief respite of a cup of coffee and perhaps a slice of toast or two, while Mr. Darcy informed her of the objectives he would be pursuing for the day, and inquiring after hers.

Afterwards, they would separate--he to ride, a dual purpose

served to not only benefit his health and pleasures, but also to inquire after his tenants and to confer with his steward, before the day truly started, Mr. Lamb--and she and her new sister, Miss Georgiana would meet outside in the gardens for a walk among the grounds.

Miss Georgiana had confessed to her, shortly after they had begun their ritual, that she was not an avid walker, and so Elizabeth took great pains to limit their exercise, despite her eagerness to explore the grounds of such an estate.

Three days a week though, she and Miss Georgiana would walk alongside Mr. Darcy's horse, and take their turns visiting the young, sick, and elderly, dispensing medicines and making sure the doctor had come when needed, and so forth.

Breakfast would commence, and then Elizabeth would go to her duties as mistress of Pemberley in the manner that she had for the past three months.

Towards the end of the midday, Miss Georgiana, Mr.

Darcy, and Elizabeth would meet and together they would venture out from Lambton and into other counties, attending the various functions that they had been invited to, although being that they were so newly married, Mr. Darcy had thankfully used it as an excuse to spend much of their time at Pemberley, nor to receive much themselves.

And then the day would end, with each of them embarking on the lone trek to their respective rooms. The first month, Elizabeth had laid awake for most of the night, waiting for Mr. Darcy to open the door to her room. Each night she waited in vain.

She did not comprehend herself. She should be glad that he was not forcing his attentions upon her, when he had realized that she had clearly been uneasy at the prospect of their marital relations, yet he had not breathed a word about it to her, except to bid her good night.

Elizabeth sighed to herself.
"Elizabeth?" Miss Georgiana queried, noting that her new sister had been distracted for a few moments.

"Are you well?" she repeated dubiously.

"Oh, I am sorry my dear," Elizabeth allayed Miss Georgiana's unsaid fears, "I was simply lost within my own thoughts, would you repeat yourself?"

Miss Georgiana smiled dreamily.

"I had only asked," and here her voice grew quiet, and she looked around the room as though someone might be standing in plain sight and they were unaware, "if you were, perhaps, with child." She gazed at Elizabeth expectantly.

"A-and why should you think that, my dear?" Elizabeth stammered, wondering if she was unaware of a piece of information that Miss Georgiana had perceived before her.

Miss Georgiana blushed furiously, from her neck to the roots of her hair.

"It is simply that I have noticed that you have been holding your belly more frequently, that is all, and I wondered---", her word tapered off and Miss Georgiana looked at her sister in embarrassment, "Oh dear, I am so sorry, Elizabeth I did not mean--."

"It is all right, Georgiana," Elizabeth replied softly. Something pressed her to continue past the usual lines one doled out to console someone. "In truth, I have been thinking of children lately, for I come from a rather noisy household, and your brother has informed me of the loneliness of his upbringing, and yours as well. And I imagine that your brother should want an heir for Pemberley." Elizabeth said practically.

She was correct. Pemberley needed an heir, in the same way that Longborn suffered without one from the Bennet family.

Miss Georgiana shot her a beaming smile, and Elizabeth fervently prayed that she had said the right thing.

***

Later that night, Elizabeth had plead a headache and had gone to bed early, book in hand. Since becoming the mistress of Pemberley, she had attempted to become more of a reader than she actually was, but she was slowly beginning to take to it--a pleasant mainstay to keep her mind occupied.

Currently she was reading her favorite of Shakespeare's plays, *Coriolanus*, a vivid mainstay in her imagination when she had first read the play at thirteen. After reading the play, with her father's encouragement, she had embarked upon a rather heavy course study in the history of Roman generals, wishing to know, in detail, if the character of Caius Martius Coriolanus had been exaggerated, or if the Romans truly could be that bloodthirsty and proud.

 These days, it comforted her, as she could almost close her eyes and imagine her papa reading it to her in the very walls of his study. She had sat in the very chair that both of the Mr. Collins had forced her to, and had fixed her gaze upon the wall, and imagined that she could hear the whispers of her father's voice, narrating his favorite books aloud.
A sharp rap was heard on her door, and Elizabeth put her book away, recognizing the knock as Mr. Darcy's particular sound. She climbed out of bed, tying her wrapper around herself tightly, and settling on the edge of her bed.

"You may enter," she said, feeling silly as she gave her husband permission to enter, an embarrassment she suffered every night.

Mr. Darcy lingered in the doorway a moment, before he cleared his throat and asked her permission to enter her room.

"Of course, sir," she said, fairly certain of his intentions. She had spoken of children to Miss Georgiana earlier today, as he was her brother, and she told him everything, and he was now here to ascertain her interest, or, rather willingness to proceed to the begetting of children.

Mr. Darcy entered her room, and with a questioning glance, seated himself at the foot of her bed.

"Georgiana informed of your conversation today. She was," he paused, trying to find the word that described Georgiana's enthusiasm, "excited about the prospect of becoming an aunt."

Elizabeth smiled nervously. "Indeed she was. I understand of course, Mr--Fitzwilliam, that you should--"

Mr. Darcy shook his head, nervously ducking down to examine the palms of his hands.

"I simply wished to--" and here, Elizabeth waited for the implications of each pause he took, "I am not unaware of the adversity you experienced while under the guardianship of Mr. Collins," here he paused again, cataloging her flinch at Mr. Collins' name with solemn, dark eyes, "and I am aware that I did not display gentlemanly behavior for the majority of our acquaintance, nor during my proposal for your hand in marriage," here he blushed to the roots, a trait he shared with his sister, "and I am attempting to make up for my deficiency in that area, and so I wished to hear your thoughts on inviting your family to come and visit Pemberley before the spring is over."

Elizabeth could hardly contain her pleasure at Mr. Darcy's thoughtfulness, and inched down the bed towards Mr.

Darcy.

"Thank you, Fitzwilliam," she said, unable to contain her happiness at seeing her beloved sisters once again, for she had soon discovered after her wedding that letter writing was not the same as seeing them in person.

"That is very thoughtful of you, sir. It is wonderful here at Pemberley and Georgiana, but I miss my sisters most dearly." she admitted cautiously.

Mr. Darcy took the opportunity of her confession to lay an arm around her shoulder, for they were nearly side by side, and Elizabeth melted at the warmth of his touch for the first time. Suddenly she felt tired. His hand was a soothing presence, lightly massaging the back of her shoulder and neck. Her head was now close to his lap, and she could feel the heat emanating from his body. This was the closest she had been to him as a married woman.

She felt compelled to speak, felt safe to do so.

"I should like children, Fitzwilliam, one called Bennet Darcy." she heard herself say distantly. Mr. Darcy's grip tensed briefly, and she turned to look at him, intent on studying his reaction.

"May I sleep with you tonight?" Mr. Darcy asked softly. She nodded her assent, bonelessly and Mr. Darcy gently enveloped her in his arms gently, and moved to the head of the bed, sliding her under the coverlet and two layers of sheets. He left the room briefly, but soon returned, sliding under the coverlet.

"Good night, Elizabeth.", and that was all she heard before she drifted off to sleep, her body warmed by the presence of his body heat.

***

"Might I sleep with you?" the surprisingly gentle question startled Georgiana out of her thoughts. She was shocked to see that it had belonged to Elizabeth's youngest sister, Lydia. The Gardner-Bennet family had arrived to Pemberley only a week ago, and Lydia had spent the majority of the week pouting and keeping her company to herself because of a set down that had been delivered by Elizabeth the second day of their visit.

Lydia, Georgiana admitted to herself, had been behaving in a rather rude manner, and had ignored the gentle correction of her eldest sister, Jane, and so finally Elizabeth had taken Lydia aside and spoken to her. When they had returned, Lydia had settled down, but was clearly angry at her sister.

She had met Lydia before, of course. During her brother's engagement period to Elizabeth, Georgiana, for the first time had been thrown into the company of girls her own age, who cared not a fig how many pounds were in her dowry, except perhaps to borrow some of her ribbons or lace, and was utterly terrified, as before. despite what her her brother may have expected of her, she had enjoyed spending time with the youngest Bennet sister. It was very refreshing, Georgiana had concluded, to meet someone like Lydia Bennet--so carefree and *fun.*

Georgiana was especially happy, for she had sensed that her new sister had desperately missed her sisters, her family.

Georgiana understood the feeling, for she had grown up hardly knowing that she had a father. After her father had died, her nursemaid had presented her to a young, serious man, and informed her that he was her new guardian, her brother. despite not bonding with her brother until she was nearly into her teens, she had quickly formed a close attachment to him, and to her cousin Richard. When her brother had sent her to school, and then to holiday in Ramsgate, she had desperately ached for her brother and cousin.

Georgiana sighed, as she recalled the outcome of the trip, of what she had almost done. But most of all, Georgiana worried for Elizabeth. She had thought that having her family here, with her, would be enough to help Elizabeth settle in, but for some odd reason, Elizabeth seemed to be even more distant, yet terse at the same time. Georgiana did not know what she could do to console or shift some of Elizabeth's burden onto herself, but she would take any opportunity to assist in any way she could.

Therefore, when the youngest sister of her new sister in law had asked to sleep with her, despite the fact that Pemberley had enough beds to house more than a score of people, Georgiana had stammered an affirmative reply, and then Lydia Bennet had skipped off without a care in the world to join the rest of their party in Elizabeth's sitting room.

Georgiana wondered what she had gotten herself into, and, as she made her way to her rooms later that night, Kitty giggled at her as she said goodnight, embracing her with a whispered "good luck!", utterly terrifying her. Elizabeth, upon learning that she was to share a bed with Georgiana, had informed her that Lydia was somewhat brash compared to herself, and that if she should become too much for her to handle, that she could always go to her, and Elizabeth would speak to her.

Georgiana thanked her sister, but privately promised herself never to go to Elizabeth, even if Lydia should throw her out of her own bed!

Lydia, who had offered to let Georgiana call her Lyddie, as her sisters did--but Georgiana did not feel comfortable doing so yet--had arrived shortly after her maid had come to help her undress and slid under the covers with a cheery "good night!", and so they had laid together.

Except Georgiana could not sleep, and so she lay awake, staring at the canopy surrounding the bed. The bed shifted,

Lydia turning onto her side to face Georgiana.

"Georgiana, are you awake?" she whispered.

Georgiana turned her head to face Lydia.

"I am," she whispered, "what is it? Are you unwell? Shall I call for a servant? Or Elizabeth?"

"No, Georgiana, just--" Lydia seemed to search for something that she could not voice, and the bedroom was silent for a few minutes as Lydia's words hung between them.

"Is Lizzie happy?" she finally asked.

"I believe she is," Georgiana replied tacitly, not wishing to deceive Lydia. "The first few months were very difficult. She was very lonely and homesick, I believe. That is why I asked my brother to invite you all sooner." she finished on a bright note.

Lydia was silent for a moment, and Georgiana watched her in the darkness.

"And Mr. Darcy," she asked hesitantly, "He treats Lizzie well?"

Georgiana leaped to defend her brother.

"He does indeed! I have heard Colonel Fitzwilliam tease my brother about his reticent nature, but I assure you he is the best brother in the whole of the world! And he is sure to be the best husband any woman could ask for!"

"That is very well," she said finally, causing Georgiana to smile at her in response. "I am simply glad that she is away from that odious Mr. Collins. I should have run away to my Uncle Gardner's had she married him!" Lydia shivered.

Georgiana frowned, aware that Mr. Collins was the name of the man that had inherited Longbourn, but unaware that Elizabeth had been made an offer by him. When she thought of it, she realized Elizabeth had not spoken much about Mr. Collins, but Georgiana had thought that to be because of the circumstances that caused them to leave Longbourn in the first place. "What do you mean? Did Elizabeth receive a different proposal?" she asked, curious about Lydia's words.

Lydia abruptly sat up, and gestured for Georgiana to do the same. Looking Georgiana up and down, she glanced about the room, as though Elizabeth or someone else were hiding in the room.

"Can you keep a secret?" she whispered lowly, "You cannot tell Lizzie I told you!"

"No, of course not," Georgiana promised faithfully, her eyes not leaving Lydia.

"As you know, Mr. Collins became our guardian while Papa was still injured and his horrible father had died," Lydia continued, ignoring Georgiana's gasp of shock at Lydia speaking ill of the dead, "and straight off, he had declared that Lizzie had to marry him when our Papa died." her voice lowered even further, "And, he tried to take liberties from her, on the very night that Jane, Lizzie, and Mary had met Mr. Darcy."

Georgiana gasped, her mind going straight to Mr. Wickham, and all that he could have done, given that he had the opportunity. She knew ladies were not to think of such things, but she found she could not help herself.

"I saw Mr. Collins that night." here, her voice turned childish and high, her mouth turned downward into a pout. "I saw him!" she exclaimed. "He thought I was stupid and ignorant, but I saw him!"

At Georgiana's frightened expression, Lydia softened her tone, aware, for the first time, that she had gone too far.

"I'm sorry Georgiana," she whispered soothingly, rubbing a gentle hand on Georgiana's shoulder.

"I--I simply wished to know if Lizzie was all right. She thinks I haven't noticed, but I have!" Lydia declared emphatically.

Georgiana said nothing, her mind swirling with the new information that Lydia had given her.

Lydia laid down again. "She is well, isn't she Georgiana?"

Georgiana clasped Lydia's hand within hers. "I promise she is, Lydia."

"You promise you won't tell, Georgiana?" she yawned.

"I promise Lyddie."

*****

Lydia relished her short lived freedom, as she browsed the shop located next to the milliner's, in which her sisters, Georgiana, and Aunt Gardner.
Lydia wasn't stupid.

She understood that there dangers that she had not even comprehended, and had outright ignored as soon as a year ago.

But all she wished forwas an afternoon to herself--a quick walk to the shops to buy a small amount of lace for her hat, blue to match her new gown--and now she was forced to wait for her aunt and sisters to finish. All because Lizzie was still angry at her for being a little loud at tea when they first arrived to Pemberley. It had been over a week ago, and she could still see the consternation in her sister's eyes.

And God knew how long they should take, she groaned inwardly, but then forced herself to stand up straight. She wished they would hurry, for Lizzie had insisted they walk the five miles, and of course Mr. Darcy had done little to dissuade her.

"Miss Lydia!"

It was Mr. Wickham. Mr. Wickham was across the street, here in Lambton! Instantly a thousand warnings flashed through her eyes, and she resisted the urge to shake her head free of them, lest Mr. Wickham think she was mad.

"Mr. Wickham." she said, giving him a low curtsey, and a charming smile. He bowed charmingly as always.

"What are you doing in Lambton, Mr. Wickham?" she asked, "I thought the militia would still be encamped in Meryton, sir." she added quickly, truly wondering what

Mr. Wickham gave her a warm smile, a smile that had caused butterflies in her stomach upon their first meeting, and something she had thought about late at night, that kept her warm as she had to cozy up to Mary, whose feet were always ice cold.
"I should ask you the same, child. I am here on business, Miss Lydia." Mr. Wickham glanced around. "You are not alone, are you?"

Lydia barely resisted the urge to pout, for if she had, then she would be doing nothing but proving Mr. Wickham's point.

"I am not a child, Mr. Wickham," she said with an upturned nose, and she quickly added on "Nor am I alone. My sisters and aunt are in the milliner's shop there, I am waiting for them." she pointed quickly to the building next to them.

"No, indeed you are not, Miss Lydia," Mr. Wickham agreed

most amiably. "But you had not answered my question, my dear lady. Are you on holiday with your aunt and uncle? Unfortunately," he continued, "I had not the time to call upon you at your Aunt Phillips', before you had gone away to London, for a short period of time before, I had been obliged to go to Bath, on a matter of urgent business. The militia is now encamped there, if your aunt and uncle could spare your company."

Lydia glanced back at the window of the shop, where her sisters and aunt were, and she debated whether or not she should move to go inside the shop, mindful of Lizzie's warning months ago about Mr. Wickham, yet they were in *public*, she reasoned, and he did not even seem to be aware that Lizzie had married Mr. Darcy.

A few minutes silence reigned, as Lydia began to tap her right foot impatiently. Mr. Wickham regarded her with unconcealed amusement.

"A bit restless are you? How about I show you one of my favorite climbing trees as a boy, Miss Lydia?"

Lydia, again, glanced back to the shop.

"I shouldn't leave my sisters, Lizzie wouldn't like it," she said edging away from Mr. Wickham. Something was not quite right, she thought. But what should be the problem? Mr. Wickham did not know that she was now the sister in law of Mr. Darcy of Pemberley, but why should he not know? They were in Lambton, not five miles from Pemberley, and Lydia had read Lizzie and Mr. Darcy's wedding announcement in the paper.

Her mind recalled back to Lizzie's warning, of the story he had told Lizzie during their second meeting, that Mr. Darcy had been jealous of his father loving Mr. Wickham, that he had kept him from his deathbed and inheritance.

Lizzie had updated them shortly after her engagement to Mr. Darcy, informing all of the Bennet sisters that Mr. Wickham was a dangerous man to be around, especially for a lady, and that they were not safe with him. That they should not encourage him.

Lydia was still angry at Lizzie, for Lizzie expected her to behave as though she were still living with Mr. Collins and *they were not,*

"Come now, Miss Lydia," Mr. Wickham cajoled, stepping forward a bit. "It is only down the street."

Lydia shook her head firmly. "No, Mr. Wickham, Lizzie and Mr. Darcy would be angry. As a matter of fact," she said lifting her chin up higher, "I am going inside, with my *sisters.* Good day, Mr. Wickham."

There now, Lizzie would be pleased with her, and then perhaps she would stop acting as though Lydia had committed a mortal sin, and cease her sermonizing.

Mr. Wickham lost a hint of his smile and regarded her coolly, "Well then, good day, Miss Lydia."

Unfortunately, Lydia had to cross in front of Mr. Wickham to enter the shop, and by the time she had recognized the intent on his face, the same look she had seen less than a year ago when she had happened upon Lizzie and Mr. Collins in the front hall at Longbourn, after the assembly, and she *knew* what was about to happen.

She did not close her eyes though, for she knew it was not the end.

Chapter Twenty-One

"Fitzwilliam?"

Fitwilliam's gaze shot to his door, as he watched his wife open it quietly and gently for the first time since their marriage. He had come to her--to wish her goodnight, inquire about her day, and the like. To this day, they had spent one night together, in her bed, and while Elizabeth had been relaxed enough to fall asleep quite easily, at his side, by the time he had woken up at his customary time, she had already been awake and seated at her vanity.

Privately he wondered if she had slept for more than a few hours that night, but knew that it was progress, the right step in their relationship.

"Elizabeth." he said hoarsely, his gaze softening as he beheld her.

"How is Lydia?" he asked, when he noticed she had not come through the door, but lingered in the doorway, unsure of whether or not she should come in.

Fitzwilliam, of course, knew his sister in law's condition, for his personal physician had waited in the drawing room for hours after treating her to inform him of her condition. Besides a minor concussion, deep bruises and scratches on her arms, Miss Lydia

Bennet was physically in a good condition. Her treatment plan included bed rest in a darkened room, to help prevent headaches, for about a week.

It was a good thing that she had so many sisters, Fitzwilliam mused, as he pictured Lydia Bennet on bed rest. He knew of course, from Miss Bingley and Mr. Collins, that Lydia had been a high spirited girl, fond of giggling, and forever chasing after officers on a daily basis before everything had changed for her, he doubted that she was so changed in principle, whatever her former behavior had been.

Elizabeth was the same. She had tried to hide it, in the beginning, but he had noticed. While she was Mistress of Pemberley, she was still Elizabeth Bennet Darcy, the woman who looked forward to completing a three mile walk on a daily basis. Fitzwilliam smiled. Lydia and his wife *did* share something between themselves, and he hoped that would be enough to console both of them.

"She is faring well," Elizabeth replied to his inquiry. "She is not terribly injured, the doctor says she has a minor concussion and some bruises, some scratches."

 Her voice trailed off towards the end of her sentence, as she considered all that might have happened, if Lydia had not screamed and attempted to fight back. If Lydia had not heeded her warning.

"She will have to be on bedrest for a week in a dark room, so I can imagine how well she will take that tomorrow," Elizabeth replied as she considered her sister's various reactions, "but for now she is sleeping."

"Good." Mr. Darcy gestured that she should sit, and with a few moment's hesitation she did, on the chaise he had set by his fireplace.

Mr. Darcy took the chair opposite her, and both sat, warmed by the flames of the fire. Elizabeth studied the face of her husband. She had gotten better at reading the minute changes in his face and temper, and although he had been nothing but kind and understanding, she still could barely face him.

"Fitzwilliam," she spoke hesitantly, wishing she knew how to broach the subject of the attack on Lydia, by Mr. Wickham.

"I spoke with Lydia, before she fell asleep, and she----." She broke off, not knowing how to continue.

Fitzwilliam studied her in concern.
"What is it, Elizabeth?"

She was having trouble getting her words out, and would not look at him.

"Elizabeth?"

"I simply wished to apologize for all that has happened." Elizabeth finally choked out, after a few false starts. Grateful that she was already dressed for bed in her nightgown and wrapper, she slumped in her chair, thankful that her sister was not seriously injured, and that Mr. Wickham would be punished for what he had done, attempted to do. But what of Mr. Darcy?

"And what would you have to apologize for, Elizabeth?" Fitzwilliam fought to keep his voice steady, as he considered the implication of her words.

In his application for Elizabeth's hand, he, Mr. Gardner, and Mr. Phillips had had a frank conversation about the circumstances that led to Elizabeth's acceptance of his proposal, and ever since then he had been painfully aware of her altered behavior.

 Before his proposal, she had been one of the few women of his acquaintance that had not attempted some form of an innuendo, or flirtation, and actively challenged him on his opinions. He had begun to look forward to being in her presence and had sought out her company, when he could no longer self flagellate himself for the desire to do so.

Fitzwilliam's thoughts drifted to their first introduction, and remembered how she had deftly handled Mr. Collins' breach of manner and common sense, without a misstep to either party. His first impression of her. He *had* noticed that she had behaved differently while in the company of Mr. Collins and himself, but thought that it had been due to embarrassment over Mr. Collins' foolish behavior and exhibition of poor manners.

After their engagement, he had foolishly believed that their sorrows were over, that Elizabeth, although she did not love him, would marry him, and it would be as simple as him showing her that he truly did love her--and thus, all of their past problems would disappear.

It would never be that way, he knew from past experiences, yet in the hope of retaining the face of his own happiness, he had persisted in believing it to be so.

It was incredibly foolish and short sighted, and now, months after their wedding, Elizabeth and Lydia were paying the price for his arrogance.

Elizabeth began to weep. "I can't, Mr. Darcy." she sobbed, crumbling into herself. Fitzwilliam knelt before her, noticing not for the first time, how delicate she truly was.

Elizabeth started to speak, feeling as though she were unable to breathe. "I *told* Lydia to stay away from Mr. Wickham, I warned her months ago that he was not to be trusted, and I further warned all of my sisters to be on their guard against him by informing them that he had attempted to seduce a young girl for her dowry! I *told* her, and she still---"

"Elizabeth," he said firmly, "none of this is your fault. Not you, nor Lydia's, nor any other member of your family's fault. The fault lies in myself."

He sighed in frustration.

"After we had become engaged, I foolishly believed that you

and I could begin from that point onward, and that if I compensated for my former inaction towards you and your family that that would be the end of it, and we would, eventually be able to move forward with our life together."

Elizabeth was confused. "I don't understand. Uncle Gardner informed of me of your intent to speak to Colonel Forster before you departed for London."

"I suggested to Colonel Forster that he should look closely at Wickham's finances, and suggested to him that it was not a sound idea to carry about a mere lieutenant with that much baggage. Nothing more, Elizabeth."

Elizabeth, by the end of his speech had dried her tears and was seated upright. Fitzwilliam stared intently into her tear tracked face, and dropped his shoulders, his strength, pouring all of it into her lap for her to hold.

"I have failed you, Elizabeth, and I am sorry." he whispered hotly, feeling his emotions betray him with the quickening of his tears. He knew why she had not asked about Mr. Wickham, nor why he had chosen to try and kidnap Lydia. The only point of control she, or any of her sisters had was with whom they associated themselves with, whom they stopped to politely greet and speak to for more than a few minutes in the street, and so forth.

A woman's lot.

A few moments passed, and he spoke, his voice soothing and more calm than he felt.

"Mr. Wickham is in jail, and is awaiting a trial. The constable assures me that with his history of debt, not just in Meryton, but several other towns all over England, and taking into the consideration of the assault on your sister, that he has no doubt that he shall be bound for Australia, when it is said and done."

Fitzwilliam hesitated.

"There is something else, Elizabeth. Something that I need to attend to directly, in the morning."

"What is it?" Elizabeth inquired, almost in a whisper.

"I questioned Wickham, before the constable sent him off to jail. I promised him that I would keep him from debtor's prison if he would tell me who was the mastermind behind Lydia's attack."

"Why should you think that he would not simply......?" here she trailed off, confused, for she knew Mr. Wickham to have little moral compunction, especially with regards to young ladies.

"Wickham is used to getting what he wants through charm, not force. If he had been on his own, and wanted Lydia, he would have spent more effort in convincing her to leave with him, not attack her the moment she refuses to walk down the street with him," he said, referring Lydia's slightly slurred speech on what had happened outside the shop.

"He was hired by my aunt, Elizabeth, and I am sure you can understand my feelings on the matter. It is my fault. I should have stopped all of this months ago, and not simply ignored it." he said in a rush.

"Lady Catherine?" Elizabeth asked with a growing comprehension, remembering the warning the lady had issues her.
"Yes. I must away to Rosings and London tomorrow."

"Are you going to confront Lady Catherine?" Elizabeth asked, placing her hand hesitantly on Mr. Darcy's shoulder.

Despite his discomfort at the position of being on his knees and hunched over, he found that he would bear it, for

Elizabeth was *touching* him, willingly.

"I will. She has gone too far, and I know why. I had not wished to say anything, for I did not wish to see her humiliated, but I have been providing her with a monthly allowance for the past nine years. Her husband, Sir Lewis, left Rosings Park under a mountainside of debt when he died."

He stood up, gently drawing Elizabeth with him until they stood face to face, hands entwined.
"I had warned her, after she had paid a visit to you, that if she should continue to disrespect you than I would cut off her finances. I thought she was content to ignore my existence, now that my marrying Anne was out of the question, but it seems it was not. Wickham informed me that she told him she would pay him thirty thousand pounds if he would grab Lydia. She did not care what he did to her afterwards, so long as everyone thought that Lydia had run away with him. It seems neither she, nor Mr. Collins thought that Lydia would resist."

"Mr. Collins?" Elizabeth echoed, looking away from the intensity of being so close to her husband, face to face.

"Yes, Mr. Collins, Wickham told me, brought him to Rosings Park. It seems my aunt wrote to your cousin, and he told her all about you and your sisters. It was decided that Lydia would be the easiest one to work on, given her....."

"Given her former behavior." Elizabeth finished for him.

"Yes."

There was suddenly a lull between them, neither of them quite able to adequately express the relief that they felt between their newfound, mutual understanding and respect towards the other, and Fitzwilliam cursed his natural reticence. However, Elizabeth spoke, unprompted.

"Would--." she paused to lip her bottom lip in worry, "would you be willing to share--?" her gaze betrayed to the large bed in the corner of the room, the curtains tied to the posts, and the coverlet downturned by the maid some hours before.

Fitzwilliam cannot hide his smile, nor his happiness at her request.

The next morning, he awakes at his usual time to find her lying next to him, studying his sleep slackened face, and he could not help but feel that this was love.

***

Two days after the attack.....

In the darkened room, Georgiana Darcy laid silently next to her friend, Lydia Bennet, taking care not to disturb her. She, Kitty, Jane, and Mary had taken turns keeping Lydia company throughout the day, although they had each reported that Lydia had not wanted them to speak, nor for anyone to even stay with her in the room.

She soon realized she did not particularly have to make the effort of not disturbing her, for not only was Lydia awake, but she was trembling with effort to keep herself from giving away the fact that she was awake.

"Lyddie? Does your head ache?" Georgiana whispered in a soft tone. Fitzwilliam's physician had warned them all that Lydia needed peace and quiet, and they were not to aggravate her condition by being anymore noise than absolutely necessary. "Shall I fetch you a cold compress?" she offered.

"No." Lydia's tone was flat and lifeless.

Georgiana reached over and laid a sympathetic hand to Lydia's side, not daring to touch anywhere above her neck, no matter what the physician said. Lydia was injured, that she could see, but this was something more. Lydia had a spark that Georgiana was sure could never be extinguished, yet here she was, witnessing its suffocation.

"Lyddie," Georgiana continued, despite the lack of encouragement she received, "no one blames you, Mr. Wickham is--."

"I know what Mr. Wickham is!" Lydia exploded harshly, and then began to sob real, fat tears that Georgiana could not see, but she recognized the heart rendering ache behind the sobs, and she rushed to calm Lydia down.

"Lizzie told me--." Lydia was having trouble getting her words out, to form without being broken up by a sob. "And I didn't listen to her, because I was so *angry*, and I--."

Georgiana had to make sure Lydia knew that it was not her fault, and she knew of only one way.

"Lyddie, remember a few days ago," she started hesitantly, knowing she was about to reveal her biggest secret, "when you asked me if Elizabeth was happy with my brother, because she had been so
unhappy and distressed while under the authority of Mr. Collins? "

Lydia nodded tearfully, an act Georgiana could barely make out through the small amount of light that filtered through the drapes around the bed.

"I-I know how Lizzie felt, Lydia, and why she felt the way she did--even after marrying my brother. That is why I was so happy that you and the rest of your sisters and aunt and uncle were able to come visit. I--." Georgiana paused to take a steadying breath. "Last year, when I took a holiday at Ramsgate, Mr. Wickham and my companion conspired together for Mr. Wickham to elope with me and gain access to my dowry of thirty thousand pounds."

The last of those words tumbled out of her mouth in one fell swoop, and Georgiana felt nothing but relief that she had finally told someone--something she had not even told Elizabeth about.

Lydia laid there, still, applying the facts as she knew them, to the story that Lizzie had told her a short time after her engagement to Mr. Darcy, that Mr. Wickham had attempted to elope with a young girl, close to her age with a large dowry, only to leave once he realized he would not be receiving a single pound. It was Georgiana, Mr. Darcy's sister!

The sister whom Miss Caroline Bingley had taunted Lyddie and Kitty and Mary over, a short time ago.
"I was utterly humiliated and dejected, Lyddie." Georgiana confessed. "I was humiliated that I did not see it--I was completely taken by Mr. Wickham, even though I knew what we were doing was improper and that a serious gentleman would not have tried to convince me to hide our courtship from my guardians."

Georgiana's voice took a tone, a tone that Lydia had never heard from her, that made her take note and listen, as though she were not already doing so.

"You saw him, Lydia. For what he truly was. I had grown up with Mr. Wickham, and had only heard whispered, half conversations of why he would not come visit me at Pemberley, and only half hearted excuses when I dared bring up the subject to him. You had only met him one time, and did not have a complete warning of his character."
"You saw who he truly was Lyddie." Georgiana repeated with tears forming, as she mourned the outcome of such an incident, of what could have been.

"Thank you." was her whispered reply.

***

Fitzwilliam had reached Matlock house, four days later, after a long ride from Rosings Park. The Darcy carriage was a few hours behind him, and he had taken it only so that he could either sleep or change horses. He would submit his terms to his aunt and uncle, and then he would return to his townhouse for the night, and return back to Pemberley the next morning.

Mr. and Mrs. Gardner, before he left had assured him that they would not cut their visit short, but were unable to extend it any further, and so he made a note to speak to them about having his sisters in law to stay with them for an extended time period, when everything had settled.

The butler announced him, and quietly informed him that the Earl and Countess were taking breakfast with their two sons.

His uncle did not look surprised to see him, nor did his aunt. Richard, immediately bowed and then came to embrace him, while the Viscount gave him a brief acknowledgement. Fitzwilliam guessed that he had over imbibed again, and was in no condition to do much of anything but drink more and eat.

"Aunt, uncle, cousin." he said, sketching a short bow in their direction.

His aunt, the Countess of Matlock regarded him with interest, her cool eyes resting on his tightly restrained form.

"I presume you know why I have come, aunt." Fitzwilliam said tightly. despite his choice in wording, it was not a question.

The Countess stood up and walked to the sideboard, fetching a cup and filling it with fresh, hot coffee, and making it the way she knew her nephew liked. She delivered it to him, and said, with no hint of malice, "Yes."

Airily, she sat back down next to her husband, and clarified her speech.

"Your aunt came to us almost directly after she had harassed your wife, at her uncle's home in *Cheapside*," she said with a small sniff, "and then again, two days after she read the announcement that you had married in the papers. She delivered a rather impressive diatribe, in which she stated that she would not stand for your marriage, nor the shame and desecration of the Fitzwilliam and Darcy name, and was not pleased when I informed her that your uncle and I held no sway over you, financially or emotionally, and that you were the master of your own home, and thus, would make your own decisions."

His aunt shrugged elegantly, "I recall some half shouted threats that she should make you regret defying her, but quite honestly, nephew, I have effectively been ignoring your aunt since before you were born."

The last sentence was delivered with such a charming smile, and Fitzwilliam forced himself to calm.

"What is it, Darcy?" came the concerned tones of his cousin, Richard. His other cousin, the Viscount, snorted into his food, ignoring his mother's disapproving glare.

"My wife's sister," Fitzwilliam's voice was low, clipped, and barely restrained, "who is but a year younger than Georgiana, was attacked by Wickham, at Lady Catherine's order!"

He ignored the fumbling, surprised blustering of his uncle, the pleas of Richard as to the condition of Lydia, and the general antipathy of his debauched cousin, to focus on the surprise that flitted over his aunt's face all too briefly.

"He attempted to persuade her to walk down the street with him, to look at a landmark, while she was waiting for my wife and sisters from inside the milliner's shop. When she would not, he grabbed her, and when she tried to pull from him, he hit her. She was lucky, for one gentleman had tried to stop Wickham from taking her, but she is bound to her bed with a concussion and several bruises and scratches from that brute!"

Fitzwilliam forced himself to calm down, as he began to grow angrier and angrier at the general antipathy his aunt had displayed. He knew she favored Richard, but he was now fully understanding where his cousin had received his disposition from

"Lady Catherine has been receiving a monthly allowance from myself for the past nine years. This has allowed her to pay off the debts that Sir Lewis left behind at his death, and not exacerbate her own. As of this moment, I have stopped her payments,and will do nothing further to help her, and have informed her of my decision. Anne, of course, will always be welcome at Pemberley, should she wish it, otherwise I shall have no dealings with Lady Catherine or *anyone,*" and here, he stressed his words carefully, "who seeks to insert their opinions of my household business without permission."

Nodding to Richard, who silently communicated that he would follow him to his townhouse, Fitzwilliam gave the assembled party a clipped bow, and was about to stalk out of the room, when his aunt's soft voice stopped him, "Fitzwilliam?"

He paused and turned to face her. Her face was wan, and it was probably the most discomforted he had ever recalled seeing her.

"I truly am sorry about what has happened to your bride's sister. You have my apologies." she took a hard look at her husband, before turning her attention back to Fitzwilliam and saying, "I understand, from Lady Catherine, that you have two new sisters who are out in society as well, and two younger ones who are not yet old enough to be out, who live with their aunt and uncle in," here she paused deliberately, "*Gracechurch Street*, which is a short distance from our home. If you would pass along our card to Mrs. Darcy's aunt and uncle, I am sure your uncle and I would be glad to meet them, and speak of their introduction to London society."

She awaited his reply, her face cool, calm, and collected as always. Fitzwilliam found that he could never *not* admire his aunt's cool head, for she never allowed her temper to rule her, and returned her offer with steps forward, hand outreached to collect her card.

It was given, and he left. He was ready to go home.

Epilogue

Summer at Pemberley....

Caroline Bingley sighed in general dissatisfaction as she strolled throughout the halls of Pemberley, admiring the portraits and picturesque landscapes that graced the walls of the fine estate.

For a time, she was able to close her eyes and imagine the satisfaction and happiness she would have felt had she been the mistress of Pemberley, and she was able to enjoy this harmless amusement until she heard a loud giggle accompanied by the animated conversation of two others, the shriek of an older woman followed, and her happy fantasy was ruined.

What had she done to deserve this? Caroline wondered.

Back in Meryton, everything had been entirely simple. Mr. Darcy, from their very first outing in the country society had gained the reputation of being a proud and arrogant man. Caroline had not minded, for it meant that he would only pay her his particular attention, or, at the very least, more attention than every other lady, and if he was unhappy as she was in that backwater town, it would have the dual motive of his influencing Charles to find a more *suitable* estate, preferably one closer to Pemberley, and the two of them sharing an intimate experience, if you will, one that she hoped would bring them closer together.

And because Mr. Darcy was a gentleman, he could afford to give the offense she could not. So she had to grit her teeth, and play the charming lady to those backwards people, which led to her having to show Meryton society that she was a generally charming, friendly woman. This meant, of course, that she should have to pick out a friend, preferably from what passed as one of the prominent families.

That led to her *befriending* the two eldest Bennet chits, for it was a pity that Jane Bennet was lame, as she had thought at the time, and she should invite her younger sister, although she had been quite impertinent, more so than good breeding permitted, but she and Louisa could hardly bear the thought of only entertaining the lame Bennet chit, so it was decided that they should invite them both.

That had been the end of her conquest, and Caroline still could not comprehend how everything had turned out.

Eliza Bennet was supposed to marry her cousin, and spend out the last days of her country existence as the wife of a foolish, backwards man to save her family from ruin.

That was what how the story was meant to end.

Instead, barely nine months later, Caroline was now a guest at Pemberley, and had to sit and pretend to be gracious about the fact that Eliza Bennet had supplanted her place as the mistress of Pemberley.

And it mortified her beyond extreme prejudice that she should soon be related by marriage to the chit!

Caroline had never taken Charles' pathetic crush on the lame Jane Bennet seriously, for she knew of his kind and generous nature. Particularly that he was *too* kind and generous, and had been taken advantage of often by penurious, grasping servants and otherwise poor people-- people who had the nerve to demand money for which they had not earned--and so she had not been surprised, especially considering Jane's beauty, that he had paid more than a cursory attention to her.

Charles was *agreeable*, she sneered, even when he was not. She and Louisa had mercilessly teased him about his delightful little crush on the eldest Bennet chit, gratified that the girl, in addition to being beautiful and easy to manipulate, was well aware of her status in life, and gave her brother no encouragement towards his attentions, only speaking to him when greeted, and showing him no particular favor.

It was *Charles* who had pursued her all the way to Pemberley.

And now they were engaged, and would be married this coming November.

Everything was ruined, everything she and her sister had agreed upon, to help benefit the Bingley name. Louisa married for connections of the Hurst name. Mr. Hurst, the drunken sot, could stand to earn a much better income if he had taken any interest in

 managing his estate, beyond the supplementing the vineyards, but his income was very comfortable, and Louisa's dowry of twenty thousand pounds had helped in that regard.

While their fortune had gotten their foot within the door, Mr. Hurst's name had granted them entrance, and Caroline had never been so proud of her brother as she had been when he had befriended Mr. Darcy, whose name opened the majority of doors that had been closed to them.

The rest of the plan was exceedingly simple, one that she had congratulated herself on when it became evident that Mr. Darcy did not allow many into his inner circle, and she had received an invitation to felicity where no other woman had been able to enter, simply because of his friendship with her brother.

And Eliza Bennet had ruined that.

How! That was what she wished to know. Mr. Darcy had been there--he had seen the idiocy of the current master of

Longbourn, and his *beloved* Eliza came from the same family! Caroline was forced to admit that beyond her troublesome tongue, Eliza Bennet was moderately pretty and pleasant enough company, if she was the cream of the crop, one had been forced to choose from.

But her sisters!

Her mother!

Her cousin!

And not speak ill of the dead, but Caroline had heard tales of what the permissiveness of the Bennet father had allowed his offspring to dabble in.

Blood always ruled out, and Caroline was sure that Mr. Darcy was going to regret his choice, soon enough. It would then be too late, she thought victoriously, but that thought could not brighten her spirits. She had made it her mission to do what no other woman had been able to do in nearly a decade--become the mistress of Pemberley.

And some country chit had stolen it right from under her.

After this visit, Caroline would return to her sister Louisa's home, and would have to start her search for an appropriate husband from scratch, because her brother had insisted on keeping his lease until it ran out, and Caroline had promised to stay with her brother, in anticipation of an extended visit with Mr. Darcy, for the majority of the lease period.

It was close to mid afternoon, Caroline realized. Soon they would be gathered for dinner, and then to meet in the music room. Of course, one of the greatest pleasures of her life had been to listen to dear Georgiana Darcy play for herself, Charles, Mr. Darcy, and Louisa during their last visit to the Darcy townhouse, the previous Christmas, but Caroline did not enjoy listening to the plain Bennet sister play her tedious, country ballads. Nor pretending to.

But she would applaud the Bennet chit with all the graciousness she could muster, and then some for she was not as nearly shortsighted as her dear Charles believed. Mr. Darcy's downfall would come soon, she was sure of it, especially given the incident that occurred some time earlier that year, with the youngest Bennet chit, the one who chased incessantly after officers.

Turning a corner, Caroline found herself at a familiar door. Eliza Bennet had offered to give her a tour of Pemberley, and Caroline had been forced to oblige, especially since her brother was present. Inwardly, she had seethed the entire time, for she had visited and explored Pemberley before that country chit was even aware of a Mr. Darcy of Pemberley, yet she was forced to make way for her, and be gracious and pleasant about it.

If she remembered correctly, Eliza had said that this was the door to her private study, where she performed her duties as the mistress of Pemberley. Caroline scoffed at Eliza contributing anything to the great estate of Pemberley, but had been very curious to see the room. However, Eliza had explained that she wished to keep such a room private.

Well, now was her chance to see inside, Caroline thought with a grin, as she gently eased the door open.

***

Later that evening, when darkness had fallen over Pemberley, Elizabeth Darcy sprawled over the bed of her husband, Fitzwilliam, watching his form through a screen as he dressed himself after his bath.

Stepping out from behind the screen, Fitzwilliam grinned in response to the mischievous look on his wife's face. "What do you find so humorous tonight, Mrs. Darcy?" he asked, leaning against the post at the end of the bed.

Her eyes glittered with amusement, and he was suddenly reminded of the very first time she had seen through Caroline Bingley, and charmingly disarmed her every inference--her first visit to Netherfield.

"Miss Bingley." she said shortly, though her voice caught a laugh, seeing no need to explain, for Fitzwilliam had been present when Miss Bingley had been alarmed to see a husband and wife holding hands and kissing in a private room.

"Would you sleep with me tonight, Elizabeth?" Fitzwilliam asked quietly.

His only answer was to watch her slide under the sheets and coverlet, and he repeated his near nightly ritual of sliding only the coverlet beneath him.

One day, they would do more than sleep under separate layers of blankets, or steal kisses as though they were an engaged couple, but for now, Fitzwilliam was content, knowing their bond would only strengthen the more time passed by.

All was well.

The End.

Contact:

Please email me at AubreyAndersonAuthor@gmail.com

Thank you for reading!

Other JA Variation Authors

Zoe Burton

I Promise To....

In this 'Pride and Prejudice' novella, Elizabeth Bennet has known Fitzwilliam Darcy since both were very young. When she flees Longbourn and an unwanted suitor, her uncle and his father arrange a marriage between the two. Will Lizzy and Fitzwilliam agree to such a marriage? Will it keep her safe from a Peer who is determined to have her? Will this young couple be able to keep the promises they have made to each other?

Promises Kept

This 'Pride and Prejudice" novel variation follows Fitzwilliam and Elizabeth Darcy through the first year of their marriage. Arranged by his father in the I Promise To... novella, their union saved Elizabeth from a persistent, abusive suitor. The couple has known each other for years and quickly come to realize their love for each other. However, not everyone is happy with the marriage, and trouble comes quickly upon them. Dealing with jealous ladies and scornful gentlemen in London as well as illness and injury at Pemberley, they grow together as a couple while Elizabeth regains the confidence she has lost.

Lilacs & Lavender

A Pride and Prejudice Novella Variation.

On her way to Kent, Elizabeth Bennet unexpectedly meets Fitzwilliam Darcy in London. Having spent time reflecting on her interactions with Darcy after the dissolute habits of George Wickham are discovered, she has come to realize her first impressions were wrong. Love secretly blossoms between the two when they meet again in Kent. By the end of their time

together, it has grown from the first blooms of love into ardent admiration, and they are determined to marry. However, not everyone is pleased and trouble follows our dear couple threatening to tear them apart.

Mr. Darcy's Love

In this Pride & Prejudice short story, Elizabeth Bennet is injured immediately after overhearing Fitzwilliam Darcy insult her at the Meryton Assembly. She loses all memory of the incident. Without her feelings of offense, their relationship starts off on a better foot, which leads them to love far sooner than would happen otherwise. This in turn leads Elizabeth to react differently to those who would try to derail their happiness. Mr. Collins, Mr. Wickham, Lady Catherine, and even Miss Bingley will soon find themselves in places they never imagined they would be. This story contains a non-graphic attempted sexual assault scene.

Bits of Ribbon and Lace

Sometimes a seamstress or a milliner requires just a little bit of something, a snippet of ribbon or of lace, to make a project complete. This little book is just that for readers: small snippets of story, all in different sizes, designed to fill a few minutes between appointments or before bed. Intended to be enjoyed over and over, they will hit the sweet spot you are looking for. Some are modern and some are Regency, but all feature the wonderful characters Jane Austen created in Pride & Prejudice.

Jennifer Joy

Darcy's Ultimatum (The Cousins Book 1)

When Fitzwilliam Darcy's arranged life falls to pieces, his father, Mr. George Darcy, gives him an ultimatum: Marry by the end of the London Season or risk disinheritance. Can Darcy cast aside society's frigid attitude toward marriage and find true love? Or will his desire to honor his deceased mother's memory hold him back?

Elizabeth Bennet faces the greatest challenge of her life: Find a husband by the end of the London Season or be forced to marry the heir apparent of her family home, Mr. Collins. A romantic at heart, will Elizabeth find a gentleman to meet her high expectations?

After a disastrous meeting, Darcy and Elizabeth determine not to like each other.
But, the London Season has only begun...

Anne's Adversity (The Cousins Book 2)
When Anne de Bourgh discovers a family secret in an old letter, she is given two choices: Burn the letter and forget about it or leave Rosings and face disinheritance. How can a sickly lady past the bloom of youth, with no prospects and few friends, hope to stand on her own two feet? How can she learn more about her family's past without causing a scandal which would forever cast a shadow over the de Bourghs?

Luc Mauvier has led a life of freedom and success as a small theater owner in town. His tragic past has taught him to enjoy life and its pleasures to the fullest. When he meets Anne de Bourgh, she is opposite to everything he has ever known and he is soon reminded of how a gentleman should behave with a real lady. Can a tradesman win the heart of a lady? Even more important: How can he win Lady Catherine's approval?

What Anne reveals about her past gives her courage, but will it be enough?

Colonel Fitzwilliam's Challenge (The Cousins Book 3)
Colonel Richard Fitzwilliam, a hopeful romantic, cannot afford to marry for love. When he is offered a new assignment with the promise of a promotion, he eagerly accepts— only to find himself immersed in a world of intrigue and lies.

Adélaïde Mauvier is a successful dressmaker on the verge of attaining everything she thought she wanted. When she is thrown into Colonel Fitzwilliam's company, she begins to think there might be more to life than her ambitions.

As the colonel gets closer to the truth, he finds out that people are not always what you believe them to be. Will he fall in love while catching a traitor? Or worse... will he fall in love with a spy?

Earning Darcy's Trust

Tragedy strikes Pemberley and Fitzwilliam Darcy must assume the role of guardian to his maiden sister, Georgiana.

When Darcy's trust is betrayed by a childhood friend, Darcy decides to take affairs into his own hands— only to find himself blackmailed by his worst enemy and manipulated by a woman who would ruin his innocent sister's reputation to suit her own wants.

Miss Elizabeth Bennet longs for excitement and a good match for her dear sister, Jane.

Hope springs in Elizabeth's heart when Mr. Bingley lets Netherfield Park and sets his sights on Jane. Victim of a poor decision, Elizabeth is forced to spend time with the disagreeable Mr. Darcy. She learns that there is more to the gentleman than meets the eye and she has the key to solve his problems... if only he would trust her.

Penelope Swan

The Netherfield Affair (Dark Darcy series Book 1 of 4

A regency romance with mystery and suspense. When

Elizabeth Bennet goes to stay at Netherfield Park to keep her sick sister company, she is surprised by eerie noises in the night and ghostly faces at the attic windows. Could the rumours about the country manor being haunted be true? Then a midnight encounter with a tall, dark stranger thrusts Elizabeth straight into the path of scandal and danger. As she races to

 unravel the mystery, she finds unexpected assistance from the handsome but arrogant Mr Darcy.

 Is such a proud, reserved man to be trusted?

A romantic Regency mystery inspired by Jane Austen's Pride & Prejudice! This is the first book in the Dark Darcy Mysteries - a Pride and Prejudice variation combining mystery and romance. * Each book in this series features a standalone mystery which is resolved, but the overall story of Darcy and Elizabeth's courtship is told over the 4 books of the series.

Darcy Revealed
An unexpected mix-up leads Elizabeth Bennet to renewing

her acquaintance with the handsome Mr Darcy during her stay in London. Amid a whirl of society balls, fashionable promenades in Hyde Park and dangerous flirtations, Elizabeth find herself unwittingly drawn to the haughty gentleman. But does Darcy return her feelings or does his heart belong to another?

Darcy's Wager

When Elizabeth Bennet discovers that her sister, Lydia, has risked her reputation by staking a wager against one of London's most notorious rakes, she races to prevent a scandal before shame and ruin befall her family. But saving her own sister could mean sacrificing another: the sister of the handsome, aloof Mr Darcy. Can Elizabeth make a choice between her family and the man she loves?

From the pleasure gardens of Vauxhall to the gambling dens of Piccadilly, join Darcy and Elizabeth as they banter, dance, and fall in love in this Regency romance for Jane Austen fans everywhere.

Darcy's Christmas Wage

Curl up with Darcy and Elizabeth this holiday season!
Fitzwilliam Darcy never forgot the little girl, with the

beautiful dark eyes, who saved his life fifteen years ago...
though he never expected to meet her again. But when he
comes to Rosings Park to spend the Advent

season with his aunt and encounters the enchanting,
spirited Miss Elizabeth Bennet again, he discovers that at
Christmastime, wishes can come true...

Rose Fairbanks

A Sense of Obligation

A chance, but meaningful, encounter in Netherfield's library
changes everything between Darcy and Elizabeth. As they
rush to the altar, Darcy's faulty memory may destroy their
chance at domestic comfort before they begin. Knowing
their obligations and no longer resisting their attraction,
they forge a foundation of trust and respect. New feelings
may not be enough, however, to overcome the
misunderstanding which lays between them. Exploring the
juncture of sentiment and reason, A Sense of Obligation,
takes Darcy and Elizabeth on a passionate, humorous and
introspective path toward happiness in marriage.

The Gentleman's Impertinent Daughter

When Fitzwilliam Darcy and Elizabeth Bennet meet in Hyde

Park, Darcy immediately finds his opinions of the world challenged by the lady. Their attraction grows at the next meeting as Elizabeth finds she has at last met a man who accepts her wit and intelligence. The budding romance may be killed, however, upon their arrival in Hertfordshire. Darcy must meet Elizabeth's family while Elizabeth grapples with the jealous Caroline Bingley, all the while a man in uniform cuts a familiar figure. Fate brought them together, but only love can overcome their obstacles. Short and sweet, The Gentleman's Impertinent Daughter is an uncomplicated romance for all who love Jane Austen Fan Fiction.

No Cause To Repine

When a simple accident is misinterpreted and threatens Elizabeth Bennet's reputation, her fate seems sealed as Fitzwilliam Darcy's wife.

While the bride is resigned, the gentleman could hardly be happier until betrayals and schemes threaten to
 entirely take the matter out of their hands. Overcoming the plots before them will take all the patience, perseverance and collaboration they can muster, but a partnership requires truth. Self-discovery and trust await Jane Austen's most beloved and willfully blind couple as they attempt to

master their own destiny in life and love.

Undone Business

One small moment can change so much. An omitted conversation from the Netherfield Ball...a shortened letter...passage aboard a ship, each forever alter the lives of Fitzwilliam Darcy, Elizabeth Bennet, Charles Bingley and Jane Bennet. Find out what happens when Jane Austen collides with one of the greatest feats of the 19th century as each character must ask themselves what their business in life is.

Upon leaving Hertfordshire in early December, Darcy feels certain he provided reasons for Elizabeth to distrust Mr. Wickham. She, in turn, believes Darcy understands Jane's feelings for Mr. Bingley.

Disappointed in her attempts to see Bingley again, Jane despairs of ever finding happiness. Yet, the business of life cannot always remain undone. When Darcy and Elizabeth meet again in Kent, both couples must face the courses their lives have taken. Undone Business explores the cost of both opportunities missed and second chances seized.

Elizabeth Ann West

The Trouble With Horses When a riderless horse interrupts Elizabeth Bennet's daily walk, she is inspired to begin the search herself. Finding a gentleman in the ravine of a creek bed, she

scares off snakes and raises the alarm to end up with the man situated at Longbourn for his recovery. Enamored with his dark curls and handsome face, her life appears to be following the fairy tale story line of a novel, that is until the proud, disdainful Fitzwilliam Darcy of Pemberley wakes up.

A Winter Wrong (Seasons of Serendipity, Book 1 of 5) When Jane Bennet's illness at Netherfield ends up not being just a trifling cold, but an epidemic that sweeps through Hertfordshire, the lives at Longbourn are turned upside down. Elizabeth Bennet finds herself lost without a cherished loved one and the interferences of one Fitzwilliam Darcy most aggravating. Combating the bombastic behavior of Mr. Collins, Elizabeth runs to London for the protection of her aunt and uncle. But acquaintances and introductions bring Mr. Darcy back into her life and Elizabeth discovers he might just mend her broken heart.

By Consequence of Marriage (The Moralities of Marriage

Book 1)When his horse throws a shoe, Fitzwilliam Darcy misses rescuing his sister, Georgiana Darcy, from the clutches of George Wickham by only one day. Now on the hunt to find them both, the gossip beginning to swirl in London forces him to abdicate the search to his cousin, Colonel RIchard Fitzwilliam, while he plays the wayward gentleman in Hertfordshire with his friend Charles Bingley. After a collision with his future, Darcy struggles to satisfy his attraction to a pair of fine eyes and keep his family's scandal hidden. Elizabeth Bennet dreams of nothing more than remaining close to her sister, Jane. When the rich gentleman, Charles Bingley, enters the neighborhood, it seems certain that Jane will make a match with him. After all, Jane Bennet is the sweetest and most beautiful woman in the county! But Elizabeth's efforts to find her own local match go awry and she feels abandoned by the first man to cause stirrings in her heart. Her parents attempt to marry Elizabeth off to

 her cousin, William Collins, who is set to inherit the estate. But when she refuses, she soon finds herself In London with relatives, forced to find her own happiness.

Very Merry Mischief

When Mr. Darcy left Hertfordshire after Charles Bingley's proposal to Jane Bennet, he promised to return in ten days. When he breaks that promise due to events outside of his control, Elizabeth Bennet is left abandoned for over a year, finally joining the Bingley household as the second unmarried sister under Charles' protection. An invitation to Pemberley brings out the merry match-making mischief as everyone has a plan for their future happiness. Caroline is convinced Mr. Darcy has loved her all this time, Mr. Darcy struggles to seek Elizabeth's forgiveness, and Elizabeth just wishes to make it through this visit without constantly embarrassing herself! There's no better season for miracles, even if it takes a few elves to make them happen!

Barbara Silkstone

The Gallant Vicar

In the GALLANT VICAR, Darcy and Elizabeth retain the same jousting banter contained in my MISTER DARCY SERIES, but they have now returned to their own time where insults are an art form and reputations the most valued of commodities.

What would happen if Mr. Collins finally snapped and

Elizabeth might be the cause of his breakdown? What if he were replaced at the Hunsford parish by a charming, unwed vicar who arrives on the heels of Elizabeth's rejection of Darcy?Darcy is desperate to deconstruct the growing attachment Elizabeth feels for the new vicar. Determined to unearth the truth about the clergyman before Elizabeth is coerced into marriage, Darcy swings into action even as he fears he will appear to be jealous.

Will Darcy save the day? Will Elizabeth accept his help? And exactly who is the Gallant Vicar?

Mister Darcy's Honeymoon
Under the guise of honeymooning, Mr. and Mrs. Darcy set off to save a quartet of domestic maids being held hostage in London and to return the legendary Red Rosary to the Templars' treasure vaults. Can they avoid Caroline Bingley, evade the sinister men from Rome, and will they ever get to enjoy their honeymoon?

Mister Darcy's Secret (A Mister Darcy series comedic mystery, Book 3)The mysterious Mister Darcy enlists the aid of dog psychologist Lizzie Bennet in his secret quest. Lizzie soon finds herself deep in his battle where familiar villains join forces to stop Darcy at all costs. Darcy's true feelings for Lizzie bubble to the surface but can she reciprocate? And what about that peanut butter kiss?

Happy Christmas From the Darcy's (A Mister Darcy series Book 7)

With the best of intentions Elizabeth Darcy plans a surprise Christmas Eve for Fitzwilliam Darcy at their London penthouse. How much chaos will little urchin Annie and her seven siblings, plus the entire Bennet clan, bring to One Snyde Park? Add two basset hounds, one borzoi, a shaggy otter hound, and a disheveled nun who bears a striking resemblance to Caroline Bingley; then stir in some holiday magic and you have a Happy Christmas wish from the Darcy home to yours.

Ayr Bray

The Illegitimate Heir The younger son of an earl often cannot afford to marry for love, so it is fortunate Colonel Richard Fitzwilliam has fallen in love with Helen Malham, who

has both beauty and wealth. Her father, however, will not allow her to marry a man without a title.

When the Prince Regent names Richard the Duke of Blachedone, it is both a blessing and a curse. His newly acquired title means he may marry Helen—assuming she will have him once the truth comes out. He was awarded the dukedom not for his service to the Crown, but because he is the former duke's illegitimate son, and soon all of London will know.

Mr. Calvin Aldrich is a rake and a blackguard and set to be one of the richest dukes in England ... until his uncle is stripped of his titles and possessions while on his deathbed. Bereft of his inheritance, Calvin will stop at nothing to get revenge on his uncle's illegitimate heir. He will strike at Richard in any way he can, even if it means ruining an innocent woman.

Blinded Recluse (Pemberley Book 3)
Ghosts from the past keep a family apart in *Blinded Recluse*, the third instalment in Ayr Bray's beloved *Pemberley* collection.

While all of Pemberley is preparing for the annual May Day celebration, tragedy strikes among the tenants. Paul Goss is losing his fight against a mysterious illness and stands at Death's door. With his blind daughter, Daisy, soon to be orphaned, he makes one last request: Find his estranged reclusive father and bring him home so Daisy will be taken care of.

Elizabeth and Fitzwilliam rush to his aid, but the far-reaching effects of a thirty-year-old scandal stand in the way of their success. Can they touch the old recluse's heart and help him see how much Daisy needs him, or will Daisy be left to rely on the charity of strangers?

In *Blinded Recluse*, the charming denizens of Ayr Bray's Pemberley learn the importance of family and security in a tale sure to tug at your heartstrings.

Cowardly Witness (Pemberley Book 1)
Matthew Poe is the only witness in a case of murder and corruption in the lead mining industry. After an attempt is made on his life, he seeks refuge at Pemberley.

Mr. Darcy, bound by honour and duty to his King and country, agrees to take him in, though his presence puts everyone at Pemberley in danger—including Darcy's new bride, Elizabeth.

When Mr. Poe's secret is revealed with disastrous consequences, will Darcy succeed in protecting his loved ones and the witness, or will he be forced to choose between family and honour?

Conjugal Obligation (An Erotic Pride and Prejudice Continuation Book 2) **adult content**

Conjugal Obligation; An Erotic Pride and Prejudice Continuation (2) picks up where *Felicity in Marriage* left off. This book can be read independently or enjoyed as a sequel to *Felicity in Marriage*.

Twenty-four hours have passed since our newlyweds married and experienced their first night of conjugal felicity. Now it is time that they leave London for Pemberley.

Conjugal Obligation takes readers on an erotic and passion filled three days as our newlyweds travel from the Darcy's London residence to Pemberley. The trip is not all romantic interludes though when twenty miles into their journey they are waylaid when they come across a disabled carriage and a woman being brutally taken advantage of.

Mr. Darcy must display courage and strength to save, not only the woman, but Elizabeth as the ruffians pull her from the carriage.

April Floyd

Mr. Darcy's Brides

Mr. Darcy has no choice but to marry his cousin in this Jane Austen inspired Regency romance! But then there is Miss Elizabeth Bennet, the lady he truly loves. Can he manage the expectations of his mother and Lady Catherine or will there be one bride too many? Anne or Elizabeth, James or Fitzwilliam? Be there and see the sparks fly!

The Parson of Pemberley

Mary Bennet, the third of the five Bennet sisters, longs to be understood and cherished. When Elizabeth Bennet suggests she would be the most suitable match for their cousin, William Collins, Mary determines that her search for love will not be sacrificed to save Longbourn. She goes to London to visit the Gardiners and meets friends who show her the regard she hopes for, amongst them one friendly parson by the name Andrew Moore. Along the way Jane and Lizzie face their own romantic woes.

Can Mary have the love she dreams of or will time and

distance intervene?

No Promise of the Kind

In this Pride and Prejudice inspired Regency novella, Elizabeth Bennet seeks to delay a marriage with her cousin, the parson William Collins, in order to marry for love. Her sister Jane's husband, Mr. Bingley, her best friend Charlotte Lucas, and the man of her heart, Mr. Darcy of Pemberley try to intervene to help Elizabeth escape the dreaded wedding day with the parson.

Just as Elizabeth and Darcy find their way Lady Catherine and George Wickham threaten their happiness. Can Jane Austen's beloved couple find their way back to one another?

Leenie Brown

Her Father's Choice (Choices: Book 1)

Sometimes a father knows what is best for his child. At least Mr. Bennet trusts he does. Seeing the potential of a good match for his beloved Lizzy but knowing her ability to hold a grudge, he puts a plan into action that forces a marriage between Darcy and Elizabeth.

Trapped in a compromise, Elizabeth Bennet has no choice but to accept the proposal of a man she is not entirely sure she likes. On the advice of her sister, she begins to question all she has heard about Mr. Darcy. When she realizes that she has been seriously mislead

about his character, she then begins to examine her own heart. What she finds there is unfamiliar. Could these strange feelings be the beginning of love as her aunt suggests? Is it possible that she can find happiness with her father's choice?

For Peace of Mind

When Elizabeth Bennet is sent to London to stay with her relatives, Fitzwilliam Darcy is the last person she expects or wants to see. On advice from her aunt, she agrees to give the gentleman a second chance at making a first impression.

Fitzwilliam Darcy never expected to find Elizabeth Bennet in town, and when he does, he is equally surprised to discover she heard his slighting remark at the assembly. Just when Darcy and Elizabeth's relationship begins to blossom, danger threatens. Action, intended to separate them, instead provokes declarations of love. Now on the path to matrimony, a new adversary creates a seemingly impossible choice, testing the strength of their bonds.

Teatime Tales: Short and Sweet Austen Inspired Tales

From Oxford Cottage

A Music Room Meeting

A look at the beginning of Richard and Harriet's relationship

From Mansfield Park by Jane Austen

With All My Love

A letter from Edmund to Fanny

From Pride and Prejudice by Jane Austen

Mr. Bingley Plans a Ball

Mr. Bingley returns to Netherfield

From Tolerable to Lovely

A ballroom blunder stops Mr. Darcy's famous disparagement

A Battle of Wills and Words

Elizabeth engages in a verbal joust with Colonel Fitzwilliam

Two Days in November

Darcy and Elizabeth embark on a plan to bring happiness to Jane

Listen to Your Heart

Anne de Bourgh has never had a coming-out. She has never had a season. In fact, she has never had a suitor. But, according to her mother, she has always had a future husband. Although Anne desires to marry, she does not wish to marry her mother's choice, and he does not wish to marry her.

With no other choices and the prime of her youth slipping away, Anne's view of her future is bleak. But when she finds some papers hidden in her father's study, that view, in the light of his wishes, changes. Her declaration to follow her heart and choose her own future causes discord and forces secrets to be revealed.

Sometimes the path to happily ever after can be strewn with danger and intrigue.

Linda Thompson

The Companion's Secret

"You must marry her," the stern voice said. "I need to gain control of her inheritance before she reaches her next birthday. It need not be a long marriage, but marry her you must."

Alone in the world, Elizabeth Bennet had to rely upon herself. She knew escape was the only way to ensure her safety. With the help of Longbourn's faithful servants, Elizabeth disappeared from her home and the odious heir. She was determined to find a way to support herself and remain hidden until after her birthday. Fortune smiled on Elizabeth when a series of events offered her the position of companion to Georgiana Darcy. In spite of her position, Elizabeth found herself attracted to her new employer. Could he ever see her as more than his sister's companion? Sometimes Elizabeth thought Mr. Darcy might care for her, too, but would his attraction—if that is what is was—survive when he learned the truth about her?

Hidden away at Pemberley, would Elizabeth be able to remain safely concealed until coming of age? What surprises did the future hold for her?

Her Unforgettable Laugh (Her Unforgettable Laugh series Book 1)

Dark curls and an unforgettably sweet laugh were all he knew of his sister's rescuer. Later, a second glimpse showed her to be lovely, and he heard her melodious laugh again. Darcy wondered what it would be like to meet this remarkable, and remarkably lovely, young woman. Would the spirit that caused her to go to the aid of a stranger be able to bring some joy to his lonely life? Would they ever meet, or would he always be left wondering?

Little did Fitzwilliam Darcy know that his trip to Hertfordshire to help his friend would bring him face to face with the lovely young woman whose unforgettable laugh had haunted his dreams for the last several years. Would she be anything like the

woman he had built up in his dreams? Would he be able to avoid Miss Bingley long enough to discover more about this mysterious young woman?

Laughter Through Trials (Her Unforgettable Laugh series Book 2)

In Book I of the series, Her Unforgettable Laugh, a trip to Hertfordshire brought Fitzwilliam Darcy face-to-face with the woman who had haunted his dreams for five years. Their chance meeting led to a courtship, in spite of those who wished to separate them. Now Elizabeth Bennet is traveling to London where she will be introduced to Darcy's family and the ton. How will Elizabeth be received? Will their love flourish and grow or will new trials overwhelm them?

Cynthia Cross

Lydia Holds Her Tongue: A Pride and Prejudice Sequel

Four intertwined love stories in one narrative, all in different stages of their Happily Ever Afters, all about characters you love from Pride and Prejudice.

If you believe

That Jane and Bingley's love story deserves a closer look...
And enduring love is not just for the young...
And even a poorly-begun marriage can bloom...
And an undervalued introvert can find understanding...
And that love has its humorous side...
Then this novella is for you.

Lydia's visit to her family at Longbourn is notable for her faux pas, overheard conversations she repeats, and even for a "loose lips sink ships" secret divulged which could harm the British in the war against

 Napoleon. Can the Bennets and Bingleys teach her to hold her tongue, or will disaster result?

"Let other pens dwell on guilt and misery," Jane Austen wrote, and in that spirit, this novella of 17,000 words, a sequel to Pride and Prejudice, is offered.

Wickham Meets His Match: A Pride and Prejudice Sequel

Is a Happily Ever After really possible, when you number

the Wickhams as part of the family?

Every family has its dirty dishes, but with the Wickhams around, not only are the dirty plates on display, but the scones and the silverware are mysteriously disappearing...

When Wickham and Lydia show up at the Darcy London townhome, asking for five thousand pounds to invest, their timing couldn't be worse. Not only is Georgiana in residence, but Darcy and Elizabeth expect a large party of guests to arrive at any moment, including Col. Fitzwilliam, Cousin Anne--and Lady Catherine de Bourgh. despite all efforts to pack the Wickhams out the door, like all dreadful in-laws, they do not understand hints. As tempers flare and sparks fly, are fisticuffs imminent?

"Let other pens dwell on guilt and misery," Jane Austen wrote, and in that spirit, this novella of 14,000 words, a sequel to Pride and Prejudice, is offered.

Upcoming JA Variation Author:

Marion Kay Hill

www.ingramcontent.com/pod-product-compliance
Lightning Source LLC
Chambersburg PA
CBHW060008180626
46817CB00015B/277